19Q

iUniverse, Inc.
Bloomington

19Q

Copyright © 2011 by Gerald Rainey.

All rights reserved. No part of this book may be used or reproduced by any means, graphic, electronic, or mechanical, including photocopying, recording, taping or by any information storage retrieval system without the written permission of the publisher except in the case of brief quotations embodied in critical articles and reviews.

This is a work of fiction. All of the characters, names, incidents, organizations, and dialogue in this novel are either the products of the author's imagination or are used fictitiously.

iUniverse books may be ordered through booksellers or by contacting:

iUniverse
1663 Liberty Drive
Bloomington, IN 47403
www.iuniverse.com
1-800-Authors (1-800-288-4677)

Because of the dynamic nature of the Internet, any web addresses or links contained in this book may have changed since publication and may no longer be valid. The views expressed in this work are solely those of the author and do not necessarily reflect the views of the publisher, and the publisher hereby disclaims any responsibility for them.

Any people depicted in stock imagery provided by Thinkstock are models, and such images are being used for illustrative purposes only.
Certain stock imagery © Thinkstock.

ISBN: 978-1-4620-4006-3 (sc)
ISBN: 978-1-4620-4008-7 (hc)
ISBN: 978-1-4620-4007-0 (ebk)

Library of Congress Control Number: 2011914246

Printed in the United States of America

iUniverse rev. date: 08/23/2011

"For the love of money is the root of all sorts of evil . . ."

1st Timothy 6:10

INTRODUCTION

Sunday April 3

"OK guys. Time to eat."

The mother beckoned for the rest of the family to gather around the dining table as she sat the last steaming dish in the center. "Hurry up before it gets cold." She placed the carving knife on the side of the platter resting against the chicken and wiped her hands on a towel draped over her shoulder. She was a middle aged woman with auburn hair tied back into a bun. Her smile was broad across her freckled face. Her pink dress was still creased from the Sunday morning church service she attended with her children. Her white apron had strawberries printed on it, with a few splatters from cooking the dinner.

"Smallest turkey I've ever seen," her husband quipped. A smile broke out across his weathered face. Though he was only forty-two, the years in the mill weighed on him. The scar over his left eye was a constant reminder of the dangers working with lumber. He looked like a lumberjack with his flannel shirt tucked into his jeans held up by wide, red suspenders. His hands were broad and calloused as he reached for the back of the chair to pull it away from the table to seat his wife. He was fit, strong, and rugged.

"Or the largest Cornish game hen ever," the mother quipped. "You are quite the gentleman tonight," said the woman as she sat in the chair held by her husband. "What's the occasion?"

"No occasion. Chivalry isn't dead, my dear," he said with a slight British accent. "It's just a bit slow, mum." Their light banter was interrupted by the scream of a young girl circling the corner of the room.

"Momma!!!!" she yelled. She was crying almost hysterically. The eight year-old girl ran to her mother's side and hugged her hard. "Johnny said I'm going to have a beard like daddy's now."

"What?" her mother replied. "What do you mean?"

A young boy walked around the corner as the drama was unfolding. The father confronted him with a scowl. "John. What did you do now?"

At fourteen, John was young but strong. He was built like his father; broad and chunky. He had sandy hair and wore glasses. "Nothing. It was nothing, dad." He strolled to his place at the table as his younger sister continued to cry and hug her mother.

"He said I was going to have a beard," the girl cried. She looked over to her brother with tears in her eyes.

The mother patted her on the shoulder to console her. "Why would he say that, honey?"

The girl composed herself and through her sniffles said, "He used a lectric razor and shaved my face. He said I would grow a beard now." She started to sob again and buried her head into her mother's bosom.

The parents looked at each other and smiled, holding back their laughter for fear of hurting their daughter's feelings. "You won't grow a beard, Lisa," the father smiled and assured her. "John was playing a trick on you, and a bad one at that." He looked displeasingly to his son.

"April Fools?" John asked.

"That was Friday. This isn't funny," the mother scolded. "You're always teasing her and this scared her." She rubbed her daughter's shoulder to calm her down.

"It was just a joke, Lisa." The boy walked over to his sister. "I'm sorry. I was just playing a trick." He leaned over and hugged her. "You won't grow a beard."

"That's better," the father agreed.

The boy mumbled under his breath as he returned to his seat, " . . . . but maybe a mustache . . ."

The girl didn't hear him, but the mother did. "Johnny, stop it."

"Ok. Ok. I'm sorry. I'm really sorry." He sat at his seat.

"Come on, honey." The mother pulled the little girl away from her bosom and wiped her tears away with her fingers. "Let's eat some dinner. You'll feel better," she said.

"Yeah. Come on, Lisa. I'm really sorry. I'll take you down to the park after dinner," he paused, " . . . if that's ok dad?"

The father was seating himself. "Sure. That would be a good gesture after tormenting your little sister." He looked over the table and at his family and smiled. "You know," the father began. "I really enjoy these Sunday dinners. Even with some of the antics that happen around here," as he playfully glared at his son.

The mother agreed. "Yes, it seems like everyone's schedule is just so crazy we hardly have time to eat, much less together and never at the same time." She reached to her right and uncovered the plate of rolls.

The young girl wiped her eyes. "Together would be at the same time, mom," she chided.

Everyone chuckled at the comment. "Way to go, sis." John reached out and high-fived his sister's hand.

The father looked at his two kids at the table. John was a leader by nature, an example of virtue. He studied hard, worked hard, played hard and joked hard. He had goals and aspirations even at his young age. His glasses made him look intelligent and mature. His daughter was young, innocent, and so dependent upon all of them. They were so different. *How can two kids from the same family raised the same way be so different*, he thought?

The father reached over and grabbed his son and daughter's hands, and bowed his head. Everyone followed his lead. "Heavenly Father. We thank you for this food and the hands that prepared it. We ask you to bless it now to the nourishment of our bodies in Jesus' name . . . . amen."

"Amen," came the collective reply.

"Son, would you pass me the broccoli?" he said as he pointed down the table.

"Sure dad." The young man made a face showing his dislike of the vegetable. "You can have it all."

The family continued to fill their plates and share stories of their day and their week; who went where, who saw whom, what was playing at the movie, how school was going . . . all of the small talk of a typical family getting reconnected.

As the tableware clinked on the dishes, the young man slowly leaned forward and took his glasses off. He put his head on his hand and said, "I think I'm getting another seizure." He had a defective chromosome that resulted in a mild seizure; a Maskill's Seizure.

"Don't worry, honey. Your treatment will work. It just takes a little time," the mother said as she pushed away from the table. She walked into the next room and returned with a small inhaler. "Here honey. This will slow the migraine."

The boy took the inhaler and sniffed the medicine into his nostrils. He tilted his head back and let the medicine slowly trickle down the back of his throat. He squinted his eyes as he tasted the bitter medicine. The rest of the family never missed a bite, and continued to talk and eat. "You'll be OK, son," said the father.

"Ugh." The boy took a big bite of mashed potatoes and then drank some milk. "This stuff is terrible."

"But it's going to help," his mom assured him.

"I know. It's just an inconvenience for me, that's all." The young boy put his glasses back on and started to dish out some more mashed potatoes. "I just don't like it when my hearing fades. It's like being in a vacuum; everything's muffled." He took another drink of milk and continued. "How long has it been so far?" he asked.

"About four weeks, honey," the mother replied. "It should start reducing the seizures and, hopefully, cure you."

No one knows what triggers the seizures. Some suspect it is stress. Others, lack of sleep. The seizures come and go, but last for a lifetime. The frequency and strength of the seizures vary with the patient but it generally occurs every few days until controlled by the medicines.

"Feeling better?" His mom was curious and wanted her little boy to get well soon, as all mothers do.

"Sort of." He paused and put his fork down. He took off his glasses again and laid them on the table. "Mom."

"What is it, honey?" The mother's concern showed on her face.

"I don't know . . . ." The young man's voice trailed off as he slowly closed his eyes and laid his head forward on the plate full of mashed potatoes, gravy, and chicken. His left arm started to twitch wildly, knocking over the glass of milk.

"Oh Jesus!!!" the mother yelled. "Johnny!" She reached across the corner of the table and grabbed her son's convulsing arm. Her chair fell backward as she jumped to her feet. Her full dish fell off the table and shattered on the wood floor. No one noticed. No one cared. "Johnny!!"

Blood started to flow from his left nostril, mixing with the gravy on the potatoes. His body was convulsing.

"Go call 911," the father yelled to the little girl as he dashed to his son's side. The girl ran to the kitchen, terrified.

"Johnny!!! Johnny!!!" The mother continued to yell his name with no reaction from the boy. He stopped convulsing and lay quietly in his food. The father lifted his head out of the food and slowly leaned him back in his chair. A small trickle of blood ran out of his left ear. His body was limp as his dad pulled him from his chair and laid him onto the floor.

The woman was hovering over her husband and son clasping her hands. "What's wrong with him?" Tears started to roll down her cheeks.

The dad had a look of terror as he wiped the blood, potatoes and gravy from his son's face and felt for a pulse on his neck. "I don't know. I don't know. Johnny!! Can you hear me?" He lightly slapped his son's face as the mother began to sob. He leaned down to listen to his heart. He could only hear his daughter yelling the address into the phone for the 911 dispatcher, and his wife sobbing.

"Do something!!" she demanded as she cried. "Do something!!" She knelt down next to the two of them on the floor.

"I am. I don't know what to do!! Johnny!! Johnny!!!!" The father lightly shook his son. "He's not breathing!!" The father tilted his son's head back, opened his jaw and looked inside. Then, he pinched the boy's nose, leaned over and breathed into his mouth.

Chaos filled the room as the father began CPR. Life slowly escaped the boy's body.

CHAPTER 1

Monday April 4

It was five A.M. The sun was just lighting the eastern sky of Antelope, Oregon. The clear morning sky was unusual for this time of spring. The plowed, rolling hills stretched to the horizon. The rich, black soil was lined by the green grass of the hills. The mountains in the distance were black from the backlit dawn. The snow capped peaks could easily be seen in the early morning light. The air was brisk. Clusters of fog shrouded the small valleys and canyons through the hills.

The yellow AIRTRACTOR AT 300 crop duster swung in low across the dirt road and circled the field. The pilot glanced down as several elk scampered across the meadow into some brush on the edge of the field. The plane leveled out and headed across the field, following the planted rows. The pilot loved this plane. It was fast and easy to handle. The closed canopy protected the pilot and his navigator from the bone chilling wind in the Pacific Northwest. It was a 40 year-old plane, but it ran like new. The 600hp Wasp engine hummed as the plane soared over the fields. The vibration from the engine was relaxing, the hum mesmerizing, the view captivating.

The pilot pulled a small map from off the dash clip. He was in his late fifties but still had his eyesight. He didn't need glasses. His wavy hair poked out from under his ball-cap with an "O" on the front. He was unshaved, rough looking. "Know what the last words of a redneck are?" A small black mutt with short hair and a curled tail sitting to his right barked. The dog had a tint of grey on his chin, just like the pilot. The flight goggles and flight cap made him look like a real navigator. In a southern drawl the pilot said, "Hey, ya'll. Watch this!" He let out a laugh as the dog barked again.

He verified his coordinates from the GPS with the coordinates on the map. "This is it, buddy." He circled the plane over the field and swooped toward the ground. As the plane leveled at twenty feet, he pulled the lever to open the applicator. "Bomb's away," he laughed.

The fluid held in the hopper mixed with water as it sprayed out the back of the crop duster and over the bare ground. The pilot left the lever open as he crossed the field. Just as he approached a row of trees, he simultaneously closed the sprayer and pulled back on the stick. The plane roared up and over the trees. The pilot circled the plane and applied the product one more time swooping in low from the opposite direction. He continued this dance until the applicator was empty and the field fertilized.

"Well, that's it baby." He looked to his flight companion. "Time to head back, Frisky." The dog lapped at the air and seemed to smile as the pilot banked the plane hard to the right. The pilot let out a hearty laugh and then a howl. The dog joined in as the pilot headed back home toward the hangar. A day's work done and the sun was just a few degrees above the horizon.

The car pulled up to the hangar just as the plane's wheels touched down on the small, gravel runway. A cloud of dust followed the plane to the hangar. The driver got out of the car and walked toward the open hangar doors as the plane taxied toward him. The man was middle aged, balding, and looked quite out of place in his sweater and slacks. It was a Monday morning sunrise in Eastern Oregon. No one wears slacks here. No one.

The plane came to a stop in front of the hangar. The pilot cut the power and opened the door. He stepped out with the dog under his arm.

"Howdy," he called to the stranger.

"Good morning. Beautiful day, isn't it?" The stranger walked over and extended his hand. "I'm James Bry from the Oregon Wheat Growers League."

The pilot placed his mutt on the ground and wiped his hand against his pants. "Nice to meet you. I'm Andy. People call me Captain Andy." They shook hands. "What can I do for you?"

"We need to use your services for some very precise spraying."

"Precise spraying? All of my spraying is precise," Andy quipped with a chuckle.

"This is a little different. We are participating in a grant program for fertilizer experimentation with wheat. We have a field that we want to spray a very small amount in a localized area."

"How small of an area?"

"About two acres."

"That doesn't make sense. Why not just apply it by hand or tractor then?"

"We want to make sure there is no damage to the crop. Because of the nature of the experimentation, we can't risk damage by machine or man as the seed germinates. It has to be applied at a very specific planting time in a very specific way." He paused. "Science, you know." The man smiled as he made his case for the job.

Captain Andy rubbed his scruffy beard as he thought about the challenge. "Well, seems to make sense. I'm not a farmer or a scientist; just a pilot. And a good one. Sure, I can hit the target. I can hit a potted plant on the back of a galloping elk if I needed to."

"Yes, we have heard you are the best."

"Where is it?" Andy asked.

"It's in Riley, Oregon, just outside Burns."

"Burns? That's almost 200 miles away?" Andy couldn't mask his surprise. "There's plenty of pilots in that area who can do the job."

"I suppose there are. But we need precision, not just any pilot. We checked around and people said you were the best. If this is something you don't feel you can do . . ."

"Oh, I can do it. There's no doubt there," Andy interrupted. He was almost indignant for the stranger to imply he couldn't do it. Andy can do anything, so he thought.

"Good. Here is a retainer. If it costs more than that, please let us know." The man handed him a cashier's check made out to cash.

"Normally I set the price and you pay it. I've never had anyone . . . ." Andy took the check and stared at it, mouth open. "Ten thousand for one short spray? Seems like a lot."

"Oh, I guess it is, but this comes from federal grants. It's not our money. We get a lot of money for experimentation through the OSU agricultural programs. Looks like you get the lucky break here. They have rules on how we have to spend it." Oregon State University was involved with various agricultural programs that often received grant money to fund research through private companies or co-ops. "Besides, the cleanup takes ten days to completely remove the residue of the spray from your application system. It won't hurt anything during that time or after the cleaning is done. We just want to make sure you are compensated for the down time, too."

"Well, makes sense. Okay. Let's go inside and fill out the paperwork. Who owns the land?"

"Mr. Bobby Joe Johnston. I have his affidavit here stating he owns the land and crop that we want to spray and is authorizing us to do so." Mr. Bry reached into a small binder he was carrying and pulled out some papers. "You will see that it is signed and notarized." Mr. Bry handed the notarized document to the Captain who studied it.

"Looks legit to me, but I'm not an attorney ya know."

"No, you're not. You're a pilot, and a good one from what I hear!" They both chuckled at the comment.

"So this is experimental fertilizer?" he asked looking at the documents.

"Yes, it is."

"I'm not gonna grow an extra ear from this stuff, am I?"

"Not hardly!" Mr. Bry slapped Captain Andy on the shoulder and a small cloud of dust rose. Mr. Bry coughed slightly. They both laughed as they walked toward the hangar office. "I brought all of the instructions for mixing, application, and clean up."

"Good. When do you want this sprayed?" Andy asked.

"It has to be sprayed this Thursday. Timing of the application and germination is critical," Mr. Bry said.

"Got it!" Frisky followed close behind the men as they entered the hangar.

The large hospital waiting room was empty except for the three people there. The smell of antiseptic and hand sanitizer was strong. A home improvement show was playing on the television anchored in the corner of the room. Bill Hammond was staring at the television. He wasn't watching it. He was just looking at it . . . waiting. His eyes were red from the tears they shed and being awake all night.

His wife, Linda, was leaning against his shoulder . . . sleeping.

Their daughter, Lisa, was curled up on the sofa almost into a fetal position with her head in her mom's lap.

They waited. It was early. He was tired. He was scared.

The doctor appeared through the doorway and whispered his name. "Mr. Hammond?" He was in his late fifties, normal build and height. His wavy, white hair was thick and full. He wore a white smock and carried an envelope and clipboard. He had the typical stethoscope around his neck.

Bill jumped to his feet. His wife and daughter woke instantly and came to his side as he stood before the doctor. Lisa wiped the sleep from her eyes.

The doctor looked glum. "I'm doctor Gobel." He paused and looked at the mother. "I am so sorry to tell you . . . ."

Linda broke out into sobs. "No. It can't be. No. Don't say it."

The doctor continued as he had many times before. " . . . . we lost him."

"What do you mean?" Bill fought to hold back his tears. He was crushed, mad, helpless. This was his son. He's supposed to protect him. How can this be? "They said it was a 'nothing seizure'. How can he die? Why? What happened?"

"Momma . . . ." Lisa clutched her mother and cried. She was so scared. She buried her head into her mother's bosom and wept.

"Johnny . . . . ," Linda whispered. "Oh God . . . . Johnny . . . ." She hugged her daughter and slumped down to the sofa. They held each other and sobbed. Linda whispered, "Oh Jesus."

The doctor continued quietly. "He had an aneurysm. A blood vessel in the brain burst."

Bill composed himself the best he could. Through his sobs he asked, "How? What caused it? Was it the seizure? He was taking a treatment for that." Bill was grasping for answers, something to make sense out of this senseless loss.

"We don't know. We are still trying to find out what happened." The doctor tried to remain professional, but the sobbing of the mother and daughter started to well up in his throat. "I truly am sorry for your loss." He cleared his throat and touched Bill's arm. "I'd like to find out what happened, too. Can we step over here for just a moment?"

Bill looked back at his wife and daughter, who were consoling each other. "Sure." He followed the doctor a few steps outside the room into the hallway.

"Mr. Hammond. We would like to ask you to consider donating your son's organs. Since he was a minor, you would need to approve the donation."

"Yesterday I asked myself, 'What if he died?' It's just so hard to believe he's gone. Parents aren't supposed to bury their children." He stopped again, and wiped the tears from his eyes. "John was older than he acted . . . in many ways. We talked about this once when he saw it on the news." He stopped to compose himself. "I realized he wasn't going to come back. When I laid him on the floor, I knew it was bad, I knew . . . . I . . . . I just don't want to believe it. This can't be happening." He ran his fingers through his hair, trying to feel something other than despair. He took a deep breath.

"I know this is hard. I'd like to find out what happened, and one way to do that is to conduct an autopsy when the organs are distributed."

"I guess he would want it done."

The doctor held a piece of paper out to the father. "We need to obtain a release from the parent to proceed. We would also need to know where to send John when we are done," he said without expression. He was back into his doctor mode.

Bill mumbled " . . . where to send him . . . ." As he took the consent form from the doctor's hand. "I better talk to my wife. She needs to agree to this."

"Sure, I understand. But, to do the procedure and have effective results, we should do so quickly. Otherwise we won't have viable organs for distribution."

" . . . . distribution . . . This sounds so sterile. He's my son!" Bill's eyes began to well up again. "Not a side of beef."

"I understand, and I mean no disrespect at all." The doctor gently placed his hand on Bill's shoulder. His concern was genuine. "I have a son. I can't imagine what you are going through right now."

Bill took another cleansing breath to compose himself. "It's surreal." He paused. "Thank you. I'll talk with her. When do we need to get this back to you?"

"Tomorrow will be fine. We can preserve the organs until then."

"This sounds complicated." Bill was confused about the entire process. "How does all this work?"

"We will continue to keep oxygenated blood flowing through John while his temperature is reduced. It's standard procedure for donors. Then, we will perform a suite autopsy as we remove the organs for donation. It's a way to see what happened without affecting the organs." The doctor assured Bill that his son would feel nothing, and that many, many people will benefit from his gift of life.

The two men shook hands. The doctor wrote his cell number on the consent form for Bill.

"Uh, doctor?" Bill paused as he searched for words. "Can we . . . . can we see him one more time?"

"Certainly." Bill took the paper and walked over to his grieving wife and daughter.

He looked at the two of them, placed his hand on his wife's shoulder, and said, "Honey. Let's go say goodbye to Johnny."

CHAPTER 2

Wednesday April 6

" . . . . and we should be landing in San Diego in three hours and fifteen minutes. So, please, set back, relax and enjoy your flight." The flight attendant placed the receiver back in the cradle and went to the galley to prepare the drink cart.

Bruce Lowell let out a sigh as he settled in for the flight. He was a big man in his mid fifties. His wavy brown hair had a tint of grey. He prided himself with staying fit after the military. The seats on most planes barely fit someone his size, except in first class. That was the only way to fly. They pamper you, care for you, and don't annoy you. That would give him plenty of time to review his speech for the conference. The young lady to his right had her earbuds in, listening to music. Bruce wondered how someone so young could afford a first class flight like this. He, of course, was rich. He could afford anything.

He was the founder and one of two partners of Biotrogen—a bio-genetic medical company that created the drugs Tegbatol and Inferon; the cure for the rapidly spreading Maskill's Seizure. The drugs were a huge success, and within months of development and testing, he and his partner became very rich. The company went public in just two years and received enough capital and government funding to expand their research and experiments in biogenetic engineering. He was one of the successful pioneers in genomic medicine. People wanted to hear from him. They wanted to hear his story.

"That looks pretty complex." The young lady to his side had glanced at his papers and saw the diagrams of the DNA molecule and its components. She had no clue that looking over someone's papers could be construed as rude or inappropriate. She was young, in her early twenties Bruce thought. She was wearing ratty looking jeans with a tight short-sleeved top. Her long, blond hair fell across her shoulders barely covering her hoop earrings.

"Huh? Oh yeah. It's a DNA molecule."

"DNA?" she asked. "Are you like a scientist or something?"

"Well, yes I guess I am . . . or something. I own a company that specializes in biogenetic engineering and genomic medicine," he said proudly.

"Whoa. Hold it." She pulled her earbuds out. "That's, like, ya know, growing fingers on rats 'n stuff, isn't it?" she asked.

Bruce let out a chuckle. "To some, maybe. To others it is hope. It all depends on your perspective and understanding, I guess." He flipped a few pages as the girl leaned closer.

"Wow. Like, a scientist. That is so cool. Where are ya goin?" she asked.

"I'm headed to a conference in San Diego to share our experiences on genomic medicine. I guess since we have a successful company and products, they want to hear from me how we did it. The world of science is all about sharing, growing, experimenting, and failing."

"Failing?"

"Sure. From our failures we gain our successes. Sometimes scientists try something a hundred times. Each time they fail, they learn something new, adjust, and try again. It is all trial and error, until they find the thing that works. One success from a thousand failures. Even Thomas Edison once said, '*I have not failed. I have found 10,000 ways that won't work.*'" Bruce laid the papers on the tray in front of him. He was proud of himself for using the saying he used a thousand times in conferences to this young girl. He could see he was gaining her attention. "Great successes don't come easy. They take a lot of hard work and persistence."

"Tell me. I had to scrap my way to the top," the girl said proudly.

"The top?" Bruce was surprised. *How could this young girl wearing torn, ratty jeans and a t-shirt be at the top*, he thought? The top of what?

"Yeah. Music." She paused, but there was no reaction from Bruce. "I'm Dee," she continued. Still no reaction from Bruce. "You know, 'Gonna Fly With my Guy in the Sky?'" she said as she snapped her fingers to the rhythm and moved her head from side to side.

"Oh yeah. That's . . . . awesome." Bruce was being polite, though he had no idea what the song or the singer was about. He felt old, disconnected. He never heard of her or her music. He was setting next to a star, maybe a Grammy winner, that thousands of kids would love to be setting near and talking to, and he had not a clue. Worse yet, he really had no interest. But he was a gentleman. And she was attractive. "I've heard the music industry is grueling to be in."

"It is. It's like no sleep, travel all the time, and no privacy." She turned downcast as she realized how bad it can be when you are very successful in her field. "Sometimes I just want to sing and not perform."

"I guess anything can be grueling if it gets out of control. You just have to take care of yourself," he encouraged.

"What about you? You are working in a really strange field, making all these mutant things," she said as she pointed to the picture. "That has to be stressful."

"Mutant things? No, not hardly," he chuckled. "It's a science. Man has been doing genetics for centuries."

"What do you mean?" she asked. Her interest was piqued.

"Okay. For example . . . . ever hear of someone taking seeds from produce, say a large pumpkin, so that they can grow one? Or breeding the best dog, a "purebred" if you will, to get a purebred of their own? Or even grafting one plant to another to make a better plant?"

"Sure, all the time. That was in the movie Dennis the Menace when Mr. Wilson was growing this really special rose." Her excitement began to well up as she connected to his thought.

"That's genetic engineering at the basic level," he said with a smile. "You see, genetics are not complicated, and they are not a 'Frankenstein' science as some would believe. They are selectively identifying, matching or altering genes to produce an outcome."

"Genes, not like these I take it?" as she pointed to her torn pair of pants and chuckled.

"No, not hardly like those. By the way, how much do jeans like that sell for anyway?" His curiosity got the best of him.

"Oh. I got these for a hundred and fifty bucks. They were on sale," she said.

"To think of all the money I've donated . . . . ," he said wistfully, thinking of the many pairs of torn jeans he gave to charity, or used for rags.

"Okay, so keep going. This is interesting." She adjusted in her seat to better face him as he spoke. "I always thought gene science was weird. I don't even really know what a gene is," she said.

"Genetic science," he corrected. "And it is weird in a way, but not scary as many believe," he continued. "It's not complicated at the basic level. DNA, deoxyribonucleic acid, carries the genetic information in the body's cells. DNA is made up of four similar chemicals called bases and abbreviated A, T, C, and G. They are repeated over and over in pairs. You see this here, the twisted spiral?" He pointed to the picture she saw earlier. "That's DNA."

"Nice!" she exclaimed. "Is that the real thing?"

"It is."

"Awesome!"

The girl was captivated by the picture and stared at it as Bruce continued. "A gene is a distinct portion of a cell's DNA. Genes are coded instructions for making everything the body needs, especially proteins. Human beings have about 25,000 genes. We scientists have discovered what some of our genes do, and have found some that are associated with disorders, like Maskill's Seizures or Huntington's disease. Even so, there are many, many genes whose functions are still unknown."

"So, DNA is grouped into things called genes. Right?" she asked.

"Close, but there's more. We know what the genes are. In 2003 The Human Genome Project identified all the human genes in DNA and stored the information in databases so all researchers everywhere could use. It is a complete copy of the entire set of human gene instructions."

"Wow! So they identified every gene a person has?" She was engrossed in the educational lesson.

"Yes. They identified the genes, but not what they do. Genes are just one more step toward knowing about the body."

"What's the next step, then?" she asked.

"Chromosomes."

"Oh yeah. I heard about those. That's what determines if we become a man or a woman, like the X and Y chromosome, right?" she asked.

"Yes. That's right. Genes are packaged in bundles called chromosomes. Humans have 23 pairs of chromosomes, or a total of 46. Of those, one pair is the sex chromosomes which determine whether you are male or female, plus some other body characteristics, and the other 22 pairs are autosomal chromosomes. Those determine the rest of the body's makeup. They are like a map of your entire body."

"That's awesome! So, DNA makes Genes which make chromosomes. Like building blocks!" She almost squealed because she was tracking right along with him. She felt smart.

"You got it!" he confirmed.

"So, how do you work with this stuff? What do you do?" she asked.

"Genes can have mutations. Going back to the DNA, sometimes the particular order of the pairs of As, Ts, Cs, and Gs is extremely important. Sometimes there is a mistake—one of the pairs gets switched, dropped, or repeated. This changes the coding for one or more genes. This is called a genetic mutation. A mutation may be disease-causing or harmless."

"So, you try to figure out what the mutation is . . . . and do what?"

"Well, there's more. Another way the DNA code could be changed is by errors in the chromosomes. Parts of a chromosome could break off, switch with part of another chromosome, or be swapped within the same chromosome. If any of these or other mistakes occur then changes, or mutations, happen in the gene coding. Sometimes there may be three or more copies of a chromosome, or only one chromosome, instead of the normal pair."

"So, genes can be mutated by either DNA or chromosome errors, right?"

"That's right. See, it isn't all that complicated, is it?" he asked.

The young lady giggled. "Need an assistant?" They both chuckled.

The male flight attendant interrupted their mini science lesson. "Care for some beverage?" He was young and smiled at the young lady.

Bruce spoke first. "Yes, I'd like some herbal tea."

The young lady nudged him. "I thought you would be ordering, like, scotch and water or something," she said.

"No, I like to keep a clear head when I fly. Never know when you'll need it," he responded.

"For you, miss?" the attendant asked.

"Cranberry juice, please. No ice."

The attendant turned toward the galley as the two continued their lesson.

"Cranberry juice?" Bruce asked. "I figured you for a coke or something."

The young lady glanced at Bruce. "Antioxidents." She paused, and then chuckled. Bruce let out a laugh.

The young lady started first. "So, what do _you_ do?"

"I deal with predictive medicine."

"Predictive medicine? What is that?"

He responded as though his audience was the conference attendees on bio-genetic medicine. "In predictive medicine we analyze genes, chromosomes, and DNA to determine if there is causation from a mutation resulting in an illness. Then we look at developing methods, such as protein attacks, to restrict or alter the effects of chromosome or gene expressions."

"Whoa, whoa, whoa. Say that again, but slower."

The attendant delivered their drink, just in time to give Bruce a break and realize to whom he was talking; a young artist, not a scientist.

He spoke slowly and deliberately. "We look for mutations in genes that could cause illness or defects. It could be the DNA, the gene, or the chromosome. Then we try to figure out a way to prevent it, or treat it."

"How?" she asked.

"By changing the gene or creating a medicine that targets the mutation and restricts the expression. That's where it gets complicated," he said.

"I guess. This is really interesting, but I think you are getting way over my head." Her interest seemed to wane. She didn't want complicated, and his answers and descriptions were getting to be a bit too much for her. She knew she was going farther than she cared, and had enough of her science lesson for the day.

Bruce also realized she was becoming disinterested. "Enough about me. Where is your next performance?" he asked, changing the topic to her interests.

"San Diego . . . at the Copely Symphony Hall. I'm doing something a little different this time," she said.

"What's that?"

She smiled. "I'm performing before a really small group of, like, 2,000 people. The hall is very cool. It's super old and I hear the acoustics are fab!" Her excitement grew.

The Copely Symphony Hall began in 1929 as part of Fox Theaters nationwide. Movies were growing, the country was booming and venues to watch and hear this new technological marvel were rising throughout the country. They were tributes to a better era. Interior galleries with fabulous acoustics, grand entry halls, chandeliers, balconies, drapes and carved wood trim throughout were common place. It was a time when couples would put on their best, strolled to the theater, and made a night of entertainment watching black and white films and newsreels.

Over the years, many of these treasures fell into disrepair. People cared more about the price of a movie than the venue. The competition for theaters escalated and was ruthless. No consideration for style, for finesse, for glamour. Soon, places like the Alhambra Theater in Sacramento, rife with marbled tile, carved wood trim, and elegant floors soon gave way to supermarket expansion.

The San Diego Symphony saw the potential in the abandoned Copely, and brought it under its wing in 1984. The Copely became the centerpiece of the symphony with magnificent acoustics to showcase their performances. Glamour and elegance returned to a small location in this world.

"I'm doing a show with some friends for a private birthday party."

"Must be some birthday," he exclaimed. He wanted her to say who it was, but she didn't budge.

"I'm so lookin forward to hearing what this place sounds like. Acoustics is what I live for. I love to find a tunnel or hallway, and just sing!" She lit up as she reminisced about some of her private venues with no one around to hear. "It won't feel like a performance with so few people there."

"Two thousand people are hardly a few," he chided.

"It is for me," she said. "I usually have concerts of twenty to fifty thousand people. Two is nothing." She went back to fiddling with her earbuds. Bruce knew the conversation was over.

"Well, I hope you do well and enjoy yourself," he said.

"Thanks. You too. Maybe I'll read about you online someday," she said.

"Yes, maybe."

The young lady placed her earbuds back in her ears and flipped through a magazine. Bruce leaned back in his chair and closed his eyes.

CHAPTER 3

Thursday April 7 ■■■■■■■

"I can't believe I'm doing this, Frisky." The pilot poured another cup of coffee and grabbed a donut. "4 A.M. We should be snuggled up together sawing logs."

The black dog yawned and wagged his tail. He loved his master, like all dogs should.

"I can see getting up this early to go hunting or fishing, but work? Just doesn't seem right, good buddy." He blew a couple of fake smoke rings with his breath. "Now that's cold."

Frisky stepped forward, put his front legs out and arched his back as he yawned. Then he pulled himself forward and stretched his back legs. When he was done, he shook his coat all the way down to the tail, and, when he finished, ran in a circle.

"Well, looks like you're ready to go. Come on. We have a long ways to go. Let's get this done." Captain Andy grabbed a small duffle bag off the counter and looked inside. "Water, map, GPS, food . . . ." Frisky barked. Andy looked at him and smiled. "Yes, your food, too." The dog barked again. Frisky probably knew a hundred words, but none as recognizable as 'food.'

" . . . . flashlight, and . . . ." Andy chuckled as he pulled the urinal from the bag. " . . . . pee pot. It's going to be a long flight." Frisky barked. "I have no idea where you will go. You'd never be able to hit this, much less in the air. Your bladder is bigger than mine anyway. You better go drain it now before we leave, pal." The dog bolted out the hangar door and over to the bushes on the side. "Boy, he's smarter than most people I know."

Andy pulled the GPS from the pouch and entered the coordinates from the map. "There, that's in and ready to go." The pilot grabbed his flight jacket from his navy days off the coat rack. The leather jacket with fur trim was one that many pilots desired, but Andy had. It was a genuine, navy flight jacket. And well it should be. Andy got it when he began flight school at Pensacola, Florida; the heart of military flight training, and it still fit perfectly.

Andy whistled and called to his navigator. The dog bolted around the corner of the hangar and stopped in front of Andy. "Up." Frisky backed up and ran as fast as he could and, with a mighty leap, flew upwards into Captain Andy's arms. "You've still got it, pal." He strolled out the door and toward the plane carrying the dog in his arm. Andy walked around the big yellow bird and spot checked all of the critical points. He double checked the applicator hoses, connections, and valves before climbing into the cockpit. "OK, Frisky. Let's go, buddy."

Frisky jumped from Andy's arms and into the co-pilot's seat. Andy closed the door and settled into his seat. Andy turned some knobs and started the engine. He checked the instrument panel. "Hopper is 1/8th full. Not much in there, but that's all they wanted. Oh well." He checked the gas, water temperature, oil pressure, and instruments. He looked over to Frisky and said, "We are a go, tower one." He leaned over and put the flight cap and goggles on the dog. "There. Now you look like a navigator."

Andy waited a few moments while the engine warmed up. Then, he taxied to the runway as Frisky settled into his spot. Captain Andy looked back at the hangar door, still open with the lights on, as the plane passed by the building. He never locked it during the day. Never had to. Why, he seldom locked it at night. Not here. Not in Antelope, Oregon. No one would mess with his stuff. That only happens in the big cities.

He accelerated as he pulled onto the makeshift runway. "Up, up and away . . ." Andy sang as he pulled back on the stick and the plane lifted off the ground and into the black sky with ease. "Riley, here we come."

Frisky barked his approval.

The alarm went off and Bruce Lowell got up from the table to walk into the bedroom and silence it. He returned to the table where his coffee and breakfast were waiting. It was 4:30, and he had been up for some time already. He was an early riser; always had been, always will be. Maybe it was the military that conditioned him to get up before dawn. Maybe it was the early morning studies from his graduate work in genetics at University of California in Davis, or maybe it was from his research in

Maskill's Seizures and subsequent success that caused him to get up early every day. Whatever it was, he was conditioned to stay up late, and get up early to succeed. He was one of those people who could function at 100% with as little as four hours of sleep a night . . . every night. He proved himself capable when he went through Hell Week with the SEALS back in sixty-nine. No sleep, extreme conditions, peak performance.

He dialed a number on the phone as he took a bite of his eggs and glanced at the paper.

"Hello?"

"Jim. Bruce here."

"I'd say it's kinda early, but I know you too well." Bruce could hear him yawn. "How are ya?"

"I'm fine. Look, Jim. I'm getting myself together for a presentation today at the conference on the Future of Genomic Medicine in San Diego."

"Yeah. I heard something about that through the grapevine. Don't you have another one right behind that?"

"Yeah. It's in Houston. Friday. I should be back in the office Monday," Bruce said as he took a gulp of coffee.

"Me too."

"That's why I'm calling, Jim. I wanted to check on your progress with the development and distribution of our product in Oregon. I want to make sure it gets to the target site before the crops sprout. You know how critical that is to the development of the crop."

"Already did, Big Bruce. I contracted a pilot Monday to conduct the spray today. He should be applying it as we speak, the day after planting from what our research says."

"That's great. Is he providing a report?" Bruce gulped some of his eggs as he waited for the answer.

"No. We agreed he would only send a receipt and summary to our post office box. Nothing more to sign off. Nothing to file. Just the general contract and application instructions."

"Great!" Bruce was pleased. "What about cleanup?"

"I gave him instructions on how to clean the hopper of residue, similar to cleaning for oil based applicants. I know he'll thoroughly eliminate all traces of the applicant because he had an older AIRTRACTOR AT300 that was as clean as my '37 Chevy."

Bruce voiced his approval. "Excellent! You are good, I must say."

"You taught me well. Anything else, because I am still a bit tired?" He yawned again. "Not everyone likes to get up before five like you, ya know."

"Bruce chuckled. "No, go back to bed you slacker. I just wanted to make sure we got the product distributed in time."

"We always have and always will. I have two more lined up next week. We should have 200 more acres covered by next month and all applications in place for the spring crop," Jim said, his excitement coming over the phone.

"Even Saskatchewan, eh?" Bruce asked with a poor Canadian accent.

"Yes, even Saskatchewan," Jim replied. "Some of these are small sprays, but the larger ones are making up some ground for us."

"Fabulous. Okay. I'll let you go. Talk to you later."

"You too. Hope your presentations go well, as I am sure they will," Jim chuckled as he hung up.

Bruce pushed the button on the phone to disconnect the call. He leaned back in his chair with his coffee in both hands and a smile on his face.

"Perfect."

The sun was just below the horizon and starting to lighten the morning sky. The sky was clear with no wind. Conditions were perfect for a quick, early morning spray.

The AIRTRACTOR AT300 soared over the field at 400 feet. Captain Andy checked the GPS for location. "OK, buddy. We are almost there. Let's make a pass and make sure we have a clean line over the target area." He looked around to verify there were no obstacles in the area. "Looks good, Rocco." Frisky barked.

Andy banked the plane into a 180 turn and headed back over the field. He dropped down to 20 feet over the ground and pulled the lever to the hopper. "Bomb's away." Captain Andy was in his zone. He loved this work. He pushed the lever in for three seconds and then released it. He pulled back on the stick as the plane roared up and over some trees. He banked the plane and turned it 180 degrees for the second pass. The dance of the yellow AIRTRACTOR was captivating.

When the job was finished after just four passes, Captain Andy leaned over and scratched Frisky's chin. "That was too easy. Let's head home."

The plane roared as he banked it to the north and started home toward Antelope. "That was the fastest ten thousand dollars I've ever made!" Frisky barked. "Okay . . . . we've ever made, but I still get 60%!" Captain Andy laughed as he turned on the music and settled in for the flight home.

Bobby Joe Johnston stepped outside the front door and onto the porch to watch the AIRTRACTOR disappear over the hill. He pulled his suspender up over his shoulder and rubbed his scruffy chin. "What the heck?" he said. The elderly farmer wasn't quite awake.

His wife stepped through the doorway as she wrapped her robe around her protecting her from the desert chill. "What is it honey?" she asked.

"It looks like a duster, but I can't tell who it is." He scratched his head.

"Probably Luke getting an early spray on his crop," she said.

"No. Too early in the season for that. Probably some yahoo looking at elk or something. Who knows?" He scratched his head trying to figure out whom and why they were out so early and over his field.

"He didn't spray anything in our field by mistake, did he?" she asked.

"No. Looks like he's just passing through. I sure hope he didn't spray close to us and have it drift onto our field. It could ruin our organic status."

"Come on. I'm sure everything is fine. I'll make us a pot of coffee." His wife wrapped her arm around his tubby waist and escorted him into the house. "I ever tell you what a stud muffin you are?"

Bobby Joe laughed. "All the time," he replied as he scratched his rear. Ethel spanked his hand and they giggled.

It was 8 A.M. Doctor Alan Gobel was reviewing patient files and dictating notes into a recorder when the assistant entered his office.

"Doctor Gobel. There is a mister Bill Hammond here to see you."

"Great." Alan placed the recorder on the desk. "Send him right in."

The assistant held the door open and Mr. Hammond entered the doctor's office. He had the consent form in his hand. His hair was uncombed.

Dr. Gobel noticed that his eyes were clear, likely because he got some sleep. "Good morning, Mr. Hammond." He extended his hand.

"Doctor." They shook hands. "Here is the consent form. I signed it." He handed it to the doctor.

The doctor looked at the form, searching for words to say. "I appreciate this. I know it was hard for you, but I think we will be able to find out what's going on and maybe save other people as a result," he said.

"I hope so. I know Johnny would want this done. He was a generous young man, willing to go out of his way to help others." Bill paused. "He was a good kid."

"And you are a good father."

"You will see we asked to have him sent to Evergreen Mortuary." Bill pointed to the document. "They will know what to do from there."

"Thank you. If there is anything more I can do, please let me know," Doctor Gobel said.

"There is."

The doctor was a little surprised to actually hear a reply from a common, meaningless request. "Oh?"

"Yes. Please let us know if you find anything."

"Oh, certainly."

Bill turned and left the office. The doctor looked at the consent form again and set it aside.

CHAPTER 4

Friday April 8

Dr. Gobel stepped out of the elevator and into the office of the hospital administrator, Grace Moore. "Do you have a second Grace?" he asked. He didn't want an answer as he approached her desk.

Grace Moore was the hospital Administrator of Mercy General Hospital in Eugene, Oregon. She was forty-seven and fit. She had short blond hair that covered her grey. Her long days showed through the wrinkles around her eyes. "Sure, come in Alan. Oh, you are in . . ." she quipped as she looked up and smiled. She could see the concern on his face. The smile quickly vanished. "What's wrong?"

"I think we have a problem brewing," he said.

"Brewing? That's an odd way to start a conversation. Either a problem is or it isn't."

"Not in this case," he said as he approached her desk.

"In what case?" Grace set her papers aside and stood to her feet. She could see the concern on his face. "What's going on?" she asked as she stepped toward the doctor who was standing just inside the door.

"We had another death."

"In a hospital this large, we have them all the time, Alan," she said matter of factly.

"Another Maskill's Seizure death," he said. Grace leaned back against her desk and folded her arms. "Go on."

Alan cleared his throat. "A fourteen year old boy with Maskill's Seizures was admitted to the hospital after suffering a severe headache and loss of consciousness. He was bleeding from the left nostril and ear with no obvious signs of trauma. He was in cardiac arrest. We continued CPR and were able to restart the heart. Breathing was shallow. Vitals were weak. We did an MRI, and found this." He handed her the envelope.

She opened the envelope and pulled out some pictures. She walked over to a monitor and placed them on the backlit screen.

Alan continued. "Several arteries in the Primary Auditory Cortex and lateral Sulcus ruptured simultaneously."

"Several?" She looked at him while he confirmed his statement.

"Yes, several." He cleared his throat and continued. "I remembered we had other patients in the last few days with similar symptoms . . . . and results. I did some digging and . . ." He paused. "Grace. We've had six patients die from similar events over the past two weeks."

"That's not too unusual," she replied.

"What is unusual is that all of them were diagnosed with Maskill's Seizures, all of them suffered multiple aneurysms of the Primary Auditory Cortex, and all of them died, including the boy."

"Maskill's? That's a benign seizure at best. Are you sure?"

"Yes. The odds of six Maskill's having similar cranial aneurysms is . . . ."

Grace finished his thought. " . . . . astronomical. There's nothing in Maskill's that would indicate severe symptoms or events. We've only known about it for six or seven years."

"Eight," he corrected.

She ignored him. "Were they on the treatment?"

"Only the latest patient and one other. The others were not."

"Have you run bacterial and viral tests?"

"Yeah, nothing. We even did chemical analysis and tox screens to see if something was ingested that may have caused the event."

"And?"

"Nothing."

"Have you obtained any autopsies to conduct a thorough analysis of the tissues?" Grace was moving through the checklist of problem resolution. She was an administrator extraordinaire. Her intelligence surpassed her peers, and her leadership was absolute. She had no qualms making tough decisions. She relished the idea.

"I have one in process now with our latest case."

"Good. We need to find out what the link is, or even if there is one." She paused for a second while looking at the images. "Are you sure they were Maskill's patients?"

"Yes."

"It may take more than our staff to figure this out." She moved around the desk and called her administrative assistant. "Sandy, get Bob Struthers from the Center for Disease Control in Atlanta on the line for me. It's important."

"Yes, ma'am. Right away," came the reply.

Grace looked at the images again. "I think we need to at least put the CDC on alert here, Alan. We don't know what we're dealing with. They may know of other cases with similarities. Besides, Bob is an old friend. Maybe he can pull a few strings and expedite the testing." She placed the pictures back in the envelope and handed them to the doctor. "I want copies of the medical records on the six patients ready for Bob by noon."

"I'm on it."

"We better both be on this," she replied.

"Miss Moore? Mr. Struthers from the Center for Disease Control is on line one."

After her lengthy call to the CDC, Grace called Alan to make sure he was available for a conference call with them at three. She told him to be ready to discuss the medical records that they sent to the CDC. She knew the importance of being prepared and thorough. Alan was a brilliant doctor. She knew he had been thinking about the Maskill's patients and attempted to locate something that would be the cause of death or point to the cause. His review of the cases would be invaluable in their discussion.

Grace, too, was troubled by the cases. She took a sip of her coffee as she reviewed the summary notes on the victims of Maskill's Seizures. Even though there were only six, they were quite different in all aspects. Different ages, different sexes, different ethnicities, different vocations. There was no common thread other than they had the disease and died in the same manner. Two used the Stacatto loxapine inhaler to mitigate the effects of the migraine; four did not. Two were on treatment with the Tegbatol and Inferon regimen; four were not. Tox screens clear. No virus, no bacterial infections, no other symptoms or medical issues prior to the onset of the events. Nothing to tie them together other than they each had the defective chromosome causing the Maskill's seizure.

Grace looked up a phone number in her contact system; someone she knew well and trusted. She turned, and pushed the button on the phone and dialed Hillside Memorial Hospital in Albuquerque, New Mexico.

"This is Grace Moore at Mercy General Hospital. I'd like to speak to Tom Ivers, please."

"Just a moment. I will see if he is available," came the reply over the speaker.

After a few seconds, a man answered. "Grace. How are you?"

"I'm doing well, Tom. It has been quite awhile since we last spoke." She smiled as she leaned back in her chair and reminisced. She and Tom were friends, good friends. They knew each other going through medical school and both graduated with honors. They went their separate ways and soon both ended up as administrators of very fine hospitals in different parts of the country. He in New Mexico, she in Oregon. They stayed in touch over the years and occasionally shared ideas and progress with each other.

"I'll say. It was last summer at the National Health Care Conference. You were on the board of the Federation of Hospital Administrators as I recall. Still there?" he asked.

"No, Tom. I left after my term expired that fall. This job is just too demanding and time consuming," she said.

"Yeah, I know what you mean. I have the same issue here at this hospital. Seems to follow me wherever I go. Too much work and too little time. Did you ever think you would be working this hard at this stage of your career?" he chuckled.

"Not hardly." She paused. "Tom, I need to see if we have another issue in common . . . one a bit more serious."

Her serious tone grabbed his attention. "What do you mean?"

"I have several cases here that are troubling me. They are Maskill's Seizure patients that . . . that died."

The phone was silent. "Tom? Did you hear what I said?"

"Yeah, yeah I heard you. I just find it ironic because we had two Maskill's patients die this week." The excitement began to well up in his voice. "I thought it was a fluke, something we may have overlooked, but hearing you ask that question . . . well . . . now I have questions. Did you say several?"

Grace leaned forward in her chair and rested her arms on the desk. "Yes. Six in two weeks, Tom. We never had a Maskill's patient die before. I don't think there is even a record of a Maskill's patient ever dying from the seizure. And now we have six. What's going on?"

"I don't know. Maybe it's just coincidence. Maybe not. Most patients just have a migraine and some hearing or vision impairment. It's not normally debilitating, and has never been deadly."

"I know," Grace confirmed. "That's what concerns me so much. What's changed?"

"I don't know. What are the circumstances of your victims?" He was taking notes as they spoke.

Grace elaborated about the dissimilarities—age, sex, race, geographical location, clean tox screens . . . all of the details she had poured over with no connection . . . . no verifiable source . . . . no link. "Tom, I contacted CDC just to let them know something may be amiss here."

Tom was writing frantically as Grace spoke, trying to capture all of what she was saying. "Grace, I'm going to give CDC a call, too. Maybe there is fire starting and we are just the spark. This disease is just too new. Maybe there's some type of maturation occurring." He shuffled some papers around. "Have you called some of the other administrators you know?"

"No. Not yet. You were the first. But I did call CDC to put them on notice. One of the Deputy Directors is a friend of mine."

"Everyone is your friend, Grace." He laughed. "OK. Why don't you make a few calls. I'll make a few, too. Let's call from the Federation list. I'll do south and east, you do west and north. That way we won't duplicate information."

"Good idea, Tom."

"I'm going to get some more details here and email the info to you. If you send me the info for your contact at CDC, I can update them, too. I don't think we should delay on this thing. It could be a significant event brewing." He wrote some notes on the documents and grabbed a small phone book.

"I agree. I'll get back to you with whatever I discover. Thanks, Tom."

"Sure, hon. We'll stay in touch. All things considering, it's still good to hear from you, Grace."

Grace could sense the romance they almost sparked in college was still there. "You too, Tom." The line went silent. Grace pushed the button to disconnect the call and leaned her head onto her hands. She pulled a stapled booklet from her desk drawer and reviewed the list of administrators. She grabbed a notepad, drew some columns and labeled some headings, and started dialing.

CHAPTER 5

Monday April 11

The Hummer pulled into the parking space at Biotrogen, and Bruce Lowell stepped out. He was wearing blue Dockers and a sweater with Birkenstocks. Every day was casual day for him since he owned the company and was very successful. He strolled into the five story building and was greeted by the young man at Reception. "Good morning, Bruce."

"Good morning, David. Beautiful morning, isn't it?" Bruce was cordial with all employees. Even though he had more than two hundred on his payroll, he took great pains to get to know as many as he could and greet them by name. He exuded confidence. He had command presence.

"That it is, sir. That it is." David smiled as Bruce keyed in his code and beeped his way through the gate and toward the elevator.

The building was five stories high. Each floor was designated to a particular area of research, development, and production. The floors were divided into two parts; laboratory and production except the first floor which housed administration. Bruce never cared much for his "corporate" office there. He liked his personal office much better.

The elevator door opened and the fifth floor was abuzz with people, computers, and humming equipment. Cubicles lined the rows of people working on computers and phones. This was one floor of Bruce's empire—people working madly at creating the next genetic medicinal cure. Bruce believed treating your employees like owners will aid in retention, so everyone had the best equipment, an exceptional view from the windows that surrounded the floor, and no clocks.

At the far end of the floor, Bruce could see the glass wall that separated the production staff from research and development. He could see several people in white smocks discussing the results of something important to them. There were microscopes, centrifuges, beakers, Petri dishes . . .

everything that made a laboratory look productive and exciting. And in this place, it was. For this is where the cure for Maskill's Seizures was discovered. The holy grail of Biotrogen. It was the seedling that sprouted the development of several biogenetic medicines for constipation, ankle joint pain, lactose interolerance, and so much more. None of the new medicines have been approved or are successful . . . . yet. Several are in various stages of testing. Some at clinical phase three. Only Tegbatol and Inferon, used for the treatment of Maskill's, has been tested, approved by the FDA and highly successful. They generated enough capital and belief in the company to provide for research and development of these new medicine darlings being created. They were the very beginning, the birth of Biotrogen.

And they owe it all to Bruce, Jim and Everett. The miracle boys of Biotrogen.

Bruce walked down the hall to his personal office. He always liked being in the middle of production. His corner office commanded a fabulous view overlooking the river and old town Sacramento. It was decorated with sports memorabilia from various teams and athletes. His prize possession was a football signed by 49ers Superbowl legends Joe Montana and Steve Young. The football was openly displayed on a golden hand resting on a cherry wood hutch. It sat next to his Navy Seal emblem mounted on a gold plated stand with his purple heart, silver star, and bronze star. At the end of the hutch was a picture of his children.

A circular table with three chairs was in the corner near the three huge bookshelves with hundreds of research books on medicine and genetics arranged neatly in their rows. Jim Anderson was setting at the table drinking a Starbuck's coffee with his feet propped on the window ledge looking over the river when Bruce walked in.

"Morning sunshine," Bruce said.

"You ever notice that boat over there at the marina with the tall sails on it? The one with the red flag at the rear?" Jim was taking in the view and really liked the boat.

"No, can't say that I have." Bruce put his briefcase next to the desk and sat down without looking out the window.

"Me neither." Jim smiled and turned away from the window and toward Bruce. "We got all the fields covered in two weeks. We sprayed 420 gallons . . . ."

"Hold it!" Bruce was obviously perturbed as he got up and closed the door. "You twit."

"Twit? I haven't heard that since middle school." Jim laughed at the silly name calling. "Twit."

"OK. OK. Look, we don't need to broadcast our successes all over the building. Try to be a little discreet, eh?"

"Are you trying to be Canadian again?" asked Jim. "If you are, it ain't working, buddy." He laughed as Bruce joined him at the table.

"Now, what were you saying, oh one of little brain matter?" He chuckled.

"I was saying . . . . we sprayed 420 gallons of 'fertilizer' over 12 organic fields covering 500 acres . . . all in a month." Jim was proud of his accomplishment, and blew on his fingers and rubbed them on his chest.

"Did you use any local pilots?" he asked.

"Nope. They all traveled a minimum of 100 miles to apply the product, no questions asked," he said proudly. "Some of the sprays were really small, but we got some larger ones in, too. Kind of mixed it up this time."

"Nice job. Nice job. I take it you took care of all of the personal matters, too?" Bruce asked, wondering if Jim did a thorough job or not. Seemed like he was always checking up on Jim's work.

"Of course. I did all the paperwork and receipts to show we sprayed the fertilizer and matched them to the cashier's checks. If anyone reviews the documents, it's just a fertilizer spray on test area. The real fertilizer we purchased has been disposed of without anyone's knowledge, but the purchase order is filed with the application records."

"Good. Looks like we can wait for another successful harvest," Bruce said with delight. "Are you working on the harvest contracts through the Internet?"

"I'll get to that this week." Jim was already planning his short vacation to Cancun right after the spring jobs were done.

"OK. We want to make sure we get the buy orders in before anyone else. Then we can resell to the processor and track distributions accordingly so we can compare the market penetration to the spread . . . ."

" . . . of the disease." Jim finished the sentence. "I know we have to track how fast this is spreading and where. Don't worry. I've got this under control." Jim reassured Bruce about his ability and thoroughness. "Look. We've gone to great pains to make this product work. I know very well we have to control the growth of patients, or it could go very sour very fast. We've been doing this eight years now without a hitch. It's all about controlling the outcome."

Bruce was worried that too many patients at a particular time could cause someone in the medical or science community to start snooping around in places they didn't want them to go. If the wheat was sold to one processor or distributor for a single product, someone might be able to trace the disease back to that distributor and product and back to them. It was critical to their success to make sure there was no pattern to the distribution, buyer, product or people to expose their plan. Diversity and integration were a must. So far, buying organic wheat to control the harvest and assure limited inspection of the wheat was genius. Reselling it to multiple processors assured control and distribution to multiple entities making multiple products, which would assure no one could trace the wheat back to them.

"Don't worry," Jim continued. "No one will ever know that we sprayed the wheat to create Maskill's. No one." He reached over and grabbed the football off the golden hand.

Bruce didn't notice. He stared out the window lost in thought.

"This is Bob." Bob Struthers was in his mid sixties. He had been with CDC for seventeen years after serving many years as a surgeon and hospital administrator. He moved into the government realm because of his passion to help the sick and protect people from illnesses. His wife died from Huntington's disease, a severe neurological disorder that eats away at its victim's memory, function, and life. It was a slow, terrible death to witness. After she died, Bob poured himself into his job and career, and was a true leader and example. He had little hair, extra weight, and tremendous energy. His quick wit and intelligence enabled him to think on the run and assign tasks in the blink of an eye without hesitation. His favorite quote hung behind him on the wall.

"Tis far better to dare mighty things . . . even though checkered with failure . . . than to live in the grey twilight that knows not victory nor defeat."

Theodore Roosevelt—A Man of Action

Bob was a man of action.

"Hi, Bob. Grace Moore at Mercy General." Grace didn't give Bob a chance to respond. She got right to the point. "I have some more news for you on Maskill's."

"What is it?"

"I spent the weekend calling some of my peers at hospitals around the country. They are also seeing some deaths occur with Maskill's patients."

"Some?"

"Forty-three so far." The line went silent. "Forty-three, Bob, in one month." Bob could hear the concern in Grace's voice.

"One Month? How many locations." Bob pulled the notepad on his desk closer, and began to take notes.

"Forty-three at twenty-one locations. What is amazing is that every one had at least one patient die." Grace ran her finger along her notes. "Fourteen states, no common denominator either. Not age, sex, race, pre existing, tox screens, bacterial, virus, nothing." She paused. "Nothing, Bob."

"Nothing? That is troublesome, Grace. Can you send me your list and information you've gathered so far?" Bob wanted to start right in and confirm her findings.

"Sure. Fax or email?"

"Email. I can easily redistribute to other CDC work teams that way if need be." He paused. "Grace, I'm really glad you worked on that this weekend. I was planning to start in today, but you just moved this up the priority pole. I don't like the looks of it."

"Neither do I, Bob. You'll have the info in a few minutes."

"Thanks."

And with that, she hung up the phone and started tapping on the keyboard to send the files.

Bob leaned back in his chair and stared at the notes on the pad. The number '43' leapt at him. He felt a shiver down his back.

Gayle Rustin was the queen of Human Resources at Biotrogen. She was young, educated, calculating, and controlling. Her experience in Human Resources spanned a decade at the top hospitals and medical facilities on the West Coast. Bruce was able to woo her into joining his new team with a promise of lucrative stock options and the freedom to do her job the way she saw fit, providing she reported directly to him and his word was final. Her task was to recruit the best biogenetic students from universities with promises of growth, expansion, and challenge. The company was growing, the stock rising, and the future bright. Bruce wanted someone at the very onset to attract bright new employees to expand the possibilities and product development for Biotrogen. Gayle was just the person for the job.

"What's lined up for today, Ralph?" Gayle liked to stand next to Ralph's desk and look down on him. He was forty-eight, fifteen years her elder, a gopher, a 'yes ma'am' to her, but he was thorough. "We have three interviews for an entry level research analyst in Biogenetics. Other than that, it's pretty clear, ma'am." Ralph always smiled, was always courteous, and had no problems with Gayle being the queen bee.

"Who's first and when?" she asked.

"Leslie Singer, 10.30. I have it on your calendar for an hour. In your office."

"Interesting. Could be man or woman. Which is it?" she asked.

"Mszzzz Singer," he said with a smile. He almost sounded like a bee.

"Great. Please call me when Mssszz Singer, arrives, will you Misszzzzzzzzzzzzzter Gresh?" she joked back.

Ralph chuckled. He liked the banter. "Gladly."

"OK. That gives me a half hour. I'm going for a walk. Please have my list of questions ready on my desk when I get back."

"No worries. Have a nice walk. It's nice outside today." Ralph wished he could go with her, but that would never happen. Besides, he had work to do keeping the office together and running smoothly.

The papers were strewn across the work table in messy piles. The huge white board on the wall had notes, dates, numbers and names listed in various orders. There was a myriad of arrows, lines, and circles scattered around the board. Bob Struthers stared at the whiteboard and glanced back at the papers. "There has to be a link. Something common to these people," he said, struggling to find an answer.

"There is," came the reply. "They're all Maskill's patients, and they're all dead." Alice Barker didn't mix words. In her business, you didn't have time to waste. An hour, a minute could mean someone's life. Being blunt was a must. Being direct was an absolute. Being rude was the byproduct. "You're wasting your time, Bob."

Alice was in her forties and suffered from a genetic disease called Becker Muscular Dystrophy. The symptoms are deterioration of the muscles of the legs and pelvis area, resulting in twisted limbs. Walking was an effort. Alice used two crutches that wrapped around her wrists. She would twist and turn as she struggled to move one leg in front of the other. There is no known cure for BMD. Treatment is aimed at control of symptoms to maximize the quality of life.

Her hard life made her a hard person. She was a fighter, never to consider giving up at anything. People told her she could never graduate college or work for a living. They resigned her to disability for life. She showed them, and received her Masters in Data Management from the University of Southern California. She later joined the CDC as the Assistant Director of Data Research and Technology Department.

"How so?"

"You need to start building a correlation model now with what you have." Alice turned to sit at the table and continue drinking her tea. "We will dig around and get more information for you." She was ready to start searching for more victims of this disease and gather all of the information she could.

The data research operation at the CDC was akin to a large scale gold mining operation. The back hoe would dig tons of dirt and put it in a dump truck. The truck hauls the dirt to a separator. From there, the dirt is shaken washed, sifted, and sorted until the smallest grain of gold is separated out of tons of raw earth. With the CDC, teams gather mountains of information from agencies scattered all over the world. The data is entered into correlation models that sift and separate pertinent information into like groups until that gold nugget appears; the piece that ties it all together, if there is one.

Her team was well equipped to search and locate cases anywhere in the world. Their correlation models were sophisticated and accurate. All she needed was the go ahead to launch her network of dozens of people contacting thousands of medical centers to get pertinent information to sort through.

Time, however, is the enemy. The longer it takes, the more people die.

"We can't waste any time on this, Bob. If we have forty-three people dead in one month at a few hospitals that we know of, there may be thousands all over the world. This could very well be a pandemic surfacing.

We could have thousands of victims in no time." Her emotions seldom showed. Her comments were matter of fact, but true.

"You sound like a drama queen."

"You know I'm right, though," she said.

"I do. That's what scares me, Alice. Get your teams ready." He buzzed his secretary on the phone. "Janet. Call Randall and set up a meeting for Alice and me. Today."

"Yes, sir," she said and the line went dead.

"Alice, we need to get Randall to issue an alert. That will enable us to gather the data we . . . . I mean you need to do a full assessment."

Alice looked annoyed. "You know how Randall is. He needs evidence before he acts."

"I know. Let's hope we have enough evidence for him." Bob glanced at the board. "I think these deaths may be enough to at least ask the question."

"Especially from a benign disease," Alice replied.

"Especially. We need to start gathering data right away so we can get it mined. Let's get Randall to agree to contact all of the normal outlets and medical points of interest first . . . ." He paused. "I hope we can get him to issue a request for information, too."

"That's really what we need," Alice agreed. "I'll work my charm on him." Alice flashed a big smile and fluttered her eyes.

"He won't stand a chance," Bob said. "You better get to it!"

She cracked a smile and snapped a salute. "Yes sir-eee."

Bob watched as Alice struggled to her feet and left the room. Then he turned to the board and became very glum as he stared at the emerging monster before him.

The young lady was smartly dressed in her sweater and slacks. Her black hair fell onto the white sweater making a striking contrast. She sat on the edge of her chair as Gayle asked questions about her interests, experience, desires, aspirations, and shortcomings. Each question opened an opportunity for excellent answers from the bright young candidate. Gayle had interviewed many people during her career, but this one was obviously prepared. She knew her stuff. She certainly had the qualifications to fit well in the genetics research department.

"Well, that about wraps it up for me. Do you have any questions of me?" Gayle always presented this question to the candidates, who often were surprised or ill prepared to ask anything. They have asked stupid, silly questions like, "what sport do you like best," or "do you like to white water raft?" As though those questions would demonstrate someone's intelligence or ability to master the job they were applying for. Idiots.

But this girl, <u>this</u> young lady was different.

Gayle was stacking her papers and preparing to stand when the young lady responded. "Yes, I do." She flipped open her notepad. "I wanted to know a little more about the beginning of the company. How was it founded?"

Good question.

Gayle was a little surprised, but settled back into her chair. "Biotrogen was founded seven years ago by Bruce Lowell, Jim Anderson, and Everett Maskill," she began. "The three men were graduates of the University of California at Davis. Bruce Lowell has a Masters in Biomedical Engineering. Jim Anderson has a double masters; one in Agriculture and the other in Finance. Everett Maskill had a PH.D. in Chemical and Molecular Engineering."

"Had?" the young lady interrupted.

"Huh?" Gayle's presentation of the great company's founders was short circuited.

"You said, 'had. Had a degree' for Everett Maskill." The young lady was showing her confusion.

"Uh. Yes. Had. Mr. Maskill was tragically killed the year after joining the company."

"How sad."

Gayle paused and continued her presentation. "The three men joined together to form a company to research and develop genetically enhanced crops for medicinal purposes. During their analysis of the effects of various proteins from crops on chromosomes, they discovered a chromosome called 19Q13.33 that had a mutated gene that resulted in a neurological disease where the victims had seizures. The newly discovered disease was called Maskill's Seizures after Doctor Everett Maskill, the man who discovered the gene mutation purely by accident. Their research in biogenetic medicinal crops complemented their discovery well, and in a very short time, they found that wrapping the gene in a particular type of protein restricted the gene expression of the chromosome and eliminated the seizures."

"I've heard of the disease. I thought the name sounded familiar." The young lady was becoming very interested.

Gayle continued. "Within a year, they were known for their success with the newly discovered disease and cure and obtained significant funding from interested investors. They branched into genomic medicine to explore genetic alterations on diseases without the use of crops. It turned into the complete package deal; cures through genetics, and cures through crops."

"I see. It is fascinating how a chance discovery could lead to a company like this." The candidate made a few notes on her pad.

"The world of genetics, in both plant and animal, is fascinating. And it's just starting." Gayle glanced at the clock and looked back at the candidate. "Do you have any other questions?" Gayle asked.

"Oh. Um. Yes, I do. Just curiosity." The young lady continued. "What happened to Doctor Maskill?"

Gayle shifted in her chair. "As the company was ready to go public, Doctor Maskill died from a fall at his home. He was working on his roof gutters when he fell off a ladder and struck his head. He died instantly." Gayle became a little restless. She was ready to end this interview.

"Oh, his poor wife!" Leslie exclaimed. "It must have been terrible for her."

"He wasn't married. There was no one at the house. Bruce Lowell discovered him on the back deck. He was pretty broken up over the matter." Gayle straightened her skirt and shifted in her chair again. She was getting uncomfortable about discussing this emotional event. "Anything else?" she asked.

The young lady flipped a page on her notepad and scanned the questions with her finger, looking for the right one. Gayle glanced at the clock again. It was time to end the interview.

CHAPTER 6

Wednesday April 13

Leslie was going through her email while enjoying some coffee and a bagel. She tried diligently to maintain her weight. In this rushed world of school, social activities, and job hunting, eating on the run was common place. She might have a meal out almost everyday, but her breakfast was always lean. She was listening to the rambling news while she scanned her messages.

"Looks like it will be cold this weekend. Thanks, Jim." The young male anchor was comfortable in front of the camera, as they all are. *"And now to Natasha Aziz for an update on the meteor shower that's happening this weekend. Natasha?"*

Leslie giggled as she read her next email. "Oh sure, a run Thursday." She started typing on the keyboard. "I can't, you silly. I have to look for a job. Some of us work, ya know. What about Saturday?"

"I'm here at the California State University Sacramento Science Department with Professor Miles Adams, professor of astronomy and avid star gazer. Professor, can you tell us a little about this meteor shower that's coming our way this Saturday?"

Leslie stopped and turned toward the television. *"Actually, the meteor shower will peak Saturday, but has been going on for several days. It is called the Lyrids Meteor shower because it originates in the Lyra constellation to the north."*

Leslie was looking for something to do Saturday night, and maybe she found just the thing. The professor continued. *"This event occurs every year at this time. It is the result of debris from a comet C/1861. The most visible meteors will occur between midnight and dawn, but you can see up to twenty or more meteors per hour if you get away from the city, from ambient light. This is going to be similar to the Lyrids meteor storm of 1982. It should be a good one."*

"That's it!" exclaimed Leslie. "That's what we can do!" She couldn't contain her excitement.

The professor continued, but Leslie was busy typing her request to some friends for a spring night out watching meteors. *"This is one of those predictive events that we have in astronomy, not like the solar storm we had last year. This shower has been recorded for 2,600 years, and returns each year at this time like clockwork."* The professor continued to educate the audience, but Leslie was lost in her email request. She reached over and took another bite of her bagel. *This will be so awesome,* she thought.

The phone rang and interrupted her life.

"Hello?"

"Hi. This is Gayle Rustin at Biotrogen." Leslie's heart skipped a beat. She dropped her bagel and wiped her mouth, as though Ms. Rustin had just walked through her door. "Is this Leslie Singer?" She fumbled with the remote to mute the television, and straightened her hair.

"Yes, yes it is. Hello Ms. Rustin." She took a deep breath away from the receiver and calmed herself down. Either it was good news or bad, but she was hoping for good. "What may I do for you?"

"Come to work for us, I hope." Gayle got right to the point. She was a busy woman. No reason to beat around the bush. "I'd like to offer you the research analyst 1 job at Biotrogen."

Leslie almost squealed as she pumped her fist into the air. She calmly replied, "Yes, I would love to."

"You haven't heard the full offer yet. Starting pay is $19.70 per hour or $41,000 a year, two weeks personal days, no sick time, stock options after probationary period of six months, medical, dental, vision paid for, and a 401k with 100% match of 10% of your salary." Each time Gayle stated a benefit, Leslie got more and more excited until she almost fell out of her chair.

"Sounds great, Ms. Rustin. When would you like me to start?" The rest of her world stopped. This was the job she wanted. To get into a growing genetic research company was a dream come true.

"Is this Saturday too early? That gives you a few days to arrange your schedule."

"That's perfect. After this week, I am pretty open because of the new semester and classes. Saturday would be great. What hours, if I may ask?" Leslie was concerned about conflicts with her education.

"The total time will be forty hours per week. You will be hourly, but can work your hours to fill the forty per week around school. That will make for a tight schedule for you, I'm sure." Leslie couldn't believe it. It was absolutely perfect. Gayle continued. "I realize this is your last semester, so after graduation and probation, we will discuss a change to your classification and get you on salary. Then, you can work whatever hours you prefer, as long as the job gets done."

"Perfect!"

"How does it sound, Leslie?"

"Like a dream come true, ma'am."

"Oh, please. Call me Gayle. After all, we are teammates now."

"OK, Gayle. I will be there Saturday. What time?"

"Seven A.M. We have a lot to go over for orientation."

"Great! See you then."

"Bye." Gayle hung up and wasn't able to hear Leslie let out a squeal of delight as she jumped to her feet and did the happy dance, clapping her hands above her head and spinning in a circle yelling, "Woo-hoo!!!!"

It was almost eleven in the morning. CDC was hopping, as it always is. "Life in the Cubes" was playing at every workstation. Phones were ringing, people chatting, documents stacked in piles on the floors, coffee flowing.

Bob was in his office reading through his morning mail and reflecting on his meeting with Alice and Randall yesterday. Bob had many years and many meetings with the Deputy Director of Infectious Diseases for CDC. This Director, Randall Sterling, was not a push over by any means. Bob often wondered how he would do in Randall's position. It was an ominous job with tremendous responsibilities. One wrong move could result in companies going broke, industries being shut down. It was imperative that any warning of any type have sufficient information to justify action. Alice and Bob pulled it off. And Bob was well pleased. It always felt good, even after all of his experience, to get someone like Randall onboard with an action.

Bob was deep in thought when Alice walked in with her messenger bag around her shoulder. She had a small carrier on the front of her bag akin to a water bottle holder that carried her travel mug usually filled with coffee or tea. Bob looked up. "Good morning, Alice."

"Here." She reached into the bag and plopped a small stack of papers on his desk. "A thousand plus Maskill's deaths so far, and rising." She paused. "I don't think I would call this a good morning." She pulled a chair up to his desk and settled in.

Bob slowly caressed the documents with a blank stare on his face. "Any common denominator?"

"Yes. They were all Maskill's. They all died within the last sixty-four days. They all suffered aneurysms in the Primary Auditory Cortex of the brain. They are primarily in the North American Continent, but we are still mining." She took a drink from his coffee. "Ick. I thought it was hot."

"Sorry. It's been there awhile."

"So I see."

"Is yours empty?" he asked.

"I wouldn't have tried yours if it wasn't, my dear." Alice smiled and fluttered her eyelashes.

Bob ignored her and hit the button on the speaker phone. "Janet. Can you get us two coffees, one with double cream, one black?"

"Yes sir."

"Oh, and hold my calls. Alice and I don't want to be disturbed."

"Yes, Mr. Struthers." The phone went dead.

Bob began. "We need to get an alert out. No telling what this is going to blossom into," he said.

"I know," Alice agreed. "We are still sifting data, but have most of the U.S. in. My team was up all night mining. We are receiving data from Europe and South America. Asia and Africa are still behind, as they always are. Their systems are just too archaic."

"No other common factors? Were they cleared for tox, virus and bacteria?" he asked.

"Cleared."

"Have you presented this to Randall yet?"

Alice chuckled. "Are you serious? I wouldn't dream of doing that without you. You need to share the love here."

Bob grimaced. "Love? OK. Let's see if we can meet with him right away. We need to get an alert distributed." He turned to the phone and started dialing.

After a few rings, someone answered over the speaker. "Yeah, Bob. What's up?"

Bob cleared his throat. "Randall, I have Alice here."

"Hi Alice."

"Randall." Alice knew Randall was busy and was always to the point. "We have a thousand plus Maskill's deaths so far."

"A thousand?"

Bob continued. "Yeah. This is just from the preliminary run Alice did last night through her normal channels."

Alice jumped in. "We expect there are more, Randall."

"Are you sure they are Maskill's related?" Randall asked.

"Yes, all Maskill's. All died within the last sixty-four days. All suffered aneurysms in the Primary Auditory Cortex of the brain," Alice reiterated.

"Locale?" Randall asked.

Bob answered, "Mostly North America."

"Randall, Bob and I believe we should issue an alert to get all of the information out there. Something is wrong here. I can feel it."

"Thanks, Alice, but you know I don't go on feelings. Can't." Randall paused for a second. "Bring up the data you have and let's take a look at it. Have Charles from HAN[1] join us."

Bob responded. "Will do, Randall. We'll be right up." He waited for Randall to disconnect the call first.

Janet walked in with two coffees. "Janet. Can you get Charles from HAN in here right away?"

"Yes, Mr. Struthers." Janet placed the coffees on his desk and scurried out.

Alice started to rise when Bob stopped her. "I'd like to have you stay and help me brief Charles before we go see Randall. We need to make this simple, accurate. I think the main issue is to just make people aware of the new situation, and to report abnormalities and victims immediately." He knew the sooner professionals around the world were aware, the sooner they could participate with gathering data, and the sooner they might be able to find the reason for the deaths. "I don't want any missteps here, Alice."

"I agree. I think it's best to have everything ready to share with Randall so he can just rubber stamp it." All Alice wanted was the data.

Bob started to work through the checklist in his head. "We'll need to get a work team together to dig into this. It could take the weekend. We have to get the autopsy results and tissue samples to the genetics, chemical and microbiology labs. I'll need complete screens re-run on all of the

---

[1] HAN is the Health Alert Network for the CDC. It was the dissemination point for critical information and bulletins from the CDC to the health and press community throughout the world.

tissues we receive to rule out mutations, heavy metals, radioactive, EMF[2], electrical, anything that they may have overlooked." Bob knew there were many more causes other than poisons, bacteria, and viruses that can kill. "We may have to turn over every rock here, Alice."

"I know. We have just scratched the surface. This could take a long time, Bob."

"It could, and that's what worries me. We don't know what this is or what it can be." Bob had enough experience to know when something significant posed a serious threat to society. He saw it with Ebola and AIDS.

Charles quickly walked into the room as Bob was finishing his sentence. "What's up, boss," he joked in a Bugs Bunny fashion.

Bob didn't smile, nor did Alice. Bob spoke first. "We have a problem."

Charles' smile immediately left his face. He sat next to Alice and leaned toward the documents spread on Bob's desk, trying to catch a glimpse. "Must be serious," he said.

Alice and Bob replied in unison, "It is."

Jim was in his corner office on the fifth floor right across from Bruce. The two owners always stayed in touch with each other even though they each managed different aspects of the company. Bruce with research and development; Jim with finance and agricultural applications.

Jim didn't have the view of the river, but the mountains looked fabulous this time of year. Their snowcapped peaks towered over the valley. He loved watching the clouds fold their way over the peaks in the spring. He couldn't wait to get away for another vacation. All this traveling around to get the sprays in was grueling. Funny, he thought, that he needed to travel to Cancun to get away from his travels. How ironic.

The sound of the printer ejecting the paper broke his daydream. He turned and pulled the paper from the printer and reviewed it. "OK. Looks like all of the fields are covered and due to harvest at the same time." He turned and logged into Tradekey, an online global product exchange system.

---

[2] EMF—Electro-magnetic Field caused by electrical currents, such as with high voltage power lines in the vicinity.

One of Jim's jobs was managing the subsidiary company that he and Bruce owned with Jim's cousin, Leonard Wristen. The company was focused on the development, manufacture and distribution of a specialized fertilizer. Jim personally managed the spray application of the fertilizer, as well as the harvest and redistribution of organic wheat from the grower to the processor. Tradekey was central to this operation. It is a website that brings worldwide buyers and sellers together to exchange products. It is an excellent way for the home farmer to sell their produce in the open market. With more than five million members, it is a massive clearing house of products worldwide. All one has to do is set up an account, and search to buy or sell a particular product. That was how Jim found the likely candidates for the spray. They were members of Tradekey and sold their organic wheat on the open market. They had small farms, small crops, and were easy to entice with big dollars to sell their products to him.

Jim went through his list of sellers and sent offers for their products due to be harvested in 130 days, give or take. He knew when they planted it, so he knew when it was due to be harvested. He made sure the offers exceeded the futures prices so each seller would be happy with his offer. These farmers liked having a sure sale rather than wait until it was closer to harvest time. In these uncertain economic times, better a bird in the hand than two in the bush. They didn't like to gamble with their livelihood. Accepting a future bid for their product before harvest was not unusual. It was a guaranteed price.

Bruce walked in, closed the door as he had a habit to do, and noticed Jim was on Tradekey. "I see you are placing the orders." Bruce knew everything about everything. He helped set the system up. He processed the first series of orders years ago. He was well versed in every aspect of this operation, as well he should be.

"Yup. Should be done today." Jim kept typing away. "I also finished the last of the shipments of the winter harvest wheat, so we can close those files." Jim paused and turned to Bruce. "Sometimes I'd just like to sell this stuff on the open market. It would be so much easier and less time intensive for sure."

Bruce seemed a bit exasperated. "Jim, you know we can't."

"I know, but the chances of anyone finding anything wrong are almost nil," he said. "It takes a lot of time to coordinate the purchase, pick up, shipping, and redistribution. If anything did go wrong, we would be leaving a little trail all along the way leading back to us."

Bruce sighed. "There's some truth there, but I think it is better to control the whole process to make sure the product doesn't go through some rigorous testing that could expose it." Bruce elaborated. "The key here, Jim, is to make sure it gets sold to a low-end processor; another mom and pop shop, if you will, and doesn't get exported. They won't have the means to test for anything more than the minimum of what they are required to do by the FGIS for domestic sales."

The Federal Grain Inspection Service, or FGIS established standards for testing the 30,000 wheat varieties for quality, content, weight, infestations, moisture content, foreign materials, damaged kernels, and more. They assure the wheat that goes to market is properly identified, properly represented and safe to consume. They didn't have the resources to test all of the wheat or in great detail, unless it was exported. That only happened on very select products, and then it was for a reason. Bruce wanted to make sure they never had a reason with his wheat.

"I know, Bruce," Jim responded. "You're right. It's safer that way. It just takes a lot of danged time to do this." Jim was almost pouting. "I'll be searching for processors after I get back from vacation."

"Like you have a busy schedule," Bruce chuckled. "When is your trip to Cancun? Tomorrow?"

"I do have a busy schedule, you know. I just got back from flying all over the west coast getting the sprays done." Jim paused and looked at Bruce. " . . . and the trip is next week." They both laughed.

"Fine. Just work your fingers to the bone before you leave. I want to make sure everything is lined up for the summer harvest."

"Will do." Jim stopped typing and turned to Bruce. "What are you working on?"

"This afternoon, I'm going golfing. You aren't the only one needing a little R and R here," Bruce chuckled. "Tomorrow I'm updating our distribution report of patients. I want to make sure we aren't spraying too much. I've let it fall behind for the quarter." Bruce liked control. He was always in control. It was well known in the medical and scientific community that the mutated 19Q13.33 chromosome was the cause of Maskill's. A few scientists were trying to replicate the work of Doctor Maskill to develop a different cure, but to no avail. Bruce wanted to be sure the spread of the disease was manageable. Having an outbreak could be catastrophic. Doctors and scientists would direct all of their resources to finding a cure. If they were successful at any level, it would undercut their market share and cause the stock to tumble. Right now, they were in control of the only "cure" for Maskill's, which was a nuisance disease, and Bruce wanted to keep it that way.

"Good. Let me know if we need to make any adjustments on our next spray this fall."

"Will do," Bruce replied. Jim turned to the computer and started typing again as Bruce walked out the door.

CHAPTER 7

Friday April 15
Deaths—1,863

Bill Hammond walked out to the mail box to get the mail. It was a daily routine for him, though usually in the evening after work. He was wearing dirty jeans, an old shirt, and slippers. His hair was uncombed. He was having a difficult time getting back into the swing of things after his son's unexpected death from Maskill's. The whole family was having a hard time. The house seemed so empty. Their lives seemed so empty.

Bill gathered the envelopes into his hand and started toward the house, scanning through them on the way. They were the usual fodder; bills, some junk mail, credit card offers and such. He came across a letter from doctor Gobel from Mercy General Hospital.

It's probably a sympathy card, he thought to himself. He stopped, opened the envelope, and read the note from the doctor.

> *"Mr. Hammond. I received this letter from a family that was an organ recipient from your son. They asked if I could forward it to you. My thoughts are with you and your family." Alan Gobel*

Bill opened the letter and read it to himself.

> *"To the parents of the boy whose organs were donated to give life to others. We are so sorry for your loss. We know how precious our children are to us, and understand the pain and suffering you must be going through. Our hearts are broken with yours."*

Bill stopped and took a deep breath and continued to read.

"We wanted to tell you that your child's heart is beating in our daughter's chest."

Bill let out a breath and caught himself as he almost broke down. He covered his mouth and nose to contain himself.

"Our daughter, Cynthia, is alive because of your child. She has been given a chance to live because of your child. We have no words to express how grateful we are that you chose to donate your child's organs, nor do we have words to express our sympathy. We hope that someday you will be able to meet our daughter, and know that a part of your child still lives."

It was signed Mildred and Lonny Daley, along with their phone number.

Bill slowly lowered the letter and sobbed.

The elevator bell rang. Bob stepped out and passed two employees who greeted him. He didn't reply. He didn't even hear them. He walked past the large glass walled room that enclosed the mainframe computers and network gear for the brains of CDC Data Processing. He continued down the hall and into Alice's office. "Where are we with Maskill's, Alice?"

Alice wasn't fazed by his abruptness, and turned to her employee setting in front of her desk. "Would you excuse us, please?" Bob didn't care that he interrupted a performance review. He was focused and needed answers.

"Certainly." The man stood and left the office.

"We are at 1,863. All in the North American continent with a few spattered in other countries." She got her crutches and walked over to the whiteboard and checked off the traits that have been mined. "Different sexes, all ages, ethnicities, health conditions. Excluding those factors, no commonalities above 6% except that the cause of death . . . ."

Bob finished her sentence. " . . . . was multiple aneurysms located in the Primary Auditory Cortex and lateral Sulcus of the brain."

"Correct. We are gathering more data from non-domestic agencies as we speak. That will take time. So far, it appears 'centralized' to some degree to the North American continent, primarily the West Coast. There is no clear geographic centralization of events. There are a few small clusters beginning to take shape." She continued checking off the white board. "Tox is clear, bacterial, viral are all clear."

"Time frame?"

Alice looked at him. "One hundred and twelve days." She knew the significance of what she was saying. "At his rate, for a new disease, we could be looking at ten thousand deaths in no time."

Bob sat in the chair in disbelief. His thoughts started to run wild. His heart started to beat rapidly. After all of these years he knew one day he may be confronted with a true pandemic; something that would shake his world. This could be it. He was going to be tested, and he was scared. He had to stay in control and continue to lead.

Alice continued. "If the disease has a contagion, it would accelerate. However, we are not finding any evidence of that through the data thus far. Any disease will reach maturity and saturation, but at what point we have no idea. Not right now at least."

"Who knows what the saturation level is? This could be another AIDS scenario." He leaned forward in his chair and clasped his hands. "We just don't know." He looked at Alice. "And there is nothing that you can find through the data you have thus far?"

"Nothing."

Bob paused as he formulated his thoughts. He knew they needed more medical information. What they had just wasn't telling the story. "OK. We need to get all of the chart notes and medical records, if possible, in digital format. I know you can prepare a conversion program if someone isn't up to the standard. I'll order autopsies on any cases that we can, and . . . ." Bob paused for a second. "I'm going to bring in genetic analysis and see if there is any commonality there. That was the original cause of Maskill's, maybe it's the cause of death."

"I think you should. We need to look at everything. I assigned most of my staff on this project a few hours ago."

"OK. If you find anything, anything of importance, I want to be updated immediately. Email it to me." He stood and started for the door.

Alice stopped him with her crutch. "I will. Did Randall get the bulletin out?"

"Yeah. He sent it about an hour ago. You should be getting information any time."

"I'll check with my staff and see if they have anything coming in yet. I think it is just going to grow, and we need to be prepared to track it accordingly." Alice pulled her crutch back and dialed her secretary as Bob walked out.

It was 10 A.M. and time to get to work, or so Bruce thought. He had already spent half a day reading the paper, getting his workout, checking the markets to see that his stock was still rising, ate breakfast, and even washed the car. Oh, the joys of an early riser.

Bruce settled in at his desk as he did every morning and started scanning his email and listened to his voice mail messages. The firewall they installed was able to screen most of the spam and junk email and send the important ones to his email account. Bruce read through the titles and mentally prioritized them as he scanned them. He made a few notes from the voice mail messages. He came across a bulletin from the Center for Disease Control, and opened it.

> From: Randall Sterling, Deputy Director—Infectious Diseases
> Center for Disease Control
> Atlanta, Georgia
>
> Topic: Maskill's Seizures
>
> Bruce turned off the phone and leaned closer to the screen.
>
> "The CDC believes that a serious issue is forming regarding Maskill's Seizures. In the past 65 days, more than 1,000 patients have died while suffering from a Maskill's seizure."

"What the . . . ?" Bruce couldn't believe what he was reading. He continued.

> "They died from multiple aneurysms located in the Primary Auditory Cortex and lateral Sulcus of the brain. The patients are primarily in North America. We are reviewing information from other countries as we expand our research and investigation. At present, the CDC

requests that any information or knowledge that you have had, or may have, regarding abnormalities associated with Maskill's patients be directed to the following contact person immediately.

Center for Disease Control
Alice Barker—Assistant Director of Data Research
Atlanta Georgia
1600 Clifton Rd
Atlanta Georgia 30333
800.232.4636
alice.barker@cdc.gov

If you have had Maskill's patients die as indicated above, please copy the chart notes and forward them to Ms. Barker immediately."

This is unbelievable, Bruce said quietly to himself. *A thousand?* Bruce picked up the receiver to his phone and dialed Jim's cell phone.

"Jim here."

"Jim, this is Bruce. We have a problem." Bruce was rattled. He was pacing behind his chair.

"Problem?" Jim asked. "We don't have a problem. I'm going on vacation. You can handle . . . ."

"Jim! Listen! I just got a CDC bulletin. A thousand Maskill's patients have died." Bruce was almost shouting into the phone. The sweat was beginning to form on his forehead from the stress.

"Died? Are you sure?"

"Yes, Dammit! You need to get in here right away!" Bruce could feel his blood pressure rising.

"Ok. I'll be there in thirty." Jim hung up. Bruce slammed the headset into the receiver, knocking over the picture of his children.

"This can't be happening. It just can't be." He walked behind his desk and ran his fingers through his hair as he looked out over the river and marina. "What am I gonna do?"

Doctor Carl Kruger was taking a break from his research at the John Hopkins Institute for Cell Engineering, or ICE. A relatively new concept in medicine, ICE supports and houses scientists working to understand how cells' fates are determined and to harness that information in order to select, modify and reprogram human cells. Dr. Kruger was working with Doctor Alfred Haley in the Neurology and Center for Epilepsy Research to analyze seizure patients and explore gene therapy. Using genome-wide linkage analysis in consanguineous families, they mapped the chromosome 19Q13.33 and identified multiple mutations in PNKP gene that resulted in severe neurological disease. Their hypothesis was that varying mutations would correlate to varying neurological dysfunctions. Their work was the product of the foundational research that Doctor Everett Maskill started almost a decade before.

Dr. Kruger laid his marker in the tray of the white board and seated himself at his desk. At six foot four and 265 pounds, he was a big African American man. He played college football and was built like a linebacker with broad shoulders and big hands. He was in his late forties and had a shaved head and a Van Dyke beard. He opened a soda and leaned back while he checked his email messages. He scanned through the numerous items, until he came to the CDC notice.

"Maskill's, huh?" Dr. Kruger was very well versed on Maskill's. After all, it was discovered by Doctor Maskill who worked at John Hopkins before joining Biotrogen. Doctor Kruger studied Maskill's, one of several diseases, with his colleagues in the Neurology Department. The onset of the seizure, affected areas of the brain, and subsequent recovery was worth studying. Since Maskill's also had a cure in place, and the disease was not deadly, the reviews were mostly cursory. There was little need to explore additional cures. Their focus was on the deadly diseases for which John Hopkins could easily secure funding. Maskill's was benign. Until now.

Dr. Kruger dialed the number in the email.

"Center for Disease Control. May I help you?" The lady's voice was pleasant and professional.

"Ms. Alice Barker, Please." He pulled some documents from his desk and laid them in front of him.

"May I tell her who is calling?"

"Certainly. Dr. Carl Kruger from John Hopkins Institute for Cell Engineering regarding the Maskill's alert." He made a few notes on one of the documents in front of him.

"One moment please." Some music came on the line for a few seconds, then Alice answered.

"Alice Barker here. Doctor Kruger?" she asked.

"Yes. Carl Kruger from John Hopkins. Please call me Carl." He wanted to make the call as relaxed as possible. His deep voice was soothing.

"And please call me Alice. I don't believe we have met?"

"No, we have not. I am calling because of the CDC bulletin that went out today regarding Maskill's Seizures."

"Yes?" Her interest was heightened. She leaned forward in her chair. John Hopkins was one of the foremost medical research institutes in the world. For someone to be calling means they likely have valuable information, and she wanted to know what it was. "What can I do for you?"

"I think it is what I may be able to do for you," he began. "I have been conducting extensive research on chromosomes that lead to neurological disorders similar to the symptoms and characteristics of Maskill's. I would like to discuss my research with you in case it opens some doors to possible reasons for the change in the disease."

"Your call is very timely, doctor. We are moving into analysis of autopsy samples to determine if there is a link amongst the victims. This is a serious matter, and, to be very honest, I don't have a lot of time to run through normal protocols."

"I'm not sure I know what you mean?" he asked.

"What I mean is I would be very interested in discussing your research . . . . here, in Atlanta." Alice was one to get right to the point.

"Atlanta?" The doctor was taken aback by the request.

"Yes. Can you fly out here this evening? CDC will cover the cost." Alice knew that getting a member of John Hopkins ICE on their team, particularly one who is studying neurological disorders associated to genetics would be invaluable. She also knew that Bob and Randall would have no problem with her taking the lead and approving his travel.

"Uh . . . . Yes. I suppose I can." He was surprised, but eager to work with CDC on this project.

"Doctor, this is serious. I know John Hopkins has the best research scientists and professionals in the world. And if you are already versed in genetics and neurology, I don't see any reason to beat around the bush. If it doesn't work, we can just fly you back. Right now, time is our enemy, and we have to hit this running." Alice knew she had him reeled in, and he would be a good catch.

"I will see when the flights are to Atlanta and catch the next one." He reached over to get his briefcase while he was still on the phone. "I'm single, so packing and permission are not an issue," he joked.

"Great. Here's my cell number. 404 555-6101. Call with your flight information and I will make sure someone picks you up." Alice was making notes on the call. She was preparing to meet with Bob and inform him of her coup.

"Fine. I will see you soon," he said.

"Looking forward to it."

Bruce was pacing by the windows as Jim rushed into his office and slammed the door. "Tell me that was a joke, Bruce."

Bruce looked at him with fear in his eyes. "Sorry, it's no joke," he said. "We have a serious problem. Look at this email from CDC." He pointed to the monitor on the desk. Jim sat down to read the email. As he read through it, he slowly leaned forward, put his head in his hands. "What are we . . . I . . . I . . . ." He couldn't finish a sentence, His mind was racing a thousand miles an hour, thinking of the sprays, the purchases, sales, medicine . . . all the pieces of the empire ready to fall like a house of cards.

"Jim." Bruce grabbed his shoulder. "We have to figure this out."

"Figure it out!!!" Jim shouted. "Are you kidding me? Figure it out!!!?" He threw Bruce's hand off his shoulder and jumped to his feet. He started pacing about the room like a caged animal. "I'll figure this out for ya. We're going to prison! That's what's going to happen!! Prison. For manslaughter!!" Jim was breaking out into a sweat as he kept pacing. He couldn't sit still. "Oh God. Oh God." He was running his hands through his hair and then shaking them and opening and closing his fists, like he was trying to get the blood flowing again.

"Would you shut up!!" Bruce yelled at him as he slammed his fist on the desk. "Get control of yourself!"

Jim stopped and looked at Bruce for a second. Suddenly, he reached over, grabbed the wastebasket and threw up.

The mall was hopping. There were people everywhere. Maybe it was because it was a Friday near the first of the month. Or that it was just before spring break. Or maybe people just wanted to get out and enjoy the weather.

Whatever the reason, Leslie was thoroughly enjoying her mini shopping spree for new clothes for her new job. She just finished her class and wanted to get a few things so she would look professional, but comfortable. Besides, it was a good excuse to shop.

She knew she would be involved with projects, files, and running errands, stuff like that. But her first day would be orientation. Then, after who knows how long, she would start working on really cool stuff. She was excited about the possibilities, and the chance to work at Biotrogen. Especially since they were willing to adjust her work schedule to accommodate her education.

Leslie held up a blouse and looked in the mirror. "Well, Miss Biotrogen girl," she giggled. "You rock in that."

A young man shopping for his girlfriend glanced at her as he walked by and crashed into a stand of clothes. Several skirts fell to the ground as the stand nearly tipped over. Leslie laughed at the site, and was very pleased she could turn a man's head so easily.

"This will most definitely do." She laid the blouse over her arm, and continued shopping.

"Are you OK now?" Bruce was perturbed about Jim's inability to handle pressure. He was always that way, and now when he needed him the most, he was afraid he would have a melt down and be totally worthless.

Bruce was different. The initial shock hit him like most people, but soon he was able to compose himself and tackle the situation. He did it in Iraq under fire. He did it in the auto accident. He could do it now. "We need to keep our heads straight and figure out what to do."

Jim was still nauseated and scared. "Bruce, what can we possibly do? We're killing people!"

"Stop right there." Bruce pointed his finger to shut him down immediately. "We are killing no one."

Jim was incredulous. "How can you say that? How can you possibly say that?"

"Jim, listen to me." Bruce took control as he always did. "We don't <u>know</u> why these people are dying. We believe it could be associated to Maskill's, but we really don't know if it is, or if there is a change in their body that conflicts with Tegbatol or Inferon, or something else causing the aneurysms. The bottom line is . . . . we don't know why they are dying." Jim was struggling to believe what Bruce was saying.

Bruce sat down in his chair and continued. "Let's start with what we <u>do</u> know and work from there."

Jim interrupted. "You make this sound so damned simple, like it's another experiment or something. People are dying, and I believe we are the cause of it. How can you take this so nonchalantly?"

"Noncha . . . are you crazy?" Bruce jumped to his feet. "I'm agonizing over this too, buddy. But going crazy and saying, 'Oh God.. Oh God' while rocking back and forth and puking in a trash can won't accomplish SQUAT!!" Bruce turned his back on his partner and ran his hands over his head while he looked out the window. He took a deep breath. Jim was downcast, embarrassed, scared. "Listen, Jim. We are scientists." Bruce turned back toward Jim. "We need to figure out what we know, generate hypothesis about what we assume, and test the theories. We have to try and work through this dilemma in an educated, controlled way. Otherwise . . . . ," he paused. " . . . we may as well just turn ourselves in, assume responsibility and suffer the consequences, even though we don't really know." Bruce paused. "And <u>that</u>, my friend, would be stupid."

"I . . . I don't know if I can. I . . . . I . . . ." Jim paused. "I guess we have to."

"What other choice do we have right now? The longer we take to start working on this, the more serious it becomes. If we can find the cause, I expect we can find a new cure." Bruce started to show signs of confidence.

Jim didn't. "Everett was the brains of this, you know. He was working at the molecular level, Bruce. The molecular level! We aren't even close to that. How are we going to analyze something that we don't have the capabilities to do so?"

"I don't know. Believe me, I'm with you on that. Everett was brilliant, no doubt. He created everything here. But we have to try. Let's start with the basics. Let's start with what we know. Let's work on the pieces that we can address." Jim was ambivalent as Bruce walked to the whiteboard, stopped, and turned back to him. "Can you lock the door? I want to make sure no one accidentally walks in on us."

Jim locked the door, and joined Bruce at the whiteboard.

Bruce continued. "Everett created the chemical to alter the wheat gene. The mutation occurs at the time of germination. The chemical breaks down as the wheat matures and is not identifiable after two months. Only the mutation of the wheat is detectible through genetic analysis." Bruce was writing keys words frantically as he spoke.

"That's somewhat of a relief." Jim continued the process. "The mutated wheat gene is absorbed into the body through ingestion, regardless of processing."

"Right," Bruce agreed. "The ingestion takes in the altered gene and proteins of the wheat which affects only the 19Q13.33A, a mutated chromosome, by destroying the CC pair in the gene, thus mutating the gene, and the chromosome, again. It works like a silk worm eating a leaf, and then dies." Bruce stopped writing. "What we don't know is <u>how</u> since Everett was the brains behind the alteration of the gene by using the mutated wheat."

"But the issue is the aneurysm of the brain in the general region Maskill's affected." Jim was jumping ahead. "How does this cause that?"

"That's what we don't know, yet. There can only be a change in two things; the wheat, or the gene in the chromosome. We know the chromosome is 19Q13.33A. We know the wheat affects 19Q. One or the other must have changed. We have to find out which one, why, and correct it." Bruce made it sound simple.

"Bruce, there's only two of us to do this, you know. It isn't like we can turn our entire staff lose to research this thing."

"You are wrong there. We can. At least we can on the gene, not the wheat."

Jim was shocked. "We can? How?"

Bruce was kicking into high gear. "Listen. It is known we have the cure for Maskill's. We have the bulletin from CDC informing us of an 'issue' with Maskill's patients. We absolutely can turn all of our resources loose on the chromosome, and will be expected to, without reservation."

"That's right!" Jim suddenly became excited as he saw a possibility of pulling out of this. "We can get some project teams on this first thing Monday."

Bruce continued. "The issue is that we, you and me, have to research the wheat to see if any changes occurred. We have to be extremely discreet with what we find if the wheat is the cause." Bruce started to see a possibility they might get out of this unscathed. "And we might have an answer to this nightmare, and how to correct it, very soon." Bruce smiled. "We might even create a new 'cure' and make even more money off this."

"Yeah! Plus save some lives," Jim replied.

For a moment, the two men forgot that people were dying and, instead, were focused on the new project and challenge at hand. They continued to discuss their plans and assignments. They were, once again, partners, working together like they had before when they created this nightmare. Now, they were working just as diligently to put it to rest.

The plane landed smoothly and on time. "Welcome to Atlanta International Airport. The local time is 7:10 P.M. The weather is partly cloudy, temperature forty-nine degrees."

Doctor Kruger wasn't listening to the flight attendant. He pulled his phone from his coat pocket and dialed Alice Barker. "Ms. Barker. This is Carl Kruger from John Hopkins."

"Yes, Doctor. Have you arrived in Atlanta?"

"I have," came the reply. "I am at the gate preparing to deplane."

"Excellent. Do you have checked luggage?"

"No, just my carry on."

"Great. What airlines did you use?"

"US Airways."

"OK. I'll have someone in front of the terminal in twenty minutes. Are you wearing or carrying something to identify you from the crowd?" She wanted to make sure it would be easy to identify him.

"Sure. I am six foot four, black, with a shaved head and goatee beard. I should be easy to spot," he chuckled.

"I suppose so. They will be there shortly . . . . Uh.. I mean . . . not shortly . . . ." Alice seldom became embarrassed by anything. But, for some reason, she was by that statement.

"Yes, shortly." Carl laughed out loud. His deep laugh echoed in the phone. "I like it."

Alice laughed. "I will have them take you to your hotel where you can settle in. I'll have someone pick you up at six in the morning."

Carl could hear the authority in Alice's voice. He didn't have a choice. "Sounds great. Six. Looking forward to meeting you."

"And I, you." Alice smiled as she placed the receiver in the cradle, wondering what he looked like. If his voice was any indication . . . .

CHAPTER 8

Saturday April 16
Deaths 2,455

It was cold and raining as Leslie got out of her car and entered the Biotrogen headquarters. *I can't believe I'm up, dressed, and miserable, and it's not even seven,* she thought. No one would have known she was tired, grumpy, and cold. She was ready for her first day on the job, so she had to put on a show, even though she was almost exhausted.

"Good morning, Miss." The older gentleman setting at the guard station, also known as 'Reception,' greeted her with a smile. "May I help you?"

"Yes. I'm Leslie Singer. I'm a new employee and was asked to be here by seven."

"Ms. Singer. Yes. Please have a seat over there while I call HR." He was already dialing as she sat in the leather chair near the window, and watched it rain.

"Doctor?" The nurse was trying to get the doctor's attention. "Doctor?"

Alan Gobel was dazed. He stood staring at the patient lying in the bed. She was an older woman in her late seventies. Her grey hair was matted, uncombed. She was thin. The wrinkles on her face showed her age. She was wearing red pajamas decorated with Scotty dogs. Her finger nails were recently manicured. *I bet she just had her nails done,* he thought. A small amount of blood was pooled on the pillow near her left ear. Blood was smeared around the mouth area where the ventilator had been connected. Her eyes were closed, almost as if she was sleeping. Another Maskill's death. That made four more this week.

The nurse raised her voice. "Doctor!"

"Uh . . . yes, nurse." Doctor Gobel looked at the clock. "Time of death, 07:13." The nurse handed him a clip board and he signed the document. The attendants were covering the body and disconnecting the machines. "Leave her here while I contact Grace. I need to see if we are going to do an autopsy."

"Yes, doctor." The nurse and aids continued to clean up and prepare the body as Doctor Gobel walked out of the room.

The room was abuzz with people. There were donuts and rolls in a large box on the side table with three pots of coffee and hot water. The whiteboard had a myriad of diagrams and phrases etched across it. People were scattered about the room discussing several topics of the day. Alice and Bob were in a deep discussion with two other CDC employees when Carl Kruger walked in. "Um. Excuse me?"

"Oh, you must be Doctor Kruger. I'm Alice Barker." Alice hobbled across the room and extended her hand to greet the doctor. She had a warm smile. "You look just like I imagined, Doctor. Welcome to managed chaos," she chuckled.

Doctor Kruger was slightly taken aback by Alice's condition, but it lasted about one second. Her smile and confidence eroded any beliefs he may have had about her disability. "Thank you, Miss Barker. A pleasure to meet you," he said as he bowed very slightly, his voice mesmerizing.

Alice turned to the group of people to introduce the Doctor. "Folks, please. May I have your attention for a moment?" Everyone turned toward the couple. "This is Dr. Carl Kruger from John Hopkins Institute for Cell Engineering. He is going to be a part of our team researching the genetic attributes of the disease. Please welcome him."

The group gave a small applause and gradually returned to their conversations and tasks. Several stepped forward immediately to greet him. Bob Struthers was the first. "Doctor Kruger, I'm Bob Struthers, Assistant Director of the National Center for Emerging and Zoonotic Infectious Disease . . ." He turned to Alice who was smiling and had her arms spread out like she caught a big fish, and continued. " . . . and leader on this project. Welcome."

Alice nudged Carl. "Pretty impressive title, isn't it?"

Carl smiled and reached out to shake Bob's hand. "Thank you. I appreciate the welcome, but, to be honest, I'm not sure where to begin?

I feel a bit lost in this type of situation. I'm not used to time sensitive research."

"I understand. This is extremely time sensitive. Let's start with a briefing on what we know and develop some actions from there." After Doctor Kruger met several people, Bob escorted him to the whiteboard to review the critical pieces of information as a summary.

Alice and the others gathered around the board and let Bob lead the presentation. "The situation is that Maskill's patients are suffering multiple aneurysms located in the Primary Auditory Cortex and lateral Sulcus of the brain resulting in death."

"Is that the only location of the aneurysms?"

"Yes. This is consistent with every death thus far."

"How many, may I ask?"

Bob paused and looked at Alice. "Just over three thousand," he said.

Doctor Kruger was shocked. "Three thousand? You mean the number has tripled from your bulletin?"

Alice jumped in. "There were just over a thousand when we sent the bulletin. Additional information came in to our mining operation and yesterday we added just over two thousand. As we continue to receive data from around the world, the number has grown, now to more than three thousand. I suspect we have a pretty accurate count of the number of victims thus far. At this point, increases will primarily be new cases and not updates."

"Are reports coming just from hospitals?"

Alice was confused. "Why do you ask, doctor?"

"If victims have died at home, and are older, and the deaths were instant or masked with another illness, then the cause of death could be construed as natural, such as a stroke. They may have been transported directly to the funeral home and not passed through the medical field."

"That's a good point, doctor," Alice agreed.

"We need to send a bulletin to the mortuaries as well, then." Bob looked to an assistant standing next to him who jotted the information on a notepad.

"What time frame are we talking about?" Carl asked.

Alice answered, "One hundred and twenty-six days. We believe this is very near the origination point of the first death. Our time frame has continued to change, but now incrementally."

"Alice's team has done a fantastic job of determining origination time and spread of the disease in just a couple of days," Bob confirmed. "We believe we have it narrowed down to about four months."

"Much of this is standard, doctor, when we encounter a situation like this." Alice politely reminded him that this is what they do, and they do it well. "The big difference here is the escalation of time. We are getting results at a much faster clip than in past cases, because of the urgency and interconnected networks."

"We can be thankful for that, Ms. Barker." Doctor Kruger was impressed with Alice's knowledge, confidence, and intelligence. She was a woman he was easily attracted to, and she to him. "So, nothing to show cause, including foreign influences."

"No," Bob replied. "Tox is clear, bacterial, viral are all clear. It does not appear to be promulgated from a contagion. We have ordered autopsies of victims where allowed. We are receiving records of the results as we speak, and tissue samples of the brain later today."

"Have you ordered a full sampling of fluids?" Carl asked.

"Yes," Bob replied.

"What about the Tegbatol and Inferon combination treatment? Any indication either of them could be the cause?" Carl asked.

No," Bob responded. "Some patients were not on the treatment. We want to discuss with you about leading a team to research genetic aspects of the samples. That was why Alice jumped at the chance to have you on our team. With the resources of CDC and our partners, and your experience with ICE and the 19Q chromosome, we believe you will be able to accelerate analysis of the samples and identify any abnormal genetic influences in the victims."

"If there are any," Doctor Kruger added.

"The only commonality that we see is geographical location, to some degree," Alice interjected.

Carl was surprised. "Geographic?"

"Yes," she continued. "The victims appear to be 'centralized' to the North American continent, mostly on the West Coast. There are a few small but dense clusters in Oregon, Washington, and California. At first we didn't think this was anything significant, but as we add more cases, the densities increased."

"Have you found any correlation?" Carl asked.

""No," Bob replied. "Not yet. If there is one, Alice's team will find it." Alice smiled.

Carl smiled. "I believe they will."

"Okay. Alice, if you can introduce Doctor Kruger to some of the other teammates and show him where his lab is. It will take him some time to get oriented to our operation and settle in."

"Sure."

"Good. I'd like to get my feet on the ground before some of the samples arrive," Doctor Kruger confirmed.

"Right this way." Alice took his arm. "May I?"

Doctor Kruger looked at his arm with Alice holding on, and smiled. "Love to." He was surprised by her forwardness, and attracted to her charm.

She escorted him to another group of employees across the room using one crutch and his arm. He was strong, and the little weight she required to stabilize her was hardly noticed by the big man who towered more than two feet above her. They looked more like a couple on a date than scientists trying to find the cause of a deadly disease that was killing people at an alarming rate.

The microscopes were lined up on the tables near the centrifuges. Petri dishes were scattered along the long counter. Vials, beakers, papers, files, and reports were strewn about. Paper coffee cups were sprinkled throughout the area. It didn't look like the pristine bio-research lab that it had once been. It looked like someone had burglarized the place and didn't find what they were looking for.

And they didn't.

They were in the genetic research lab of Biotrogen digging through boxes of records, viewing samples, comparing reports, and trying to find out if there was a noticeable change in the wheat gene. They had gone through boxes and boxes extracting the wheat kernels that had been stored for so long. They had to methodically go back in time and check one kernel from every harvest. It was grueling work fit for a peon, not for the owners of a successful biomedical genetic company. Not at all.

Except today. Today, they were the instruments of death. And they wanted it to stop.

One of the demands that Everett established when he discovered how to modify the wheat gene to affect the 19Q chromosome was for them to keep samples of the kernels from every wheat harvest from that time forward. It was a huge task requiring contacting all of the growers and processors and intercepting a small sample of the harvest. When you are dealing with twenty plus small farms over a wide geographic area, it is an extreme effort.

At the time, Bruce and Jim felt it was odd, eccentric, and unnecessary. After all, the cure was established, the product worked, and they saw no reason to store kernels from every harvest.

Now they do.

"I can't believe Everett had the foresight to know that someday we may have a reason to test all of this wheat," Jim said. "I would have thrown it out, or just kept a few samples. Not every one. I think we just got lucky."

Bruce was peering into a microscope focused on his task. "I don't."

"What do you mean?" asked Jim working at the centrifuge.

Bruce took a deep breath and pulled away from the microscope. "I think he knew something like this could happen."

"Are you kidding?"

"No, I'm not." Bruce put his glasses back on and continued. "When you're dealing with the molecular structure of a cell, and alter it in a way that causes the molecular structure of a recipient cell to change, I think the possibilities for an unplanned negative event increase. And I think Everett knew it."

"An unplanned negative event? Is that what this is?" Jim asked, almost jokingly.

"Yes, without a doubt." Bruce was very serious. "What would you call it?" he asked. His stern look caused Jim to shrink away and turn toward his work.

"I don't know. I just want to find the cause and stop it. That's all. I just want to be done with this whole thing." Jim was frustrated and scared. "I don't want to go to prison."

"There's worse things than prison," Bruce mumbled, but Jim didn't hear him. Bruce walked over to the printer attached to the DNA analyzer and read the report that was coming out. He turned to the whiteboard and checked off another sample identifier and date associated to it. "19B 20100312—negative," he said.

Jim set his slide down and turned to Bruce. "We've only gone through five percent of the samples so far. We don't even have all of the samples from the last two harvests in yet. This is going to take a month," he whined.

"It might. But what choice do we have? It has to be done, and we are the only ones who can do it." Bruce could sense Jim's near exhaustion. "OK. Let's take a break. How about if we take two hours off and get back to it later?"

"I could use some rest. I think we both could use some, otherwise, we'll start making mistakes," Jim said.

Bruce looked at Jim with a snicker. "Yeah, we don't want to make any mistakes," he said. *We already made enough to last a lifetime*, he thought.

Alan Gobel and Grace Moore were setting in Grace's office. The director of Pathology, Howard Allbright, was with them. He was a young man, thirty seven to be exact. He was a brilliant, ambitious doctor. He graduated high school when he was fourteen, college with a Masters at eighteen. He was one of the youngest graduates from South Carolina University in Medicine at the age of twenty-three. He did his residency in pathology at Harvard School of Medicine, and became a doctor of Pathology at twenty-nine. His southern drawl was slight, but combined with his intelligence and command of the English language he captured his audiences.

Doctor Allbright was leaning back in the stuffed chair with his legs crossed. "There is a high probability that we have more deaths than what is currently represented."

"How so," Alan asked?

"The nature of the symptoms suggests other victims could have succumbed to this disease but been classified under a different cause of death, such as a stroke. I believe the issue is to accurately assess whether a patient is truly a Maskill's victim or not."

"I agree," Grace said. "I think we need to research each patient's death and anyone with any type of stroke, aneurysm, or seizure needs to have further testing for Maskill's associations."

Alan was troubled. "How far do you want to take the testing, Grace? You know there's only so much we can do without proper authorization or release."

Howard raised his hand. "I can answer that. The primary indicator of Maskill's type deaths is the aneurysm in the brain in the audio cortex.

A simple MRI will reveal that. It is the perfect non-invasive test." He reached over and grabbed a piece of candy from the dish.

Alice was thinking. "OK. Let's test every patient we have in the morgue." She looked to Howard. "How many are there and how long will it take?"

The doctor didn't hesitate. "Twenty-eight and four days."

"OK. By Thursday we will know what we are really working with here." Grace knew Howard well enough to know that was absolutely the fastest turn around time he could guarantee. She also knew that if he said it, it would happen.

"Yes we will," assured Howard.

CHAPTER 9

Monday April 18
Deaths 3,162

Bob was setting at the table reviewing the results of some tests he recently received from his analysts when Alice walked in. "We have the results of the autopsies, Bob." Leon Alford, Chief of Pathology was with her. They had several binders in their arms as they walked to the table and laid them down. "My team worked non-stop through the weekend. It isn't a huge success, but we have something to start with," she said.

"What is that?" Bob asked as he pushed some papers to the side.

Leon answered. "It's genetics, Bob."

"Of course it's genetics. We knew the 19Q chromosome was part of this from the beginning. How is that any different?' Bob was becoming upset at the cause the Chief of Pathology proposed. As Director of his division, he expected more from every person working on the team. The flippant manner Leon answered angered Bob.

"Because nothing else is the answer."

"What? What do you mean? We don't have time to play games here."

Leon raised his hands to motion to Bob to settle down and continued. "Process of elimination, Bob. We had samples from seventeen victims to initially work from. We ran through everything over the past forty hours, non-stop. Absolutely everything. There is nothing there, Bob. Nothing. Therefore, it has to be genetics."

"It seems like that is a premature assessment of possible causal factors, Leon. We need more evidence before we jump to a conclusion like that. We can't take action on a deduction." The idea of Bob going to Randall with this as evidence was ludicrous. Bob was more than a little perturbed by Leon's quick conclusion.

"I don't agree," Alice jumped in. "Bob, we have a situation that is serious, and the potential is unknown. Leon and his team have reviewed the tissue samples for everything and nothing is there other than what we already know; genetics. We can keep analyzing samples and running the data we receive, but so far everything, from the information abroad to our own pathology, suggests there is no other cause other than genetics."

Bob took a deep breath and looked at Leon and Alice, whom he well respected. He knew they did not take this lightly. The stress of the situation was beginning to wear on him. Each day they delayed, people died. He wanted an answer, and he wanted it now. It felt like he was making no progress. And now, to move forward based on a deduction seemed ridiculous. It would be so much easier if something other than genetics was the cause for this significant change in Maskill's patients. The truth was the longer they delayed with identifying the cause, the longer it would take to address a cure, and more people would die. Bob hated that.

"Ok, then. I need to move this up to the next level. Continue to run analysis on the data and the samples. I'm going to talk with Doctor Kruger to see how we can expedite his research and see if genetics are the cause."

Doctor Carl Kruger was right at home here. The bank of equipment that enabled him to view into the inner cell workings of his samples was remarkable. It was expensive, first class equipment. It rivaled John Hopkins research institute for sure. Of course, the government has unlimited funds and can pool their money where they choose, not like JH.

CDC provided him with a small team of analysts to prep and process the myriads of tissues coming into the facility. Their assignment was to analyze the samples and determine if any genetic mutation was the cause of the new disease. This type of research could take months, even years. It was painstakingly detailed. They had been at it for two days, working around the clock in shifts, and have made little progress. His preliminary research with the 19Q chromosome expedited many of their tasks. His team at ICE shipped his reports and samples yesterday. He should be receiving them first thing this morning. They will aid with comparative analysis of the current chromosomal structures of the victims compared to his prior research. Any changes should be glaring and soon discovered.

So he hoped.

Carl was not a gambler. He used all of the resources available and didn't rely on one process or outcome. He was methodical and deliberate in his actions. That was why he was in total agreement when Bob called to suggest he contact Biotrogen and use their research information to expedite his analysis of the 19Q chromosome. After all, they created a cure to suppress the effects of the gene and eliminate symptoms. Who better than to have them be a part of his research?

Carl also knew that the scientist accredited with the discovery, Everett Maskill, was dead. Many in the medical field, particularly those in epilepsy and genetic research knew it. But the information that he had amassed through his research prior to his death could be extremely valuable to this project.

Bruce answered the call transferred to him by his secretary. He knew it was a doctor from John Hopkins. "This is Bruce Lowell." His voice was strong and emphatic.

Carl introduced himself. "Mr. Lowell. I am Doctor Carl Kruger from the John Hopkins Institute for Cell Engineering."

"Yes, Doctor Kruger." Bruce stopped fiddling with the papers on his desk and gave full attention to the call. The Institute for Cell Engineering at John Hopkins was a well known research entity in the field of genetics, and very well respected. "To what do I owe the pleasure?"

"I am temporarily on assignment with the Center for Disease Control in Atlanta. I am working with them on the Maskill's events that recently surfaced."

Bruce's stomach turned into a knot. He thought he was going to vomit. He had to control himself. He took a deep breath to calm himself down. Maybe it was just a question, a courtesy call. "Yes. I read the notice from the CDC. What can I do for you?"

"I would like to know if we can meet to go over some of your information on the 19Q chromosome and Maskill's seizures."

A small bead of sweat formed over Bruce's eyebrow. He wiped it away. "Certainly. I would be happy to provide what I can. Unfortunately, since Doctor Maskill's death, we haven't made much more progress in our research. It almost came to a standstill."

"Yes, I understand. However, I believe your information, combined with my prior research, and the present tissue samples of the victims, will enable us to rule out any genetic mutation of the chromosome as a cause for these events. Is there any way that we can have access to your research material on Maskill's?"

"Uh . . . certainly, doctor." Bruce hesitated. He was searching for the right words. "I'm not sure how to facilitate that request, though. You are in Atlanta; we are in Sacramento. There's quite a distance between us."

"I understand. I'm sure you have much of your research and information in digital format. You can just transmit that to us."

"We do. The analysis that followed the initial discovery and mapping is all digitized. The records are very detailed. I am quite sure they will be of great help." Bruce sounded eager to assist with the research.

"Well, that's fine. Fine." Carl paused. "But what I really need is the discovery data."

Bruce's stomach fell. "Discovery data?" Bruce could feel his heart rate rise rapidly. He didn't have time to think of a good reason why they couldn't see the data pertaining to the discovery of Maskill's, other than he didn't want them snooping around their creation. He knew he wouldn't be able to allow them access to the documents because they would show how they experimented with various wheat genes to alter the 19Q chromosome and thereby develop Maskill's Seizures. They created the seizures; how could he possibly allow them access to the information that revealed it? His blood pressure spiked and he could hear ringing in his ears as little white dots started to float across his vision. He thought he was going to pass out.

"Mr. Lowell?"

"Hm? Oh, yes, sorry." Bruce shook his head and regained some composer. "Someone interrupted me."

"Oh. Well, how can we gain access to the discovery data on Maskill's?" Doctor Kruger saw no harm with asking for the information. Often in the field of genetic research, scientists share information in the hopes of advancing research toward a common good. What could be more of a common good than stopping this disease?

"Is there someone that you could send here? We could provide them with the information for your research and access to our facilities." Bruce couldn't believe he was saying this.

"Yes, there is. Let me check with our team and see who we can send out. I expect they will be there tomorrow. Is that OK?"

"That is pretty short notice. I'd like to gather the information for you, and have time to review some of the critical components with your team. I'm booked tomorrow, gone Wednesday. How about first thing Thursday?" Bruce was buying precious time. He knew he needed time to figure this out. But he didn't know what he was going to do.

"Yes. Thursday it is. In the meantime," Carl continued, "if you could send the digitized records of your research to me, I would deeply appreciate it."

"Yes, Yes I will. If you could wait while I get my secretary on the line to get the secure FTP[3] instructions from you."

"Sure."

Bruce punched the hold button and slammed his fist on the desk. "Ugghhh." He couldn't even think of the right cuss word to say. He took a deep breath and pushed away from his desk. He kicked the trash can out of his way as he walked around his desk to the door to get his secretary.

Jim was reading the printout of the gene analysis of the latest batch of wheat when Bruce walked in.

"Jim, we have a problem."

"Don't I know," he snipped.

Bruce ignored his remark. "CDC is sending a team here to review our discovery files on Maskill's."

Jim stopped what he was doing and looked at Bruce. "Discovery files? Are you kidding me?"

"I wished I was. They'll be here Thursday." Bruce started pacing toward the window and back. "Two days! Two days to cover our asses." He looked at Jim. "We need to make sure all of the data that ties the wheat and 19Q together is destroyed."

"We can't destroy that, Bruce. What if that is the only answer to how to fix this mess? We'd be putting countless more lives at risk," Jim pleaded.

---

[3] File Transfer Protocol—a secure way to transmit large files over the Internet from one server to another.

"Right now I'm only concerned with one life and that's mine!" Bruce wasn't timid about watching out for himself. "If this gets out, we will certainly be charged with some pretty serious crimes, partner, and I'm sure you don't want to see that happen."

"No one does, Bruce. But this just doesn't seem like the right thing to do."

"Right thing. Right thing. So what is the right thing? Turn ourselves in, say we're sorry, go to jail, do not pass go?" It was easy for Bruce to be cynical. "There is no right thing here beyond self preservation. Unless you have a better idea."

"Run."

"Run!?" Bruce laughed. "As I said, self preservation." He mocked Jim again through his laughter. "Run where? You don't think they'd catch up to us?"

"I don't know. I don't know anything anymore. This is just too screwed up. I don't know what to do." Jim was lost.

"I'll tell you what to do!" Bruce barked. "Make sure the data is separated. That will give us time. Then we can find a way to stop this thing and get back on track."

Jim just stared at Bruce. He bought in. He didn't know what to do, or to say. Deep down he knew it was wrong to try and cover this up. Instead, they should be trying to find a cure. But he didn't want to spend his life in prison, either. Maybe he could get away in a couple of days and eventually work independently of Biotrogen and find the cure. Then he could be a hero and still stay wealthy. He'd go along, but he was hatching his own plan of self preservation, and Bruce didn't need to know. "OK. I'll get right on the wheat files and make sure everything is moved to a safe site."

"Good. Now you're talking." Bruce was pleased with the turn around. "I'll get a team together to pull files for the CDC team. Then, while they are digging through the data, I'll be able to remove any incriminating files or data." Bruce sat down across the table from Jim, and looked him in the eyes. "All we have to do is search everything older than March 2003 and clean it up. That's when Everett discovered the mutation, and the world was on notice. What we did after that is science."

Bruce looked around the room at the piles of boxes, vials, and papers. "We'll have to put the wheat analysis on hold." Bruce looked directly at Jim. "All you have to do is make sure <u>all</u> of the wheat samples are 'secure'."

"I don't like this," Jim replied.

"Neither do I, partner."

CHAPTER 10

Tuesday April 19
Deaths 3,226

Leslie was working in her cubicle gathering the reports off the laser printer. She was checking the pages and patting the edges on the desk top to make nice, neat stacks of reports. She had just spent the last two hours photocopying reports and files for the CDC team per Bruce's instructions. She knew this was an important project, and she was excited to be a part of it.

Bruce was clear with his direction to her; pull all files on research of the 19Q chromosome and bring them into his office for review. Start with the oldest files and work forward. He would pull the appropriate documents, and they would photocopy them for CDC.

The copiers on the third floor of Biotrogen were humming. Leslie had just finished her first box and was wrapping up the reports. Her assignment was to pull the oldest boxes and then photocopy or scan whatever Bruce told her to. The other two analysts were working together pulling the most current boxes for Bruce and preparing his reports for the CDC. Once completed, the boxes and samples were returned to storage. The copied reports were filed in binders and labeled for the CDC. They were stacked in boxes in conference room A for the CDC team.

Bruce sat at the table in his office and scanned the documents from the boxes quickly and efficiently. He knew what he was looking for, but no one else did. And they didn't ask. A small pile of documents were forming a stack on the table in front of him. These were pulled out of the boxes and not returned. Leslie thought it was odd, but she thought Bruce might be pulling the really important stuff for CDC to share with them personally. So, she never gave it a second thought, and she never asked. It wasn't her business.

Bob Struthers stood before the group at CDC. He was their leader, their 'go-to' guy, and had been for years. The room was hushed. He scanned the crowd and looked at the faces of the people, his employees, who had worked day and night through the weekend to find the cause for the Maskill's deaths. They were friends. They were tired, anxious, and scared. So was he. They were talking quietly amongst themselves before the meeting started.

He stood and cleared his throat. "Folks, I need to have your attention. Please."

Instantly, there was no sound.

"I need to inform you that . . . . The Maskill's deaths are accelerating." A couple of people adjusted their positions to get a better view of their leader. "In just one week, we have four hundred and seventeen more deaths from cranial aneurysms associated to Maskill's. We do not believe they are prior deaths and, in fact, are newly reported. These are confirmed, real time deaths."

A couple of people gasped. They understood the implications. That would mean thousands would die. They saw it with AIDS and Ebola, now this.

"We do not have a cause for the change in the Maskill's patients. We have received autopsy information on several victims, and have had our director of pathology review samples of tissues and fluids with no success. We have checked everything from living organisms to materials and chemicals; nothing." A few people leaned over and whispered to their counterparts. "I realize this is troubling because, at present, we have no direction." Bob felt so inadequate saying that. He was their leader and they expected direction. "Our last hope is the genetic research that Doctor Kruger and his team are conducting. We will continue to keep you apprised of any developments. For now, please continue to work your cases and process the information that you have. Double check your findings and, if anything sticks out, I want to know about it right away."

The group dispersed and employees went back to the offices, workstations, and labs throughout the building. "Alice, I want daily updates each morning on the real-time and total death count."

"You've got it," she replied.

"Carl, I need to know about the chromosome. I don't care what we have to do, we need an answer if that is the cause, or at least some indication that it could be the cause other than the process of elimination."

"Of course. We are working through the samples, but have no variances or mutations to confirm. We are also obtaining the original samples and reports on the Maskill's discovery, which may help us isolate discrepancies with current chromosome or gene structures." Carl was confident and organized, and Bob liked that.

"Good. I need to know what you know every hour." Bob looked at the small team in front of him. "Folks, I'm going to discuss this situation with Randall to convince him to contact the FDA to request a cease order be issued for Tegbatol and Inferon. Since we don't know the cause, and the efficacy of the medicines is now questionable, I think we should have them pulled until we sort this out. I may need you when I meet with Randall, so be ready."

The group unanimously agreed.

Bob clapped his hands. "OK. Let's get back to work, then. And let's find out why these people are dying."

The office of the Deputy Director of Infectious Disease for the CDC was impressive. All of the furniture was made of rich cherry wood. A large desk was framed by three large book shelves containing hundreds of volumes of medical literature, reference manuals, and books. The table had four chairs with leather trim surrounding it. The sofa was dark leather with tan pillows. The sun shone through the large windows and reflected off the glass coffee table. Atlanta was beautiful this time of year, and Randall Sterling got to see it every time he looked out the windows.

Randall was a master of government protocol, and a brilliant doctor. He excelled through medical school, his own practice, and into the corporate world of medical research. He joined the CDC eleven years ago and quickly worked his way through the ranks to Deputy Director of Infectious Disease. He knew how to form alliances, to play the politics, and to enroll people in those ventures he deemed significant.

Alice and Bob were setting on the sofa while Randall finished the phone call. "Please hold my calls and appointments for a bit," he said as he pushed away from his desk.

"Yes sir," came the reply.

"OK, Bob. I'm all yours," he said as he sat in the overstuffed chair next to the sofa.

"As I was saying, we have a significant event developing. We know the cause of the deaths is not related to toxins, organisms, or environment. I think we should pull the medicines until we have a clearer picture."

"I agree with Bob, Randall." Alice leaned forward. "If we pull the medicine and nothing changes, it takes another variable out of the picture."

"It may take a variable out, Alice, but it will likely take a company out, too." Randall walked over to the window. "You know one notice can bring a company to its knees, financially."

"I understand, Randall," Bob replied. "But people are dying, the rate is escalating, and we don't know why."

"I don't think that is reason enough," Randall replied. "Unless we can show cause directly related to the medicines, it's a tough sell."

"Randall. We have more than three thousand people dead from a disease that should have zero fatalities." Bob could feel his blood pressure rise. He didn't like it when he knew he was right, but Randall would challenge his position.

Alice could see Bob was getting upset. "We believe they were all Maskill's patients. We know they all died the same way, Randall. Many were on the regimen of medicines. At a minimum we should be able to contest the efficacy of the treatment," Alice suggested.

The room was silent as Randall was pondering Alice's comment. Bob was angry at himself for allowing his emotions to get the best of him. He should have made that statement to Randall; not Alice. "OK. I'll see what I can do." Randall didn't look up as he continued thinking. "I'll call Don at the FDA." He walked over to his desk. "Put a formal request together, showing your concern for efficacy and justification, and I'll run with it. I may call you later for a conference call with Don if he needs an explanation, so be ready."

"Randall," Alice continued. "We also need more information."

Randall turned back to Alice and smiled. "Why does that not surprise me, Alice?" he said cynically.

Alice laughed. "Predictable?" She closed her folder and continued. "Can we send a follow up notice requesting Maskill's patients do testing, and to have any chart notes or files on deceased patients forwarded to us?"

Randall knew why Alice wanted the information. She was trying to establish a base from which to compare changes. You can never have too much information in this field. "I don't think that would be too intrusive if it goes to the medical field and testing is voluntary. I'll see what I can do."

Alice and Bob both stood. "Thanks, Randall," Bob said.

Randall pushed the button on the phone and didn't look up or respond as they exited. "Can you get Don Sinclair for me?"

"Yes sir."

Tuesday, April 19, 2011
From: Randall Sterling, Deputy Director—Infectious Diseases
Center for Disease Control
Atlanta Georgia

Topic: Maskill's Seizures

"The current situation with deaths associated to Maskill's Seizures is intensifying. At present, we have 3,162 reported deaths which occurred in the past four months.

The CDC requests that any person with a current diagnosis of Maskill's be evaluated and tested for changes in vitals, chromosome mutation, or other known abnormalities or symptoms. Please direct your findings to

Center for Disease Control
Maskill's Project
Atlanta Georgia
1600 Clifton Rd
Atlanta Georgia 30333
800.232.4636
ms.project@cdc.gov

If you have had patients die or suffer from an aneurysm in Primary Auditory Cortex and lateral Sulcus the brain, please copy the chart notes and forward them to Leon Alford—Chief of pathology immediately." (leon.alford@cdc.gov)

"May I help you?" The receptionist was polite and courteous, as she should be.

"Yes. I'd like to speak to Richard, please."

"And your name, sir?"

"Jim Anderson." Jim was nervous and anxious to finish this business.

The voice came on the line. "Jim. Good to hear from you." The Investment broker sounded excited to hear from him, though he had rarely ever seen or spoken with him over the years. Jim was a whale, a large account holder with lots of funds in many investments. Each investment earned the broker a nice commission on the size of the portfolio they managed regardless of the activity, and Jim made him a lot of money. "What can I do for you?"

"I'd like to make a withdrawal, Rick. A pretty substantial withdrawal, I might add."

The broker pulled the pen from his shirt pocket and grabbed a notepad. "Sure. How much do you want to withdraw and to whom?"

"Well, I'd like to close my accounts, to be honest." Jim cleared his throat.

The broker froze. "Close?"

"Yes, close."

"Uh, sure. Is there anything wrong?" Rick was surprised by the request.

"No. I'm going to transfer some large amounts to some banks in Europe in anticipation of an extended vacation there. I think I need to take a sabbatical from the business, and I'm considering moving to Europe."

Rick adjusted his seat. "We have branches all over the world . . . ."

"I know," interrupted Jim. "I think it's time for a change for me." He paused to regain composure. "You have done well, and I appreciate it, but I think this is the best move for me at this time in my life. I'd like to close my accounts."

Rick imagined the drop in his income just when one of his kids was starting college. He needed to try and save this account. "What if I put you in touch with our Director of European branches to see which branch . . . ?"

"Rick!." Jim slapped his hand on the desk. Rick could hear the slap on the other end of the call. Jim spoke slowly and purposefully. "Close . . . . my . . . . accounts."

"Uh. Sure." Rick didn't say another word to try and convince him to keep the accounts with the company. He knew Jim had his mind made up. "Cashier's checks or wire transfers?"

"Wire transfers. I will fax you all of the wiring instructions including routing number and account numbers." Jim fiddled with a piece of paper on his desk.

"I see. What about your equities and bonds?"

"Liquidate everything and transfer the funds." Jim was clear and controlled.

"Everything?" The broker stopped typing.

"Yes, everything," Jim replied.

Rick lowered his head and his voice. He felt like he had just been punched in the stomach. "OK. We have some papers to file with the SEC, and it takes three days to settle, so funds should be wired and received by Monday next week. Can you stop in later this morning and sign all of the documents? I need them executed by eleven to make the deadlines."

"Sure. I'll be there at 10:30." And with that, Jim hung up.

Rick sat in his chair and listened to the dial tone as he stared at the phone.

It was 6:30 in the evening. The team had already put in eleven hours of near non-stop work pulling boxes, files, samples, reviewing reports, and copying, copying, copying documents. You could almost picture them feeding a tree into one end of the copier and reams of reports out the other. The boxes of reports were stacked in the corner of the conference room under a handmade sign that read "For CDC."

Bruce told the team to take a break and meet back in one hour to wrap up their work. Everyone went down to the street vendors to grab a bite, chat, and just catch their breath. It was a pleasant spring evening in Sacramento, and the downtown mall was filled with couples strolling the old buildings, restaurants, and clubs. Even Bruce found himself escaping the chaos and stress of his world. The aromas of the restaurants, the music drifting into the streets were soothing to his soul. He stopped at a small, fast-food deli and ordered a broccoli and mushroom quiche with a microbrew beer. He sat outside at the table and watched the people stroll by while he ate his first real meal of the day and enjoyed the drink.

Leslie was finished first and was eager to get back to work. She wanted to show her new boss that she could tough it out and outwork anyone. She walked into Bruce's office with a box of files and placed it on the table by a large stack of reports ready to be copied for the CDC. She looked out the window at the evening scene of the Sacramento River and the state Capitol.

"Must be nice being the owner," she whispered out loud.

She walked over to the large desk and ran her fingers across the back of the leather chair like she was caressing a cat when Bruce walked in.

"Well, back already?" he asked.

"Oh. I'm sorry." Leslie was startled by his presence. "I was done with dinner and wanted to get back to work." She was trying to impress him.

"Well, this is my office, not the conference room. I think you made a mistake." He was annoyed and concerned that she may have seen something she shouldn't have. Of course, that would be almost impossible since he eventually shredded everything he wanted hidden.

"I'm sorry. I Just wanted to bring this box up from records." Leslie walked over to the table. "It was peculiar."

Bruce stopped and turned toward her. "What do you mean, 'peculiar'?"

She turned the box so Bruce could see the labeling. "It's a box labeled Gene Expression Research."

"That's related to the Tegbatol and Inferon studies." Bruce waived his hand and dismissed the significance of the box as he returned to his desk. "Just leave it there and I'll go through it." He wasn't concerned. It was what he expected to set aside for the CDC to show the research that was done after Maskill's was discovered.

"But the reports are dated 2001." Bruce froze when he heard the words. "In orientation they told us Maskill's was discovered in 2003."

"It must be a typo. There was no research being conducted before the discovery of the disease. Must be 2004." Bruce walked swiftly toward the table and took hold of the box. Bruce laughed as he moved the box over to his desk.

"Even some of the reports inside are dated 2001," Leslie added.

"Then they are referring to something else." Bruce was starting to show his displeasure with her persistence. "I'll go through this and sort out the documents into their right dates and topics." He dropped the box on the floor and turned back to Leslie. "Look, we are all tired. Sorry. What I need are the records for the right dates, not these."

"Yes sir. I didn't mean to cause any problems."

"It's OK." Bruce smiled as Leslie apologized again and left his office in a hurry.

Bruce opened the box to see what Leslie may have seen.

> Report: Test of Chromatin and Microtubules Coil Elasticity
>
> Subject: 19Q13.33 Chromosome
> Duration: 43 days
> Universe: 25 samples
> May 16, 2001
> Dr. Everett Maskill

He flipped to the next report.

> Report: Identification of mutation in PKNP gene that results in neurological disorder
>
> Subject: 19Q13.33 Chromosome
> Duration: 162 days
> Universe: 36 samples
> March 22, 2001
> Dr. Everett Maskill

Bruce threw the papers into the box with disgust. "Dammit!!!"

It was almost 9:00 P.M. The team had a long day in, and made tremendous progress. They were in Bruce's office as he was wrapping up their progress, and laying down the plans for the morning.

"I appreciate the work you folks put in today. It has been difficult. The CDC made a huge request, and you all came through." Everyone gave a slight clap and a couple of high fives. Nothing like getting praise from the boss to lift your spirits. "Tomorrow, we need to start back in at eight, so I apologize for the short night. However, this weekend you all have off, and I'm going to credit your vacation bank with three extra days, as well as the overtime pay you earned." A couple more high fives. "You did great. See you back here at 8 A.M. sharp."

The group started to filter out the door, saying their goodbyes and thanks, when Bruce asked Leslie to stay for a second.

This is it, she thought. *He's going to fire me.*

"Leslie?" Bruce started.

"I'm sorry Mr. Lowell."

"No, no. That's ok. I'm already past that. You worked hard today." He smiled and reassured her.

"I did? I mean . . . ." She was flustered by his remark.

"Yes, you did. I appreciate anyone who wants to learn. Knowledge is power. I wanted to thank you, and say I am happy you are here." He moved a little closer to her. "I'm glad you are a part of this team."

"Why, thanks, Mr. Lowell." Leslie blushed.

"Please, call me Bruce." He smiled.

"OK. Bruce. I'm not sure what to say."

"Don't say anything. Just be back here tomorrow morning, 8 A.M. sharp."

"Yes sir, will do." Leslie was excited that the boss recognized her good work. "I'm going to pick up some egg rolls and pot stickers, head home to be with my cat, and get a good night's rest so I can be sharp for tomorrow."

"Chinese, eh? Where do you get your takeout?" Bruce wanted to know more about her.

"Over at China Moon on Florin Road. It's the best," she said.

"I'll have to try it sometime. Have a good night, now." Leslie started to the door when Bruce stopped her. "Uh, by the way. Where did you find that mismarked box?"

"Oh. Second floor research records, about the third aisle over. It was way in the back on the bottom shelf."

"Good. I want to check them out and make sure that if there are any others with mistakes, I get them corrected. It just takes a few minutes, and this box was a mess."

"I can bring them up first thing tomorrow," Leslie said.

"That would be great. Thanks." Bruce was done. He turned away from her signaling the end of their trite conversation.

Leslie was too excited to be offended. "Thank you, Bruce." And with that, Leslie left the office.

Bruce sat at his desk wondering what to do about the girl.

It was dark and the night was cool. The sign to the China Moon restaurant was partially lit. The parking lot was bright and Bruce could easily see Leslie's car. He was setting in his parked car in the lot adjacent to the restaurant, but had a clear view through the bushes. No one noticed he was there. He wasn't moving a muscle, just watching. His hands gripped the steering wheel like he was in a race.

The restaurant door opened and Leslie bounced out to the parking lot carrying a bag and her purse. She fumbled for her keys as she approached her car. She didn't look around. There was no one else in the lot, but she didn't care. Her car beeped, the lights flashed, and the door unlocked.

Bruce watched her climb into her car. When her headlights came on, he started his car.

Leslie pulled out of the parking lot and turned east on Florin Road.

Bruce followed a few car lengths behind her.

CHAPTER 11

Wednesday April 20
Deaths 3,314

The record vault had boxes of documents stacked on shelves, sorted by date and topic. In the bioagricultural row, Jim was working feverishly. It was 7 A.M., but he had to get an early start. He was almost done pulling all of the documents and samples related to the wheat mutation and spray application. Many of the documents he already shredded. He wasn't worried about pulling out specific documents. He just wanted to make sure anything associated to 19Q was removed. So, if it related to the time frame of their development of the wheat, he set it aside.

More problematic, however, was pulling records related to the continued spraying, harvesting, and distribution of the wheat. These were intertwined with many other files. At first glance, they would look like any other agricultural application of fertilizer for their subsidiary company, but the volumes, locations and dates could be questionable. Jim tried to separate the companies when they first began, but over the years he became lax and allowed them to slowly integrate, never once imagining they would have a situation like this. Many of the records were now a part of their automated chemical tracking and accounts payable systems. Even though they were labeled fertilizer and other benign products, the ultimate harvest, purchase and distribution could lead back to them. The shell company was not separated far enough from the parent company. And Jim knew it.

He really didn't care much. He arranged for a flight to France tomorrow night. His funds were being transferred, his investments liquidated, and his local assets he could care less about. He could at least make it really difficult for someone to find all of the links if he destroyed some of the files. And that he did. It would buy him some valuable time to eventually get to the right country and lay low. But he was struggling with the idea that he might be destroying the only means to find a cure. It ate at him, constantly.

"Jim." Bruce interrupted his thought. "What's the latest on your project?"

Jim spun around in his chair. "Going great!" he said. "I've got all of the hard copies destroyed, and am working on the remaining samples and digital files. I should have everything in place by tonight." Jim wasn't used to lying so blatantly. "How about you?"

"Same. My team has done a fantastic job of getting the files to me so I could separate the data. I'm just about done, too." Bruce smiled. He didn't want to tell Jim about Leslie and her possible discovery. Not yet. That would just set Jim over the edge, and he didn't need another crisis to manage. Not now.

Both men had their little secret.

"Well, good." Jim laughed and turned back to his monitor. He was already mentally on his flight to France with millions waiting for him. He didn't care what Bruce was doing.

"CDC will be here tomorrow," Bruce reminded him. "We don't have much time."

"No problem. We have enough time, I'm sure. I'm almost done here."

Bruce was surprised to see this turn around in Jim, from someone puking in a waste basket to a man calm, collected, and in control. "Good. You sure seem perky this morning."

Jim didn't look up. "Yeah. I guess a good dinner, a good night's sleep, and a new perspective that we can beat this thing made the difference."

Bruce was suspicious. "Hmmm. I guess." Bruce turned to walk out the door with Jim watching him in the reflection of his monitor.

"Good morning, folks," Bruce said as he entered the work area.

"Good morning, Bruce." Leslie smiled at him. "Looks like another busy day."

"Yes it will be, I'm sure. Can you have someone bring me a couple of boxes so we can get this wrapped up?"

"Yes sir. I have one right here." Leslie picked up a box and followed Bruce down the hall and into his office. She sat the box on the table. "I looked for some other mismarked boxes but didn't find any."

Of course you didn't, thought Bruce. "That's good. If you do, just let me know." He started to sort through the box as Leslie left the office.

"Doctor Kruger. Will you look at this, please?" The analyst stepped aside and pointed to the microscope before him. The doctor walked over and looked at the sample on the slide.

"It appears they are two like chromosomes." He turned to the analyst. "Am I missing something here?"

"Yes sir. If you look at the upper right edge, you'll see a slight variation in one of the chromatids." The analyst drew a simple diagram on a sheet of paper to reference where the doctor needed to look. "Right about here." He circled the area.

The doctor looked again. "Yes, I see what you mean." He increased the power of the microscope and looked more closely. He turned to the analyst. "Is this cell in the early stages of mitosis?"

"No sir. The cell has divided." The analyst paused. "The chromatid is torn."

The Doctor looked into the microscope again. "Are you sure this is not the early stages?"

In the early stages of mitosis, or cell division, the chromatin strands of a chromosome become more and more condensed. They cease to function as accessible genetic material and become a compact transportable form. This compact form makes the individual chromosomes visible, and they form the classic four arm structure, a pair of sister chromatids attached to each other at the centromere. The shorter arms are called p arms and the longer arms are called q arms. This is the only natural context in which individual chromosomes are visible with an optical microscope.

During divisions, long microtubules attach to the centromere and the two opposite ends of the cell. The microtubules then pull the chromatids apart, so that each daughter cell inherits one set of chromatids. Once the cells have divided, the chromatids are uncoiled and can function again as chromatin. The process repeats itself over and over.

A tear in the chromatid is a mutation; one they could be looking for.

"Yes sir. I have verified it with other samples from the same subject." The analyst replied.

"Is this the 19Q13.33 chromosome?" the doctor asked.

"It is. But this is not the type A mutation that we know about."

"It isn't?"

"No, sir. It appears to be a new mutation."

Carl looked at the chromosome again. He pulled away from the microscope and slapped the analyst on the shoulder. His big hand knocked the analyst a little off balance. "Good work. I'd like you to run DNA and gene maps of these chromosomes right away. I also want samples and chromatid analysis of the other victims to see if they have the same mutation. We need to find out why the tear occurred. Good work." He slapped the analyst again, who braced himself for it.

The analyst sheepishly continued. "One more thing, doctor."

"What is it?"

"This sample is not from a Maskill's patient."

Carl took his glasses off slowly and stared at the microscope. His smile quickly vanished. "Are you sure?" he asked.

"Yes. I verified the results and the original sample . . . . twice."

Carl looked at the analyst and back to the microscope. He picked up his notes and his cell phone and started toward the door. All of a sudden, he was in a hurry. "Let me know immediately if anything else surfaces."

"Yes, doctor."

The sun was setting over the river. Bruce was pleased with their progress to clean up the files and remove evidence of pre-Maskill's work that would incriminate them. After all, he only had to provide the information to the CDC team that he wanted to provide. They wouldn't know if anything else existed or not if he didn't tell them, and he wasn't about to.

His plan was going perfectly. Jim had his end cleaned up. Records on the wheat mutation testing, spray, harvest and subsequent sales were destroyed. They had it well planned out even from the beginning by using a shell company, fake identifications for the banks in remote areas, employer identification numbers, separate books, separate computers, everything. He couldn't see any loopholes if Jim just shredded the records they had and made sure any links between companies were scrubbed or destroyed.

Except Leslie.

"Mr. Lowell. The team from the Center of Disease Control is here to see you," came the voice over the phone intercom.

"Now? They aren't supposed to be here until tomorrow!" Bruce looked around his office to make sure nothing was in the open that he wanted hidden. "I'll be right out." Bruce stood and walked out the door to greet them.

The two men and two women were sharply dressed, and quite formal.

"I'm Bruce Lowell." Bruce extended his hand to the lead person to shake.

"Mr. Lowell. I'm Theodore Ito, project leader here."

"Mr. Ito. Welcome to Biotrogen." Bruce motioned for them to have a seat. "I didn't expect you until tomorrow. Did you have a good flight?"

"Yes, we did. We thought we would come here tonight and get right to work, if possible." Mr. Ito was very direct, and his concern showed. "We have more than 3,200 people who have died from Maskill's to date."

Bruce was stunned. "Thirty-two hundred?"

"Yes. And rising rapidly."

Bruce stayed focused and controlled.

Mr. Ito continued. "We need to gain access to your research records right away."

"Certainly." Bruce shook off the impact of the number of people dying from his creation. "We've pulled everything pertaining to pre-Maskill's research and development as well as reports on the development of Tegbatol and Inferon to expedite your research. These drugs are patented, you know, so they can't be divulged beyond your scientific research."

"With all due respect, Mr. Lowell. With the people dying at this rate, these drugs have little to no value to us unless they are the cause, and they don't appear to be at present. We don't care to share your secrets, we only want to find out why this is happening, and how to stop it."

"As do I." Bruce sounded sincere. "Whatever you need, please let me or my team know."

"Thank you. We will. Where can we set up shop?"

"You want to start tonight?" Bruce had a long day and expected they would start in the morning. He wasn't ready for them to start right now.

"Yes. We plan to work the next twenty-four hours straight if need be to make sure we have all of the data to take back to CDC." Mr. Ito was checking his text message as he spoke.

"You can use conference room B on the third floor. But, this creates a bit of a problem. I have no staff here, other than one analyst, who can assist you through the night and security. Portions of the building will be locked down. Some samples will not be accessible, nor the entire system."

"I see. What if we start at five tomorrow morning? Would that be better?" Mr. Ito asked.

"Yes. Much. I can make sure we have you situated and a team assigned to assist you by six at the latest. That will give you a little time to settle in. I will meet you here myself to get you started." Bruce was relieved. He didn't want to work all night again. He had been working almost non-stop for a week. But now, with the CDC, Leslie, and the work he had to do, it would certainly be another all nighter. "I'll rearrange schedules to make sure we have 24-hour assistance and access for you tomorrow."

"Fine. We will see you at five." Mr. Ito and his team grabbed their briefcases and left together.

Bruce walked back into his office and sat at his desk. "Thirty-two hundred!" He put his head in his hands. "What the hell am I going to do?" he said out loud. He stood and paced about the room for a few minutes, pondering what he could possibly do to fix this mess. He walked over to the window to see the lights of downtown reflect off the river. He looked toward the parking lot and saw the CDC group walking toward their car. Then he saw Leslie approach them.

He grabbed his jacket and keys and ran down the hall.

It was dark when she left and dark when she got home. Leslie pulled her car up to the front of the duplex. There were two cars in the driveway, so she had to park on the street, again. It was a long day and she was so tired. She grabbed the two bags of groceries, her briefcase and purse, and closed the door with her leg. Her porch light was off, but the neighbor's light was on providing just enough light for her to search for her key to the door. She fumbled through her keys looking for the door key.

The figure silently stepped out of the shadows and across the grass. Without making a sound, he walked up behind her. In a second, he placed his left arm around her neck in a headlock and pushed with his right hand against the side of her head, instantly snapping her C3 vertebrae. She made a muffled sound as she fell to the concrete. The bags of groceries fell with a crash as several glass bottles broke. The man reached down, grabbed her purse, and briskly walked around the side of the duplex and out of sight.

Leslie laid motionless at the doorstep.

CHAPTER 12

Thursday April 21 ▭■▬■▬■▬■▬■
Deaths 3,476

Bob Struthers stared at the paper Alice handed him. "Are you telling me the death rate is still accelerating?"

"That's right. We are over thirty three hundred total. We had seventy-four deaths reported yesterday. It's climbing, Bob." Alice pulled some more papers out of her folder. Here's what it looks like graphically."

Bob studied the graph carefully. The upswing of the curve was frightening. It started at zero and rapidly grew to 200,000. His hands became sweaty as he realized this represented people dying. "You mean we could have 200,000 deaths in less than six months?"

"Yes. According to the growth rate and discovery, it appears so. These are new cases and continued discovery of existing. We are receiving reports that the funeral homes likely have victims, and have asked the local medical examiners to conduct a low level analysis to verify cause of death, if possible. That's adding to our totals."

"This is remarkable considering it does not appear contagious. How can it possibly be spreading through the population like this? Are there any reports of recoveries?"

"No sir. One hundred percent fatality rate from the aneurysms, from what we can deduct." Alice pulled out another report. "The majority of cases are on the West Coast. There are concentrations of cases in Oregon, Washington and California. This confirms our previous assumption."

"Any report on the efficacy of the current treatment for Maskill's?"

"Ineffective," she replied.

Bob stared at the documents, flipping back and forth, studying them. "Alice, this is huge. If the growth assumptions are any indication of what we are facing, this is bigger than AIDS."

"I know."

"Ok." Bob sat the papers on his desk and gently spread them flat with his hands. He composed himself and continued. "Have we heard from our team at Biotrogen? Any discoveries there?"

"No, sir. They just settled in and are gathering the information. They should have summaries to Doctor Kruger's teams within hours. Samples will be brought back in hand for analysis. They won't return until tomorrow." Alice took a sip of coffee.

"All right then. We need to see how the good doctor is doing. I need to get out of this office for a minute and get some air anyway." Bob stood and grabbed his sweater. "Carl said he has something to show us." Bob paused for a second and continued. "Looks like we have something to show him, too."

"Most definitely. I need a refill anyway." Alice picked up her file and travel mug, placed them in her messenger bag, and they left.

"Here are your coffee, juice, and rolls." The receptionist was a wonderful host. "You can access an outside line on these buttons. The copier is right outside the door. No code is needed for copying. Supplies are in the cabinet there." She paused to think. "That should cover it. Let me know if you need anything more."

The CDC group thanked her as she left the conference room.

They settled in and started to open boxes. Two people sat up their laptops, scanners and satellite wireless connections.

Bruce walked in looking a little disheveled. He had circles under his eyes. Two analysts were right behind him carrying two boxes. "Good morning folks." He shook hands with Mr. Ito. "I trust you had no problems getting in and settled?"

"No, not at all. Your security staff and receptionist were very helpful," Mr. Ito replied. "We are ready to go."

"Good," Bruce replied. "I have two senior analysts here, Al and Landry. They'll help you in any area you need. They have full clearance to access everything for this project. Just ask them and they should be able to take care of anything."

"Good." Mr. Ito pulled out his notepad and a few files and sat at the table. He was ready to start.

Three analysts and Doctor Carl Kruger were seated at the head of a large table. They were shuffling some documents back and forth, putting them in order for the presentation. The centrifuges on the counter in the background were spinning creating a mild hum. The lab was not the best place for a meeting of this type, but should anyone want more information, it was readily available.

Doctor Kruger looked tired, worn. He had worked many hours every day trying to find the cause for the new disease. Trying to stop the dying. They were close, he believed, very close. Their discovery of the new mutation of the 19Q chromosome was troubling. He asked Bob and Alice to meet with them. Several people stood at the sides of the table looking on. Alice sat in a chair while Bob stood next to her.

"Folks, thank you for coming here this morning." Carl jumped right into the presentation. There was no need to waste any time. "We found a new mutation of the 19Q13.33 chromosome."

Bob spoke first. "Are you sure?"

"Yes," Carl answered. "Without a doubt. We discovered this yesterday and spent most of the night verifying the tests. We had to be absolutely sure our results were accurate." He looked at each person, and continued. "They are." He turned to the whiteboard.

"As I told you before, I was doing research on the 19Q13.33 chromosome at John Hopkins, and believed multiple mutations in the PNKP gene could result in a severe neurological disease." He drew the name 19Q13.33 and an arrow to PNKP. "PNKP is the polynucleotide kinase 3'-phosphatase gene. This locus represents a gene involved in DNA repair." He continued to write the key words on the white board, 'locus,' 'DNA repair.'

"In response to ionizing radiation or oxidative damage, the protein encoded by this locus catalyzes 5' phosphorylation and 3' dephosphorylation of nucleic acids. What this means is the mutations at this locus have been associated with microcephaly, seizures, and developmental delay. Are you tracking with me?" he asked.

"I think so," Alice replied. The others nodded their heads.

Carl continued. "Our hypothesis at John Hopkins was that varying mutations would correlate to varying neurological dysfunctions. Everett Maskill pioneered this research at John Hopkins."

One of the analysts spoke up. "So, what you are saying is that the level of the ionizing radiation or oxidative damage could result in the type or level of mutation, thus the level of the seizure. Correct?"

"There is not a direct correlation to the level of the seizures from the levels of ionization or oxidative damage, but there is a correlation to the number and types of mutations. In essence, we don't know how bad the seizures could be, but, in theory, the multiple variations suggest severe."

Doctor Kruger sat his marker down and leaned against the table. He folded his arms and continued. "The inference that ionization or oxidative damage can cause multiple types of mutations opens the door for multiple types of neurological disorders, primarily seizures. The work that was performed at Biotrogen was on the 19Q13.33'A' chromosome. It was a mutation that was limited to a very small percentage of the population, about .1%. The mutation resulted in mild seizures that caused headaches, audio impairment, blurred vision, and other mild symptoms, none which were deadly or considered severe."

He leaned over and grabbed his soda, took a sip. Several people were reviewing the documents that were handed out to follow along.

"Two medicines working in tandem were able to control the effects of the seizures and eventually suppress the expression of the PNKP gene. Tegbatol—a chromatin targeted alkaloid—was taken over a six to eight week period with Inferon, a T type protein derivative. The chromatin in Tegbatol bombards the 19Q13.33'A' chromosome with Inferon proteins and coats the chromosome, which hinders the gene expression, resulting in reduced or eliminated seizures. The medicines were highly successful and effective . . . until now."

He drew a diagram of a chromosome on the board. It was a large 'X' with squiggly lines creating the form. "This is a replicated and condensed metaphase chromosome." He drew the number one. "This is the Chromatid—one of the two identical parts of the chromosome after S phase. Number two is the Centromere—the point where the two chromatids touch at the intersection of the 'X' and where the microtubules attach. Here we have the Short arms, number three, and the Long arms, four."

He turned to the small group. "You all know that when a cell divides, the microtubules attach to the centromere and the two opposite ends of the cell and pull the chromatids apart, thus creating a set of chromatids for each new cell. Once that occurs, the chromatids are uncoiled." He paused and put the marker down. "We have discovered a mutation where the chromatid tears immediately after separation."

He drew the PNKP gene on the whiteboard. It was a long oval shape with markers at varying intersections. He drew an arrow between markers 13.32 and 13.33.

He turned to the group and folded his hands. "The inability of the chromatids to pull apart and uncoil without tears has revealed two different causes, and two different PNKP genes. We have discovered two new mutations of the 19Q13.33 gene. They are now labeled 'B' and 'C.'"

"Two?" Bob asked.

"Yes, two," he confirmed. "The mutations are between marker .32 and .33. But that is not the most troubling discovery. The new mutations occurred both in Maskill's patients and normal subjects."

Alice was stunned. "What? Are you saying that anyone could have this mutation?"

"Yes, I'm afraid I am."

Bob stepped in. "Do we know how the genes are mutated?"

"No. Our research suggests it is a type of oxidative damage . . . . but we don't know how."

Alice was very upset by the report. "So, anyone can get this mutation, and we have no idea how it occurs. How can someone . . ."

Bob cut her off. "Alice!"

The analysts started to ask questions. The voices were mixed together and started to escalate.

"Please, please," Doctor Kruger tried to calm them down. "Let me finish, please."

The group settled down, unwillingly, and listened to his explanation.

"Thank you. I know this is unsettling, but we must look at it strictly from a scientific perspective, and take the emotions out, please," he pleaded. "Otherwise, we won't make progress. Our judgment will become clouded."

"You're right," confirmed Bob. "Please continue, doctor."

"Thank you." He took a breath, and continued. "The samples of the victims we analyzed indicated they had, at one time, either normal 19Q chromosomes, or the type A mutation. Somehow, they were mutated into types B and C. The mutation is recent from the levels in the body."

"How can that be, doctor?" asked Bob.

"We don't know, yet. What we do know is the mutations appear to have been formed between seventy and one hundred and fifty days from the comparative samples we have. They could have been construed as being new Maskill's patients because of the mutation of the same chromosome."

"So, what we thought were all Maskill's patients may very well have been the new mutations. Correct?" Bob asked.

"Yes. We have been working under the assumption they were Maskill's patients with the type 'A' mutation when, in fact, they likely were not," Carl answered.

"So, to ask the question again, are you saying anyone could be subject to this mutation?" Alice wanted an answer this time.

"Until we do further analysis, we won't absolutely know for sure." He licked his lips. His mouth instantly went dry. "However, current analysis suggests . . . . Yes. Anyone."

> FDA Notice: Concerns About the treatments for Maskill's Seizures and FDA Recommendations
>
> Issued: April 21 2011
>
> 14:45 EST
>
> To: Medical Professionals, Pharmacists, and Healthcare Facility Administrators:
>
> The Food and Drug Administration (FDA) is providing this notice to inform you of important information regarding the use of TEGBATOL—a chromatin targeted alkaloid—and INFERON, a T type protein derivative. These medicines are used for the treatment of Maskill's Seizures.
>
> The FDA has received reports that the effectiveness of these applications for the treatment of Maskill's Seizures

19Q

is in question. There have also been reports of Maskill's patients dying from unknown causes. The Centers for Disease Control has launched an investigation into the causes of Maskill's deaths. Until their report confirms the drugs TEGBATOL and INFERON are not associated to the risk of death, these products are hereby to be immediately removed from the market and discontinued administration to patients until further testing validates their efficacy in a repeat phase three clinical trial test.

FDA is therefore sending this letter to make recommendations on actions that you should take.

FDA Recommendations

If you have any TEGBATOL or INFERON in your supply, please package these immediately for disposal according to FDA guidelines. Please report all disposed products to the FDA. Standard epileptic medications, such as Phenobarbital or Dilantinum, may continue to be prescribed for the appropriate patient.

For additional information, including information on FDA cleared or approved epileptic medications, see the "Questions and Answers" document[2] on the FDA web site.

Please note that user facilities, including hospitals, are required to report suspected Maskill's related deaths to FDA and the CDC immediately

Contacting FDA

Answers to many of your questions are contained in FDA's "Questions and Answers" document. In addition, FDA will host a call during the week of May 12th for healthcare professionals and pharmacists prescribing TEGBATOL and INFERON for Maskill's patients. Healthcare professionals and pharmacists that wish to participate in this call should contact Jason Dupree, Office of Special Health Issues, by phone at 301-555-4460 or by email at jason.dupree@fda.hhs.gov.

Sincerely,
Timothy A. Beringer
Director, Office of Compliance
Center for Pharmaceuticals
Food and Drug Administration

"Seven? Are you sure?" Grace was reviewing the documents in front of her. Doctor Allbright was setting across from her desk.

"Yes, I'm afraid I am. We have verified that seven of the victims in the morgue died from Maskill type aneurysms. They all died within the last week. There is no identifying commonality amongst them." He sipped his drink as Grace thought about the implications.

"This is a bit overwhelming to say the least." Grace paused. "Thank you, Howard."

"My pleasure, ma'am." Howard started toward the door and stopped. "I will continue to review all death cases and report the results to you daily." He didn't wait for a reply as he exited.

Grace hit the button on the phone. "Alyssa? I'd like you to set up an emergency board meeting for this evening."

"Yes, ma'am. Shall I let them know the purpose of the meeting?"

Grace thought for a second. "Yes; Disaster Preparedness Review."

The phone was silent for a moment. "Yes, ma'am."

"And please get Bob Struthers from the CDC on the line for me. I need to talk with him."

"Yes, ma'am. Right away."

Grace walked over to her window and stared at the sprawling city of Eugene, wondering why people were dying in her beloved city.

"Where's Jim?!" Bruce was frantic.

"He stepped out for lunch. He said he wanted to . . . ." The receptionist didn't have time to finish before Bruce fired the next question.

"Where did he go?"

"I don't know . . ."

Bruce turned and stormed into Jim's office and closed the door. The desk was eerily clean. No papers, no trash, no boxes of files and samples stacked around the room like in Bruce's office. He pulled out his cell phone and dialed Jim as he walked toward the window. He was sweating, breathing hard.

The door opened and Jim walked in. "Bruce. What are you doing here?"

"Jim! Have you seen what's going on?" Bruce was frantic. He walked over to the credenza and grabbed the remote to turn on the flat screen television on the wall. Jim often watched the stock market and wheat futures early in the morning as his first task at work. "Look at this!!"

Bruce flipped a couple of channels until he came to the market news. *" . . . . and is currently at $16.42."*

"Thanks, David. Now to look at the top stories. Biotrogen has become a market leader in genetic stocks over the past six years, and it is still a market leader, but not the way most companies prefer." The commentator snickered as he tried to inject a little humor. *"Biotrogen is in a freefall. It is leading the other genetics companies to a fifty-two week low."*

Jim moved closer to the television.

"The stock has dropped 91% to twenty two dollars and forty-five cents." Bruce sat in the chair behind him, mouth open, and stared at the TV. The commentator continued. *"The FDA issued a 'cease and desist' order on the company's two darling products; Tegbatol and Inferon. It seems like some of the Maskill's patients have died, and the FDA wants another phase three clinical test conducted before it allows consideration of placing the products back in the market. These two medicines were the cause for the rise of Biotrogen stock, but now they look like they are their demise. Investors have dumped five million shares in two hours!!"*

"Are you kidding me?" Jim almost smiled as he listened to the news. The commentator continued in the background.

Bruce was pacing the office. "Ninety-one percent." Bruce put his head in his hands. "I'm broke. I've lost it all. One hundred and eighty million dollars . . . gone!!" He jumped to his feet. "Why didn't we know about this?"

"The only notice I saw was the request for information. I've been too damn busy for the past week to check my email or calls," Jim replied.

"This is unbelievable!" Bruce continued. "Jim, we've lost everything. EVERYTHING!!"

"Not we, buddy." Jim smiled. He finally felt like he had one over on Bruce. It was about time.

"Huh? What do you mean, 'not we?' What's that supposed to mean?" Bruce started to turn red.

"Sorry to drop this on you, 'ol buddy,' but I sold most of my shares two days ago." Jim was almost gloating. He didn't care. He was leaving, soon. He had two tickets to France in his coat pocket for the red eye flight leaving in just six hours.

"You sold your shares?" Bruce was shocked. "How did you know? Why didn't you tell me?"

"Bruce, when it comes to investing, you do your thing, I do mine. It's always been like that, and we agreed we wouldn't let each other know because it could be considered insider trading, and we don't want to break the law now, do we?" Jim chuckled as he gloated over his keen financial move.

Bruce walked over and gave Jim a big shove in the chest. "You stupid. . . ."

Jim stumbled backwards against the credenza. "Me? You're the fool here, buddy. If you can't see the writing on the wall, then you're blind, or dumb, or both." He waved his hand as though he dismissed Bruce and walked past him.

Bruce grabbed his shoulder and spun him around so he could talk face to face. "The writing on the wall? You arrogant bastard. If it wasn't for me you wouldn't have anything. I've protected us from getting caught years ago, and you didn't even know it, you stupid son of."

"Protected? And just how did you do that, oh mighty one?" Jim was getting angrier each moment as the argument raged. "You didn't create the cure. Everett did. He's the one who made us millions, not you." Jim poked Bruce on the chest and walked off.

"And he was going to stop the program."

Jim stopped cold, and turned to Bruce. "What? Stop what?"

"You heard me. He was going to stop the program. He got second thoughts. He wanted to pull the plug and stop everything after we had it tested and in place." Jim looked at Bruce, stunned. "That's right, smart ass. I stopped him and kept the program running so we could get rich."

"You stopped him?"

"Hell yeah. You didn't really believe Everett, the 'basketball junkie', fell off that ladder, do you? Are you that naive?" Bruce was gloating now.

"You killed him? Are you kidding me?" Jim was shocked.

"Oh, don't go all Mr. Clean on me, you hypocrite. You knew he was wavering and even said we had to stop him. So I did."

"I didn't mean kill him. I meant to talk some sense into him, or something. I thought he changed his . . . ."

"That's what I did . . . or something," Bruce smiled.

Jim grabbed his briefcase and started toward the door. "I'm leaving. This is crazy."

"Like killing a few thousand people isn't? You're not going anywhere." Bruce grabbed Jim and pushed him into a chair. "You think you can just walk out now? After what I've done to Everett and Leslie to protect you?" Bruce's face was red, and the veins on his neck were bulging.

"Leslie? Who the hell is Leslie? What are you talking about?"

Bruce realized Jim didn't know anything about Leslie. He stared at Jim. His eyes were wild, face red. He was breathing heavy.

"I'm outta here. I've got a flight to catch, and I'm leaving. This is crazy. YOU'RE CRAZY."

"Flight? You're jumping ship and leaving me here to take the fall? I don't think so." Bruce grabbed Jim again and threw him to the ground.

Jim realized he had to fight his way out. He swung his briefcase at Bruce, who deflected it out of his hand. Jim struggled to his feet, grabbed a chair and yelled as he pushed Bruce back against the wall, knocking a picture off the wall.

Bruce became enraged. He kicked the chair out of Jim's hands and grabbed Jim by the arm. He swung him across the room like a rag doll . . . . and into the window. The window shattered as Jim flew through. Bruce could see his eyes wide with terror as he flew out into the open air, five stories up. The glass cut him so deep Bruce could see the blood begin to flow across his face as he sailed into the sunlight in slow motion.

Bruce was breathing heavily. He walked to the edge of the window and looked down. He could see Jim lying on the concrete, trying to move his leg and arm as he lay in pain. He was twisted, bloody, barely alive. He was looking up. Bruce could see his bloodied face. It seemed as though Jim was looking at him. The cool breeze came in through the broken window. Jim's leg twitched, then kicked. He stopped moving. Bruce could see the airline tickets in his inside coat pocket, spattered with blood.

" . . . . *this was quite the Cinderella story. The question now, Maria, is if Biotrogen will be able to make a comeback from this, or not.*"

"Mr. Lowell. Are you OK?" The door was locked. "This is Security." The man outside banged on the door again. Jim and Bruce had special locks on their doors to protect their secrets, so no one, not even security, could come in unless they allowed it. They lived lives of secrecy, but it was all coming unraveled and being exposed. "Mr. Lowell. If you don't open the door, we will force our way in."

The ambulance siren had just turned off as it entered the main driveway of Biotrogen. The police sirens could be heard in the distance as they made their way across town. Bruce had a glass of scotch setting on the desk. His eyes were red and swollen. He mumbled to himself, "The years I put into this company. I never wanted anyone to die. I just wanted to get rich. And I did," he chuckled. "For awhile, but now." He took a big drink of scotch and filled the glass. He glanced at the television that was broken and still smoldering.

"Mr. Lowell? The police are on their way up, sir. Please open the door."

"I'd rather wait until they get here," Bruce yelled to the door. "Three thousand!" he whispered as he took another full drink. The bottle was almost empty. He could hear the sirens approaching the building. The guard continued to knock on the door and plead. It had been ten minutes or so from the time Jim fell out the window. He had finished most of the bottle of scotch and was feeling its affect. But it didn't kill the pain.

Bruce got up and staggered a little. He walked over to the edge of the window. He saw a small crowd of people standing around Jim. One paramedic was crouching next to Jim. He had some instruments in his hands trying to get a pulse or something. The small crowd of people were standing around staring at the body. A few people looked up and saw Bruce, and pointed.

A police car pulled up to the front door. The guard pointed to Bruce standing at the broken window. The officers rushed into the building with their hands on their pistols.

Bruce took another drink. He closed his eyes and felt the breeze on his face. The warmth of the sun felt good. He felt good. He could hear a meadowlark sing in the distance. He opened his eyes and looked down to the twisted body with two paramedics hovering over him. "We could have pulled through this, Jim." He raised his near empty glass. "Cheers, partner." He emptied the glass.

The policemen approached the door. "Who's in there?" one officer asked.

Bruce Lowell, owner of the company," the guard replied.

"Does he have any guns?"

"He's been known to have a pistol in his office, but this isn't his office. I'm not sure. He was a Navy Seal," The guard replied.

Both officers pulled their weapons. "One, two, ..."

The door to the office burst open. "Police," the officer shouted. His weapon was drawn. He crouched at the doorway. The other officer peered around the corner behind his partner. Bruce turned around, and the crouching officer shouted, "Don't move." Bruce lowered the empty glass, and looked at the officers. "Put your hands on top of your head," one of them ordered.

Bruce looked at the crouching officer, then to his partner. "I'm sorry."

"Get your hands up!" The crouching officer shouted. "Now!"

Bruce dropped the glass, looked at them, and slowly closed his eyes. "God. Forgive me." And with that, he tilted his head back and fell backwards out of the window. A woman below screamed.

CHAPTER 13

Friday April 22
Deaths 3,476

The CDC team would have wrapped up their work by noon. They were planning on returning to Atlanta by night. All of the files and physical documents had been shipped. The samples were being escorted back with some members of the team. Myriads of information had been scanned and transmitted to headquarters for the "Maskill's Team" to review and process. They felt they had covered everything, until both Bruce Lowell and Jim Anderson flew out the fifth story window yesterday. Now, they were in a holding pattern, waiting to get back into Biotrogen to finish the last few boxes of files and wrap up. The building was closed. Only key employees and the police were allowed inside.

Obviously, something more than just tumbling stock values were at play. One key owner had a one-way flight to France the day he died. He had just liquidated a large portion of his investments and transferred the funds out of the country. One doesn't just do that on a whim, especially a few days before their stock value tanks into the toilet.

Theodore Ito was at the hotel waiting to hear from headquarters when he and his remaining team would be able to return to Biotrogen and gather the remaining information, files and wrap up. CDC was in contact with the police and the Executive Vice Presidents at Biotrogen. They expected to have access before the end of the day, so the team's flight was postponed until Saturday. For now, Mr. Ito was told to stand by.

And stand by he did. He decided to go to a restaurant near the Biotrogen building. He hailed a taxi and asked him to drive by Biotrogen on the way to the restaurant. The parking lot was almost vacant but for two vehicles; a police car and a pickup. Yellow caution tape encircled a small area in front of the building. Two large blood stains were still visible on the concrete. The window to Jim's office was boarded up.

The taxi drove across the river and let Mr. Ito off in front of Sally Mae's Deli. It was an old Victorian house that had been restored and outfitted as a restaurant/deli. Mr. Ito ordered a sandwich and sat at a table in the back overlooking the river. He noticed a newspaper on the adjoining, empty table, and picked it up.

The front page had a feature story on Biotrogen. It showed the pictures of three people from Biotrogen; Bruce Lowell, James Anderson, and Leslie Singer. *That's the girl who told us about the restaurant in Sacramento that night.* He read the article and learned about the creation of the company, the education of the partners, the tragic death of Jim Anderson, and the remarkable survival of Bruce Lowell. Bruce was critically injured, in a coma with swelling on the brain, broken bones and internal injuries. His prognosis was grim.

Toward the end of the article was the reference to Leslie; a young woman killed on the doorstep of her home two nights ago. It appears a case of robbery. Her purse was found two blocks away. Her neck was broken. Murdered. Police suspected someone tried to strangle her and snapped her neck, killing her instantly. She worked at Biotrogen as a research analyst for less than a week.

Ted pulled out his cell phone.

"Centers for Disease Control, may I help you?"

"Yes. Bob Struthers, please. This is Theodore Ito."

"One moment, please."

After a few seconds, Bob came on the line.

"Hello, Ted. What's up?" he asked.

"Hi, Bob. I'm not sure. Something very odd here." Ted's voice showed concern.

"How so?"

"Well, you know the two partners, Bruce Lowell and James Anderson? Well, they apparently got into a fight of some type and one ended up dead yesterday. The other is in a coma."

"Yes, I heard. Tragic."

"There was also a new research analyst killed two days ago; murdered on her doorstep."

"Murdered?" Bob sounded surprised.

"Yeah. The paper says it was a case of robbery; someone took her purse."

"What's odd about that, Ted?"

"Her neck was broken," he said

"Her neck?"

"Yeah. Bob, I'm not a detective, but wouldn't you think a robber would use a gun, knife, baseball bat, something to scare her to give up her purse, or even just take it, knock her down and run, without breaking her neck?"

The phone was silent for a few seconds. "Yeah, I would. Hold on for a second, will ya?"

"Sure." Ted continued to glance over the article, puzzled by the picture of the young woman.

"Ted? Still there?"

"Yeah."

"I'm going to contact the FBI on this. I asked Alice, and she agrees something is off. This case is too big, and too many people are at risk to pass on anything that could be important. The least we can do is let them know, and they can decide how far to take this."

"I agree, Bob. Why the FBI and not the local police?"

"If it's tied into this Maskill's thing, then we are talking about a lot of dead people in varying states. That's federal," was Bob's reply.

"I see. Well, let me know if you need anything from me or my team." Ted wanted to be involved, to find answers.

"Sure will. Thanks for the information, Ted. Keep me posted." Bob hung up the phone.

Ted looked at the sandwich and iced tea that the waitress brought. He didn't know when she brought it. He laid the paper down and started eating.

The doors for the ambulance entrance to the emergency room burst open. The paramedics pushed the stretcher into the room. "We have a female, eight years old, BP eighty over sixty, pulse . . . ." The paramedics continued to rattle off vitals as they wheeled her past the other patients in rooms and into a stall in the center of the emergency ward. Nurses came to their side. "We have a code blue here," one nurse shouted. The emergency room doctor walked up and leaned over the patient. He used his stethoscope to listen for a heartbeat while the nurses hooked her up to the machines. The monitors started beeping, erratically. The girl's chin was blood soaked. The side of her head was bloody. "What do we have here, folks?" the doctor said. "Talk to me."

The nurses were working frantically hooking up tubes, wiping off the blood, checking for broken skin, head trauma, anything that might explain the blood.

"Apparent seizure or stroke. Playing in the yard, fell over. That's all we know," the paramedic said.

"History?" the doctor asked.

"Unknown. Her parents are in the lobby," one of the nurses replied.

"Someone go see what they know." The doctor continued to view the monitors and the patient. "Trauma?"

"Nothing visible," one of the nurses shouted.

"Paddles . . . ." The nurse had just pushed the cart to the side of the bed. She handed the defibrillator paddles to the doctor. "Two fifty. Clear." Everyone lifted their hands off of the patient. THUMP. The body convulsed.

"Nothing," a nurse said.

"Clear." THUMP.

The drama repeated itself several times.

The machine beeped a steady rhythm. The lines peaked and fell with the heartbeats. The ventilator kept its steady hissing pace; up, down, up. Two bags of fluid were suspended from the wire racks. The room was empty except for the patient.

Bruce Lowell was in critical condition. His head was wrapped in bandages, his eyes swollen closed. His right arm and leg were in casts, his back in traction. Tubes protruded from his mouth. A mask covered his nose.

He was still alive, barely.

A police officer walked in with the nurse. He looked around, saw the condition of the patient, and jotted some notes. The nurse whispered something to him, and they left the room.

A few minutes later, Bruce slowly opened one eye. He rolled it around in his head, trying to focus on something, anything. The lights were blurred. *Where am I? What is this? It hurts. I can't move.*

He was thirsty, sore, confused, paralyzed from the waist down. His lungs were punctured and had filled with fluids. His brain traumatized and swollen.

He tried to talk, but nothing came out. Just a slight whimper that no one heard.

The nurse walked back in and saw that he had an eye open. She was surprised and leaned over in front of his face. "Well, hello there sexy. Can you hear me?" she asked as she reached over and adjusted his blanket. She glanced at the monitors.

He tried to talk, but barely grunted. He looked at her and slowly blinked his eye twice.

"I guess you can see me. You're looking right at me with that pretty blue eye." Bruce slowly blinked his eye twice again and looked at her. "Does that mean yes?" He slowly blinked his eye twice again. "Looks like we are figuring a way to talk here, honey. So, is one blink no?" He blinked his eye twice again. "OK. Say 'no' now." He blinked his eye once. "Good." She got a big grin across her face as she reached over and adjusted his pillow.

They were talking.

"Are you in pain, babe?" she asked.

Blink, blink.

"OK. I'm going to increase the drip a little. This will help some. I'll let the doctor know, too." She reached over and adjusted the drip. "I imagine the pain is over most of your body?"

Blink, blink.

"OK. This will make you a little sleepy, hon." She looked at the monitors again and glanced at his wrappings. "Would you like me to open the window shades hon?"

Blink.

"OK. We'll just leave them closed for now. You get some rest dear. I'll be right back." She patted his unbandaged hand.

Blink, blink.

The nurse walked out to the emergency lobby. "Mr. Hammond?" she called.

"Here." Bill Hammond was standing by the window with his wife, Linda. They quickly turned and walked to her. "What's happening to my daughter?" he said.

Linda Hammond was stunned. She could barely talk. "How is she? I need to see her. Is she . . . ?"

The nurse stopped him. "We don't know, yet. They are working on her." The nurse touched his arm. "I need to ask you a few questions."

"Sure." Linda sat in the chair by the window. She was in shock, stunned. She was slowly rocking in her seat holding herself with her arms. Any other mother would be fighting to get into the room with her daughter. Linda was sullen, withdrawn, dysfunctional. Bill stood next to her, hand on her shoulder. "Our son just died two weeks ago from the same thing," he said.

Linda broke down. Through her sobs she said, "I can't lose Lisa, too. I just can't bare it, Bill!" He leaned down and hugged her to try and console her.

The nurse was startled. "What? Did you say your son just died from this?"

"Yes," he said. "He had the same thing. Bleeding from the nose and ear after a seizure. He had Maskill's Seizures and one killed him." Bill Hammond became agitated as he remembered his son's death, how he was having dinner and soon was wiping gravy and mashed potatoes from his son's face after a seizure. The trip to the hospital, the autopsy authorization, the funeral, the letter from the organ recipient, it all came back like a flood. "But she doesn't have Maskill's. I don't understand. We can't go through this again. You've got to do something. Please."

"Mr. Hammond." The nurse tried to calm him by speaking softly. "I know this is difficult. We need some information to be able to determine how to treat your daughter."

He became more agitated as his wife continued to sob uncontrollably. "What's going on in there?"

The nurse again tried to reassure him. "Mr. Hammond, we are doing everything we can. Does your daughter have any history of illnesses or disorders that . . . ."

"No! She was never sick. She had no disorders or diseases. She didn't take medicines. She was in great shape."

Linda stood up. She stopped crying and suddenly became angry. "She was a healthy little girl, for God's sake!" People in the lobby began to back away from them. She started to walk past the nurse. "What are they doing in there? What's going on?"

"Ms. Hammond." The nurse was beginning to get nervous. "I need to ask you to please settle down."

"Settle down?" She pushed the nurse out of the way. All eyes in the emergency room were watching her. "Settle down!? My son died two weeks ago and now my daughter is dying and you want me to settle down?"

The receptionist at the check in station saw the commotion building. She picked up the phone and called security.

The nurse tried to stop her. "Ms. Hammond . . ."

Bill grabbed his wife's arm. "Honey . . ." She pulled away from him and pushed the nurse again. "You need to get back in there and take care of her. Right now!!" Her face was turning red. She was beginning to sweat. She was yelling.

"Ms. Hammond. Please calm down. We are doing the best we can in this . . . ."

"The best you can? Well, that isn't good enough." She pointed to the door to the emergency ward. "I need to get in there and see my daughter." Several people nearby moved away from the door. The nurse tried to block the door, but Linda pushed her away. Bill grabbed her and hugged her in a desperate attempt to stop her. Linda started yelling and flailing. "Let go! She needs me. I can hear her calling me." They stumbled over a chair and she broke free from Bill just as two large men came around the corner. The nurse behind the station did not buzz the door open. She just watched in disbelief. Linda pulled on the door handle. "Open up," she yelled. "Open up right now!!" She began beating on the door with her fists.

One of the guards ran up behind her just as she turned around. He grabbed her arm, and she instinctively grabbed a lamp and swung it, hitting the guard on the side of the head and knocking him to the ground. The other guard instinctively grabbed her free arm. She yelled and started swinging wildly, hitting the nurse and knocking her down. The guard on the floor started to stand and Bill Hammond pushed him back to the ground. "Stop it!!" he yelled as the guard struggled to get back to his feet.

There was chaos in the lobby as people scattered to get out of the way. Linda Hammond was yelling and flailing with anything she could grab. Bill Hammond was fighting with the guards.

One guard eventually grabbed Bill's arm and forced it behind his back. He pushed him into the wall as another guard came around the corner to help subdue him.

Linda continued to yell and flail. She tripped over a chair and fell to the floor. The guard jumped onto her back and held her down as he fought to get her arms behind her back. She continued to kick and yell.

"Get off of me!!! Let me go. Where's my daughter!? Lisa!!!! Get off . . . ." She was twisting and shouting and yelling and suddenly, started shaking. "Whsper'ss my . . . daught . . ." Blood was spurting from her mouth and nose. "Lisssaaa . . ." Her eyes rolled back into her head and she started convulsing. The guards let go of her as she lay in her own blood shaking uncontrollably. A lady in the emergency lobby screamed. A little girl started crying.

"Linda!! Linda!!" Bill tried to pull away from the guard who had a strong grip on his arm. "My wife! Help her, please!!"

The nurse ran to Linda's side as she lay twisting and bleeding all over the floor. Suddenly, she stopped. Blood trickled from her nose, mouth and left ear. The people stared at the dead woman lying in the lobby of the emergency room with the nurse attempting to revive her with CPR. The doors to the emergency room ward flew open.

Bill Hammond yelled. "Noooooo!!!!"

CHAPTER 14

Saturday April 23
Deaths 3,711

Doctor Kruger was reading the reports that the analyst just handed him. He kept switching from one document to the other, back and forth. "This just doesn't make any sense."

"I know," replied the analyst. "I felt the same way."

Carl picked up the phone. "Bob Struthers, please. This is Doctor Kruger." He waited for a few seconds. "Bob? I think you should come down to the lab right away. I'll explain when you get here." He hung up and turned back to the analyst. "I want gene maps run on all of the samples you can."

"Yes sir. The analyst spun and exited the room. Carl continued to glance through the pictures and reports when, a few minutes later, Bob Struthers came in.

"Sounds serious. What's up?" he asked.

"It is serious. We discovered two more mutations of the 19Q chromosome."

"Two?" Bob sat in the chair next to Carl. "Two more? Is that even possible?"

"From our limited understanding, no. From the evidence, yes." Carl handed Bob the photos and documents. Carl took his glasses off and rubbed his eyes. They were burning from days of little sleep, constant eye strain over reports and microscopes. Fatigue was setting in, but they had to find out why the chromosomes were mutating. "The implications of this are horrendous, Bob."

"I know." Bob paused and sat the papers on the table. "I need to get every available resource on this. Do you have any idea why this is occurring?"

"No, none." Carl was dejected, but not defeated. "We've run every test we can think of. The only variable is that something foreign is causing the mutations. I don't know if it is radiation, oxidation, or what. But it isn't from the body; that we know. The mutations are new. They were not in these bodies before, and now they are. They mutated recently, maybe in the last sixty days. It's as though they are going through some type of metamorphosis before our eyes."

"That's impossible."

"Normally, I would agree with you, Bob. But I am seeing it. It's right here." Carl pointed to the papers on the table. "It's almost as if the gene is breaking down and mutating in front of us, but we don't know why. It looks like something is eating away at it, or portions are dissolving. I don't know."

Bob studied the images. "This could explain why we are seeing the rapid increase in deaths."

"It could." Carl paused for a few seconds. "This thing is changing rapidly and dramatically. We just don't know what it is."

"OK, Carl. What's the next step?" Bob asked.

"I need to conduct a comparative molecular biological analysis of the membrane transport of the genes. We need access to an electron microscope."

"You've got it. We have access to several. The Emory University School of Medicine is the largest and closest if ours does not suffice." Bob could command any piece of equipment needed for any study.

"That sounds fine. We can use both, I'm sure. We have a lot of work to do, so the more access we have, the faster we can get the analysis done," Carl said.

"I agree. Time is critical. I'll call the Director of the Office of Research Administration at Emory right away." Bob paused for a few seconds and looked at the pictures again. "Carl. I know you can figure this out."

Carl didn't say a word as Bob walked out of the room. Instead, he picked up the photos and stared at them. "Amazing."

The doctor looked over the chart. The equipment continued to beep and hum while it monitored the patient's vital signs. Bruce Lowell was off the ventilator, but nothing else improved. The nurse was adjusting the pillow, checking the bags of solutions dripping into his veins. Every few seconds she would glance at the monitors. "He isn't going to make it, is he doctor?" she asked.

"Difficult to say, but in this case, I suspect not. There's just too much damage." He continued to glance through the chart when the man walked in. "May I help you?"

"I'm Agent Jamille Larson from the FBI. Is this Bruce Lowell?" The agent showed his identification to the nurse who approached him, and then to the doctor.

The doctor replied. "It is, but he is in no condition to carry on a conversation right now."

"I see." The agent looked at the equipment keeping Bruce alive. "Do you know if or when he will be? This is very important."

"I don't. You could try back later, but I doubt his condition is going to change much." The doctor said. He turned away from the agent and studied the chart notes.

Jamille was accustomed to people being dismissive toward him because of his color. This time, though, he didn't believe the doctor was being rude because he was black.

"Would it be all right, doctor, if I had someone call Mister Larson if the patient woke?" The nurse was pleasant and wanted to help, which was her nature.

"Yes, that would be fine." The doctor turned to the agent. "Please keep in mind any questioning needs to be brief, short, to the point . . . ."

The doctor was interrupted by a moan from Bruce. "Doctor," the nurse called. "He's coming around." She leaned close to his face. "Hello, Brucie. I'm right here." She took hold of his good hand. "Open your eyes, hon."

Bruce struggled and slowly opened one eye and rolled it around trying to focus. He coughed so slightly.

"There you go. Hello there, sweety. Welcome back." The nurse smiled. "We're having a little party here for you."

The corner of Bruce's lip twitched very little as he tried to smile. She was beautiful to him. He tried to speak, but couldn't form the words. He rolled his eye around trying to see who else was in the room.

"Do you think I can ask him a couple of questions?" the agent asked.

The nurse became irritated by the request and spun toward the agent. "Do you think he is in any condition to answer right this moment? At least give him some time to wake up."

"This is serious, ma'am. We have two dead people at his business, and thousands dying all over the world from a disease that his company has the only 'cure' to, so his condition is not as important as me getting some answers." Jamille turned to the doctor. "I think he may know something that could help either the investigation or the research. We don't have a lot of time here."

"Well, truth is, he probably won't remember anything. The brain trauma he suffered likely caused some amnesia, so I don't think he will be much help," the doctor responded.

"Give me two minutes. At least let me ask a couple of questions. If it is more than he can handle, then I'll back off. You call the shots, doctor." Jamille was willing to do anything to try and get some answers, even one answer that could help them.

"OK. Nurse . . . ." The doctor motioned for her to step aside and allow Agent Larson to get close to the patient. "When I say it's enough, you stop."

"I will, doctor." Jamille leaned over near the face of Bruce Lowell. "Mr. Lowell. Can you hear me?"

Bruce looked at Jamille with his one eye.

"Do you understand me?"

Bruce replied in a very weak voice, "Yes."

"Good. I just want to ask you a couple of questions." Jamille paused to think of the right questions. "What happened to James Anderson?"

Bruce's eye looked at Jamille, then to the nurse and doctor, and back to Jamille. He coughed slightly. Jamille repeated his question. Bruce didn't say anything. "Do you remember why you are here?"

Bruce licked his lips. "Fell."

"Yes!" They were making progress. "Yes, you did. You fell out of a window. Can you tell me what . . . ."

"preees . . . ." Bruce mumbled something, but Jamille couldn't understand.

"What? What did you say? Please? Please what?"

Bruce struggled to get the word out clearly. "Priest."

Jamille was taken back. "You . . . you want a priest?"

Bruce slowly blinked twice, and closed his eye.

The analyst was reading through documents that were shipped to CDC from Biotrogen. She was surrounded by piles of papers, folders, and booklets arranged by date and category. Her task was to review files specifically for information related to the mutation of chromosome 19Q13.33A and the research regarding suppression of the gene expression. The theory that Doctor Kruger had was that any information that would point to how the suppression of the gene expression functioned could be analyzed backwards to determine why the expression existed. It would be like looking at a healthy azalea bush with one yellow leaf and determining the plant lacked nitrogen at some time. Further research may show the plant was in nitrogen poor soil and dying, and was corrected by the introduction of the proper nutrient. Find the result, and look at the possible cause that was addressed.

    The analyst glanced over document after document. She pulled a small report from the box that had something stuck inside the pages. She opened the report and found a folded piece of paper. She opened and read it.

TradeKey
Buy Order
May 18, 2003.
10,000 bushels
Wheat
Live Earth Organic Farms
$2.68 per bushel

Online Signature—James Bry

"That's odd." She mumbled to herself. "Looks like someone used this for a bookmark or something." She set it aside and continued to read through the documents.

    Alan Gobel walked into Grace's office. "Grace, did you hear what happened in emergency yesterday?"
    Grace was setting at her computer typing. "Yes, Alan. I did." She turned and looked at him. He could see the concern on her face. "Please, sit down, Alan."
    Alan sat in the chair by the window. "I was off and heard about it when I came in. It's horrible, Grace. That was the woman . . . ."

Grace interrupted him. ". . . . who lost her son a few weeks ago. Yes, I know. Mrs. Hammond."

"What happened? I heard she just went nuts and had a stroke in the lobby."

"Not quite. She suffered a Maskill type aneurysm, Alan." She gave Alan time to respond, but he said nothing. "She apparently suffered the aneurysm while under extreme stress. They brought their daughter in with the same symptoms as their son and . . . ."

"Wait. Their daughter, too?" Alan was shocked.

"Yes. Daughter, too. Lisa Hammond. She died from the same type of aneurysm, Alan. Three in one family in less than three weeks."

"Oh, Lord." Alan had to compose himself. He thought about the father. "What about Bill, the father? How is he doing?"

"Not sure. We were going to charge him for assault, but considering the circumstances, we just let him go home. We offered some sedatives, but he refused. He was calm when he left. Almost ambivalent." Grace paused for a moment while she shuffled some papers on her desk and handed Alan a document. "This is a notice from CDC. Thirty-seven hundred cases and climbing."

"All confirmed deaths?" he asked.

"Yes."

"All Maskill's?"

"No."

"No?" Alan was puzzled. "What do you mean, 'no'?"

Grace walked over to the window and looked out at the city. "I spoke with Bob Struthers at the CDC earlier today after . . . 'the event'. I told him what was happening, and the increase we are seeing in cases." Grace turned to Alan. "Alan. I trust you more than anyone in this hospital, and what I am about to tell you can not be shared with anyone. Absolutely no one. It would serve no purpose." Grace was adamant. Alan had never seen her this way. She was scared and he could see it in her eyes.

"It won't leave this office. What is it, Grace?"

Grace took a deep breath and looked back out the window. "The CDC has discovered new mutations of the 'Maskill's' chromosome 19Q. They now have five types."

"Five? Five types?" Alan leaned forward in his chair. "Why didn't anyone bring this up before?"

"Because it didn't exist before." Grace turned to Alan. "The mutations are new, and they don't know why."

"What do you mean, 'new'? How can that be, Grace?"

"Bob said the new mutations were caused by an external agent of some type. He has a doctor of genetics from John Hopkins ICE team doing the analysis. They don't know if the agent is contagious, though they believe it is not. They narrowed the time frame for the new mutations to three months or so. The mutations are not inherently in Maskill's patients . . . ." Grace paused. " . . . . so, theoretically, anyone can have it."

Alan was stunned. He leaned back in his chair. "Anyone?"

"Anyone. And now we have three cases in one family. One Maskill's patient, two not. Causes one to stop and consider, doesn't it?" Grace looked at Alan. He was oblivious to her. He was deep in thought. "Alan, I'm not sure what we are dealing with here, but I know this is just the beginning. I can feel it." She rubbed her arms.

Grace continued to look out the window as Alan stared at the floor.

The man was setting in the chair in Bruce's room. He was reading a bible and listening to the sounds of machines. He had been in this situation many times before. He was the 'on call' minister for the hospital. Ministers, pastors and priests all volunteered to serve at the hospital to be available to those in need, usually those who were dying. Sometimes someone just wanted a religious person there to feel better. Sometimes they wanted them to pray for their recovery. Sometimes it was the family or friends asking the religious person on call to come by. Whatever the reason, it was for a need. And in this case, the man could see the need was dire. The patient lying before him was in very bad shape. He had seen many. And he knew he might not wake while he was there. But, he had plenty of time. No one else needed his services right now, so he thought he would wait.

"Unngghhh," Bruce groaned as he tried to move.

"I'm right here, Bruce." The man leaned in, closer to his face. "Can you hear me?"

Bruce's eye rolled open. It took him a few seconds to locate the man. "Yes."

"Good. I'm Pastor Ray. You asked for a priest. I know and believe in God, too. Are you Catholic?"

Bruce struggled to talk. "No."

"Can you tell me your belief?" The pastor wanted to meet the man in his area of belief. Even though he was a Baptist, the responsibility of the 'on call' minister was to meet the religious needs of the patient before them. Sometimes, that was a tall order because of the numerous and conflicting beliefs.

Bruce half licked his lips. "Forgive me."

The pastor lowered his head, and took hold of Bruce's free hand. He looked up at Bruce. "Are you asking for forgiveness of your sins?" Bruce squeezed his hand slightly.

"Yes" he whispered. A tear formed in his good eye.

The pastor leaned a little closer and whispered into his ear. "Do you want Jesus to forgive you of your sins and cleanse you, Bruce?"

Bruce tried to talk. "..ssss" He squeezed the pastor's fingers.

The Pastor laid his other hand on Bruce's forehead, and prayed with him. A tear rolled down Bruce's cheek.

Biotrogen was still closed. The executive team felt that it was better to keep the entire company closed for the weekend and allow investigators time to go through the records without interrupting business. They had the proper court orders and warrants for investigation into a possible homicide. The implications of the deaths being tied to the rising Maskill Seizure deaths caused great concern for the CDC and now the FBI. The government wanted to step in and use all of their resources to try and stop this emerging plague.

But they didn't have much to go on. Two dead founding partners of the company. Both from a fall through the window in the office down the hall. One died Thursday. The other earlier today. Agent Larson didn't get any answers to his questions. In fact, he really didn't get to question the man. Now, he had to resort to searching through his records, computers, files, receipts, and anything that might provide a clue.

Agent Larson was used to this. He had his system of what information to gather. First, get all the bank account records. Second, all the computer records. Last, anything else in printed or physical format that might relate. The interviews are helpful, but the information usually tells the story of the case. Once his team sifted through the documents, he could make a second pass and get the rest of the information. It was like following rabbit trails from one piece of evidence to another to another. He was confident that he would eventually tie it all up into a nice, clean web. He always does. It always works. No reason for it to fail this time.

"Make sure you get the backup disks off the servers and make copies for us," he called to one of his agents. "I need backups of everything, business records, research records. Everything."

"Yes, sir."

"We're going to the other partner's office after we are done here." He turned to the executive VP standing next to him who was assigned to be on hand while the FBI exercised their subpoenas and gathered the information and records. "It won't take too long," Jamille said. "We should be done by tomorrow."

The executive team was unsettled about the amount of information requested from the FBI. After all, they had significant research data and private information stored on their systems. However, they were assured the information would be protected and confidential and only used in their investigation. Besides, it was better than shutting the company down for a couple of weeks and not allow any production at all.

"Feels like you are raping the company. First the CDC. Now the FBI. Who's next?" the VP asked.

"Don't know. All I know is I have to get this stuff now and conduct the interviews. So, if you don't mind, I'd like to start with this list of employees." He handed the list to the VP. "Can you have someone contact them? I need to interview them this weekend. It's best if they just come here to this office so they don't see the broken window."

"Yes. I'll get right on it."

The VP left the office. Jamille looked around and saw the signed football. He picked it up and noticed the signatures on it. "Hmm . . . , Montana and Young. Wow!" The thought of holding a football signed by two legends of the game made him almost giddy. He smiled like it was Christmas morning and he was ten. Then, he looked to the side and saw the U.S. Navy SEAL Emblem on its stand with the medals. He reached over and ran his fingers along the edge of the emblem. "A SEAL and a hero, huh?"

CHAPTER 15

Sunday April 24
Deaths 4,087

FBI office—Sacramento, California

It was 8:30 in the morning. Agent Jamille Larson had already been at work for two hours. Being single made it easy to get an early workout in before work and still make it there long before anyone else showed up. That was his 'study' time. He would regularly take the quiet time of the morning and just review the evidence that was amassed on a single case. Today, the case was new and fresh—the Deaths at Biotrogen; over a coffee and apple fritter from VooDoo Donuts.

Jamille was an ambitious young man. At thirty-three, he was an up and coming young agent. He felt he had to work harder than the other agents to prove himself. Maybe it was his history of struggling through school as a black child in the inner city. Maybe it was his mother always telling him to work harder, be smarter, and get an education. Maybe it was his dad telling him he'd never make it. Whatever the motivation, Jamille surprised everyone, including himself, when he received his degree in criminal justice from Stanford University and went on to join the Federal Bureau of Investigation. He had a knack for investigation. He was naturally a curious man who needed answers.

He wondered why this case was such a big deal when he was first assigned to it Friday afternoon. His boss put him on the case while he contacted the court for search warrants and orders. Seemed like overkill to him. It was only a couple of deaths. That happens all the time in a city of a couple of million people. What made this unusual is the people were very, very wealthy partners, except the girl. She was a complete opposite and unknown. There were no ties to the two partners, except the company. She had only worked there for about a week.

And that was his case. The company was in some way associated to some kind of disease or something that was killing people. He was supposed to find out about the murdered girl, Leslie Singer. But after a few hours of reviewing the players in this case, he knew there was something more. Three deaths at the same time were more than coincidental, in his professional opinion. They were related. Had to be. How, was the question.

Jamille continued to look through the reports, printouts and documents that they retrieved from the offices of the partners when the door opened.

"Mr. Larson. We have something." The agent was excited, but professional. "We found some hairs and saliva on the coat in the partner's office you singled out, and ran a DNA test on it last night. The hairs were a different color than the partner. They were black. The DNA on both came back positive for Leslie Singer, the vic."

"Tell me they were on the left sleeve." Jamille sipped his coffee.

"How did you know?"

"The medical examiner's report indicated the girl's neck was broken by force from the right side pushing the vertebrae out of alignment to the left." He demonstrated the moves and holds in thin air. "Our partner, Bruce Lowell, was a US Navy Seal. I also found out he was right handed."

"A SEAL?" The agent was surprised.

"Yeah. I saw his emblem on his desk. And a hero. We ran a background check yesterday to confirm it. He served as a SEAL for eight years." Jamille took another sip. "He saw a lot of action somewhere. That's how he got those medals. He knew how to kill. If anyone could kill her that efficiently, it would be a SEAL."

"But, why?" asked the young agent.

Jamille lifted the apple fritter and admired the glossy, sugary coating. "That's what we don't know, yet." And he took a huge bite.

The room was dark. A beam of sunlight streamed through the crack in the closed curtains allowing just enough light to illuminate the cluttered dining table. The curtains were closed keeping the afternoon sun out of the house. The dining table was cluttered with dishes, silverware, glasses. The cooked ham was still on the platter. Several flies were buzzing around enjoying the feast. The mashed potatoes were beginning to get crusty. The milk was sour. The table was littered with the leftovers of that eventful day when Lisa and Linda both died at the hospital.

Bill loved the Sunday family dinners. Not anymore. There was not going to be a Sunday dinner today or ever again.

The Hammond family had just finished a nice ham dinner Friday when Lisa went outside to play on her slide. She was standing at the top, waving to her mother who was watching her through the kitchen window as she was washing the dishes and beginning to clear the table when, for no reason, Lisa slumped down to her knees, fell forward, and slid down the slide face first ending in a heap at the bottom.

Bill was sitting in the living room getting ready to watch the news when he heard his wife scream and a dish break. He thought she had dropped a plate. "What's wrong, honey?"

He heard the door open as Linda ran outside, yelling for her daughter. Bill jumped to his feet and ran behind her . . . . and the dining table sat ever since.

Bill was sitting in the living room, again, but he wasn't watching the news. The room was dark. Several beer bottles were strewn about the room. The sofa had been his bed for the past two days. He didn't want to go upstairs to an empty bed. He would have to pass by the kids' rooms, and he couldn't do it. The pain was overwhelming. His whole family, gone.

There was no sound in the house. Only a ticking clock, his breathing and the beating of his heart. He occasionally heard noises outside, but they didn't concern him. He was dirty and unshaven. His hair was a mess. He hadn't changed his clothes or bathed since that day. He hadn't eaten. He only drank. He didn't care.

The phone rang and the machine immediately came on. "This is Bill. I'm gone for a few days. Call me next week." He didn't invite the caller to leave a message. He didn't want to hear any more, *"I'm sorry for your loss,"* or *"If there's anything I can do."* He heard enough. There was nothing anyone could do.

He was the only one who could do anything about his misery.

He looked over at the rifle leaning against the sofa. The walnut stock was smooth and shiny. He took another drink of beer as he admired the shiny wood grain of the stock. The swirls and colors were mesmerizing.

He took another drink. He was drunk, and he didn't care. No one cared. He was drowning his sorrows the only way he knew.

He reached over and ran his finger from the sight of his rifle down the barrel toward the stock. The steel was smooth, cold, hard. He pulled the barrel toward him and placed it pointed into his face. The scope looked like a giant glass eye staring at him. He could see his reflection in it. The small hole of the barrel invited him. He could see the grooves at the tip of the barrel. He moved his face closer for a better look. Then, he closed his eyes and slowly placed his forehead on the muzzle of the barrel. He was breathing heavily, sweating, and his hands started to shake. Tears rolled down his cheeks.

"I can do this!" He said through his gritted teeth. He slowly started to slide his hand down the stock toward the trigger. His fingers reached the curved edge of the trigger guard. The hard steel protected the trigger. He opened his eyes for a moment, gasping for a breath, and saw a Bible on the floor next to the sofa. It looked like someone had kicked it under the corner of the sofa as they were walking by. He recognized it. It was Linda's bible. Her name was inscribed in gold lettering. The last time he saw the bible was when Linda was setting on the sofa with her legs curled under her, reading a passage to Lisa. Lisa was leaning against her mother listening intently. It was just a few days ago.

"Ughhhhhhh!" He pushed the rifle aside and it went off, firing a round through the wall and into the kitchen. The sound was deafening.

Bill leaned forward and put his head in his hands and wept loudly as the smell of gunpowder filled the room. "God, help me."

CHAPTER 16

Monday April 25
Deaths 4,586

It was almost noon. Alice Barker was refreshed after having a full day off. She was eagerly wading through the reports and analysis. The number of Maskill's deaths continued to climb over the weekend reaching almost 5,000. The additional information from the mortuaries and hospital research was adding to the totals. Her team continued to receive reports from all over the world. Most peculiar, though, is that the concentrations on the West Coast were becoming more defined and dense.

Bob was looking over her shoulder as they both looked at the topographical maps overlaid with the death locations. "Looks like there are four cluster areas on the West Coast." Alice pointed to the four clusters of red dots.

"There are. But, there is something very unusual about these clusters." Alice pointed to the Los Angeles basin. "This is the most populated area on the West Coast, yet it has almost no cases."

"I see."

"The cases per 100,000 are off the charts in the cluster areas." Alice pointed to the central Oregon and Washington clusters. "These clusters occur in low density population zones. The occurrences are one case per 2,000, compared to one case per 200,000 elsewhere."

"Why?" Bob asked.

"Ha. If I knew that, we'd be done, honey." Alice smiled and poked him in the arm.

Bob started thinking out loud. "We know it's not geographical in the sense that the cause is the environment. We've eliminated foreign materials, minerals, and chemicals that appear in the environment."

Alice continued. "We know it's not industrial. We ran correlation analysis on all industries in these areas with no hits. In fact, some had no industry, except agricultural."

"What is it?" he asked. "What is causing this? There has to be an answer."

"There is. We just don't know what it is yet." Alice spun in her chair to look at the monitor. "We have almost 5,000 cases. I expect tomorrow we will pass that mark easily. Bob, the number of cases is increasing everyday. It looks like—whatever it is—is starting to take hold and claim more victims. It's maturing. The origination date of first occurrence hasn't changed at all." She looked at Bob. "Is Carl making any progress?"

"Some." Bob took a few steps away and turned back. "He's discovered the multiple mutations of the 19Q chromosome, but no reason why, other than it is foreign induced." Bob scratched his head. "We've looked at everything foreign that we can think of. These new mutations must be causing the increased deaths. We're missing something, Alice. We have to be."

"Bob, we've been at this for more than a week. We have teams of people digging around the clock through everything from samples to documents to who knows what. It's there, you know it. We just haven't found it yet. But we will. I know we will. We're going to figure this out." Alice was adamant.

"How many people will die before we do? That's the question, Alice."

Doctor Carl Kruger took his glasses off, tossed them on the table in disgust and leaned back in his chair. He quickly stood to his feet and kicked his chair out of the way. He put his hands over his face trying to wipe the strain away from his eyes. His head hurt. He was tired, frustrated. He remembered the excruciating practices he had when he played football. Continuous drills, injuries, dehydration, headaches; but nothing compared to this. He felt like a failure. The analysis of the 19Q chromosome just exasperated him. He had never seen anything like this before. Under normal circumstances this would be a fantastic opportunity to build a Ph.D. thesis around, or experiment with alternative influences of chemicals on membrane transfers. But today, it was the bane of his existence. He was pressured to find the reason with no idea of where, how, or when this dreaded disease was created.

Bob walked in and saw the doctor at his low point. He walked over and casually up righted the chair. "You look beat, Carl. How many hours have you been at this?"

Carl glared at him. "Today or from when I first arrived?"

Bob looked at him with a puzzled look, then they both broke into laughter.

Carl put his glasses back on as he stopped laughing. "About a thousand, I suppose."

"Or more," Bob said.

"Yes, or more." Carl stood and walked to the window. "We have nothing concrete, Bob. Nothing. After more than a week of dissecting and analyzing everything we can think of, down to the molecule, we have nothing as a cause for this."

"You have something," Bob replied. "You have multiple mutations of the same chromosome. That, alone, is significant and will lead to the cause." Bob was confident, much more so than Carl. He knew Carl needed a little encouragement to keep him focused. "I know it will."

"Glad you do, Bob. I'm not quite as optimistic." Carl sighed deeply. "I've never seen or heard of anything like this. I'm beginning to think . . . ." He paused for a long few seconds. It was long enough to make Bob uncomfortable.

"You think what? What is it, Carl?" Bob's curiosity spiked. "What?"

"I'm . . . . I'm even wondering if . . . . if an alien source of some type is a possible cause." Carl was almost embarrassed to mention it.

"Alien, as in outer space?" Bob almost laughed. Carl looked at him sternly. "You're serious!"

"Yes, I am," Carl said indignantly as he walked back to the desk and put his glasses on. "Listen, an alien influence is anything not from this world. It doesn't have to be a living alien being, but an alien source . . . an unknown chemical . . . bacterium . . . something we have never seen before." Carl started to get excited as he spoke. "Maybe it is a new type of wavelength or x-ray emitted from a comet or a distant star, a type of gamma ray. Maybe it's microscopic to the degree we wouldn't know how to recognize it if we saw it. Maybe it's a new element that we didn't know existed." Carl almost sounded like a mad scientist listing the possibilities.

"Carl. Carl." Bob put his hand on his shoulder. "Settle down." He smiled at Carl as he continued. "Maybe it is any of those things. But to know for sure, more testing must be done." He paused. "Science will find it. Create the hypothesis, test for it, analyze the results. Keep working methodically through this. You'll get it." He patted Carl on the shoulder and walked out. How ironic, he thought, that he was now encouraging Carl in the same way Alice encouraged him. Maybe there was something contagious.

The white board had pictures of Bruce Lowell, James Anderson, and Leslie Singer taped to it. Under each picture words were written that described key points about each:

> Leslie Singer
> 28 years old, single, employed seven days, Research Analyst, murdered by Lowell, last assignment—Maskill's research with Lowell, genetics student at CSUS
> James Anderson
> 49 years old, single, partner and founder, University Calif. Davis masters in Agriculture and Finance, killed by fall, stock sales two days prior, recent three day travel to Oregon—unknown, one-way ticket to France.
> Bruce Lowell
> 56 years old, divorced, partner and founder, UCD masters in Biomedical Engineering, suicide, murdered Leslie Singer, Navy Seal, recent 4 day travel to San Diego and Houston—speech, no stock sales

Jamille Larson leaned back in his chair as he studied the pictures and the words underneath. He mumbled to himself. "Why would one partner have major stock sales, and the other none?" he asked. "Why would one partner go to Oregon for an unknown reason during the week? No relatives, no interests, an overnighter to Portland. Did he have a girlfriend? Business?"

"What's that?" Agent Melvin Walker walked in as Jamille was thinking out loud.

"Doesn't it seem odd to you that one partner sells a chunk of his stock two days before he is found dead, and the other doesn't?" Jamille asked.

Agent Walker grabbed a donut as he walked by the table. "Sure. You would think they would be in sync with the company performance and plans. I understand he had plans that didn't involve the other partner, like a one-way ticket to France."

"That speaks for itself, doesn't it?" Jamille didn't give Agent Walker a chance to respond. "He goes to Oregon for basically an overnighter, returns, and the next week sells his stock and gets ready to fly to France with no plans to return. Why? What did he find out?"

"Must be tied into the Maskill's deaths and notices from the CDC," Walker said.

"Those are notices. That's business. Unless . . . ." Jamille paused for a second. " . . . . unless he knew something more about the deaths."

"What do you mean?" Agent Walker asked.

"Look." Jamille grabbed a marker and walked over to the white board. "What reasons would a person leave in a situation like this?"

Agent Walker thought for a second. "OK. He knew it would destroy the company."

Agent Walker wrote 'destroy.' "But wouldn't this give them an opportunity to make a new medicine and research? That's how they got rich in the first place." He wrote 'opportunity' next to 'destroy.' "Try again."

"What if . . . what if the medicine was the cause for the deaths?"

Jamille wrote 'cause' on the board. "Yes. If the medicine was the cause, he would be inclined to run. But he wouldn't know it was the cause unless some testing was done and revealed it. This is a new event." Jamille wrote 'know' on the whiteboard. He circled 'know.' "If he knew the medicine was the cause, he would certainly sell his stock and run." Jamille put the marker down. "I don't think he would run if he thought the medicine was the cause. He might sell his stocks to avoid losses, but run? The medicine would just be pulled off the market." Jamille walked over to the window. His mind was working. "I think he knew something was amiss with the deaths, and that somehow they were culpable. The question is, how did he know before any testing was done?" He paused, then snapped his fingers. "Unless they tested this stuff before and something like this was revealed . . . and they hid it."

"Maybe that's what happened to the girl. She found out something and they had to kill her to keep her quiet." Melvin grabbed another stale donut out of the box on the table.

"I don't think it was 'they.' I think it was him." Jamille pointed to Bruce's picture. "He killed her."

"That doesn't make sense. If they both knew about something with the medicine, then why would one sell his stock and try to run, and the other kill the girl. Wouldn't they be working together?" Agent Walker continued to consume his donut.

"I know. It's a disconnect." Jamille sat back down and stared at the pictures. "Then we have the question of why Bruce killed James, or at least it looks that way."

"Agreed. I can't imagine someone selling their stock, transferring funds, purchasing a one-way flight, and then jumping out a fifth-floor window because they were distraught. Doesn't add up," Agent Walker said.

"Well, then why did he kill his partner?" Jamille asked.

"To keep him quiet?"

"No, he was leaving. No reason to threaten your partner about revealing something. Just get away."

"Because he was mad?" Walker asked.

Jamille thought for a second. "Yeah . . . . He found out he was leaving and a fight broke out. Push, shove, out the window. It fits."

"He probably found out he cashed out his stocks and was splitting."

"Probably." Jamille stood up and wrote the word 'fight' between Jim and Bruce's pictures with a line to each and a question mark. "That would explain a lot." He sat back down in his chair. "Let's assume they both know something about the medicine and the deaths, somehow, before testing reveals it. They get these CDC and FDA notices. One sells his stock, books a flight to France. The other maybe doesn't know about the 'thing' with the medicine, or he knows and thinks he can fix it. Jim comes in, they fight because Bruce finds out Jim is leaving. It probably started that day because the bottom fell out of their stock and Jim was gloating or something. Bruce went broke, but Jimmy boy is fine since he sold all of his stock. A fight breaks out, one is dead. The other is distraught and now broke, plus he killed a girl the night before, so he decides to fly. It fits."

"But why kill the girl?" Walker asked.

"She must have found something." Jamille put the marker down. "We need to find out what she found." He hit the button on the phone. "Tisha, can you have the team report to conference room six right away, please?"

"Yes Mr. Larson." He turned back to Agent Walker, who was grabbing a maple bar. He acted like he just got caught.

"Lunch!"

The people were formed in a half circle around the whiteboard. Agent Jamille Larson addressed the group.

"OK. Here's what we have." He explained the theory that he and Agent Walker developed thus far. All the pieces fit. It made sense to everyone. "There are still some holes that we need to fill in." Jamille drew two columns on the white board. He labeled one Agent and the other Tasks.

"We need to find out why James Anderson went to Oregon. Thomas, I want you to dig this up."

"Yes sir." The agent's name and task went on the board.

"The other hole is their last jobs at Biotrogen; the tasks or projects that they were working on the week before they died. I want to know about their reports, meetings, files, papers, whatever they were working on. This goes for each of them." Jamille looked at the group. "Richards. I want you to get a team on the girl. Walters on Jimmy boy, and Lisa on Bruce."

They all acknowledged their assignments by nodding.

"The rest of you continue to sort out the financial info and data off the servers. Let me know if you find anything." Jamille put the marker down as the group walked out the door. He sat back in his chair and looked at the board. "We're gonna find out why." He reached over and took the last stale donut in the box.

It was night in Atlanta. Bob Struthers was standing at the window . . . . staring. He was exhausted, disappointed, mad, frustrated. So many emotions were running through him. He knew there was a reason these people were dying, and he wanted it stopped. He felt so helpless. It seemed he was doing everything he could, but they were missing something. He started questioning if he had the right people. Maybe he should meet with Randall and explore recruiting new scientists. Maybe there was a particular field he was missing that should be represented. Maybe . . . .

The phone rang.

"Bob Struthers."

"Mr. Struthers, this is Agent Jamille Larson from the FBI office in Sacramento, California."

"Well, hello there." Bob cleared his throat. "What can I do for you, Agent Larson?"

"My director assigned me the Biotrogen murder case. He said you approached him about it and expressed some concerns. He assigned me to be the Lead Agent on it."

"That's great. What can I do for you?"

"I'm investigating the deaths of the partners and one employee."

"Good," Bob replied.

"I have some theories about this case that might involve the Maskill's deaths and their medicine." Bob leaned forward as he listened to Jamille's theories. "One theory is that the partners knew something was wrong with their medicine and tried to hide it."

"How do you mean?" Bob was intrigued.

"In your research so far, is there any indication that the medicine is the cause for the Maskill deaths?" Jamille asked.

"No. None. We don't know what's causing the deaths."

Jamille scratched his head. "Hmmm. That kind of blows my theory."

"What have you found out so far?" Bob asked.

"Not much." Jamille explained what they have discovered so far and how he thought the medicine being the cause of the deaths would lead to a cover up, fight, and possible murder.

"Well, we are convinced it is not the medicine because it was pulled from the market several days ago and the cases continue to increase." Bob paused. "Sorry to take the wind out of your sails, agent," he said dejectedly. He, too, wanted an answer.

"No problem, sir. Can you let me know if anything develops on your end?"

"Bob quickly replied, "Absolutely . . . . and vice versa."

CHAPTER 17

Tuesday April 26
Deaths 5,255

The sun was just peaking above the horizon when Grace Moore pulled into the parking lot at Mercy General Hospital. The news truck was parked in the lot. Several people were standing outside with cameras trained on them. They were speaking into microphones when they saw Grace pull into the Administrator's parking space. Grace stepped out of the car and started toward the entrance.

"Ms. Moore? Ms. Moore? Do you have a moment, please?" The young lady approached Grace with a microphone in hand. The cameraman followed the young lady as she stepped to Grace's side.

"Are we on the air?" Grace asked.

"Yes, we are," the young lady replied.

"Then no comment." Grace turned and headed toward the building.

"Ok, Dave. Turn off the camera," the young reporter said as she turned and caught up with Grace. "No cameras. Just me. I'm Rebekah Crawford. Channel eleven. Do you have a moment?"

Grace stopped and looked at the aspiring young reporter. "OK. No cameras," Grace said as she glared at the cameraman.

"None. Thanks." The reporter pulled out a notepad. She cleared her throat. "We had a report that a local family recently had three members die from an unknown disease. Is that true?"

"No, it is not. They did not die from a disease," Grace said directly.

"Then, what did they die from?"

"I'm sorry, that is patient confidentiality. However, I can say they did not die from a disease." Grace knew how to not answer questions, but still give answers.

"Ms. Moore. There was a notice from the Center for Disease Control that was issued last week indicating a problem existed with Maskill's patients dying from seizures. We understand one of the family members was a Maskill's carrier. Is that true?"

"Again, patient confidentiality."

"What about the CDC report? Haven't you had fifteen people die from Maskill's seizures in the past few weeks?"

Grace's mouth opened slightly. *How did she know? Who was telling her?* "I don't have that information readily available. Now, if you'll excuse me, I have a hospital to run." Grace turned and darted toward the door.

"Ms. Moore. Ms. Moore. Just one more question." The young lady tried to stay up with her.

Grace continued to walk away, never looking back.

The reporter returned back to her cameraman who raised the camera, flipped on the lights, and started filming.

Four agents were setting at the table with Jamille Larson. Agent Larson spoke first. "Let's start with Agent Walker. Report."

"We've analyzed about 75% of the data from the servers and the backups. There is a corporation under a different EIN[4] with the state of Nevada on the backup. It wasn't on the main server, but a backup server. It is not a sub corporation of Biotrogen. It stands alone and apparently operates here from Sacramento."

"It was on the backup and not the main, hmmm? Did you say Nevada?" Jamille was intrigued.

"Yes."

"The only reason someone would open a corporation in Nevada and operate here when they have a corporation already operating is to hide something." He looked at the agent. "What are they hiding?"

"Commodities," replied the agent.

"Commodities? That makes no sense. What commodities?" Jamille asked.

"Wheat. They buy and sell it through the out of State Corporation using an online system called 'TradeKey.' It's a global internet market that connects buyers and sellers for a variety of products." The agent pushed a few papers to Jamille and continued. "This corporation has been in

---

[4]   EIN- Employer Identification Number for tax purposes

place about eleven years. It's filed under Jim Anderson's cousin's name. Leonard Wristen. He lives in Vacaville. We are tracking him down to see what he knows about this. We are also reconstructing deleted files to see if anything else exists that might be important."

Jamille smiled. "Good. Find out more about their purchases and sales, and let me know what else you find on the server. Oh, and what the cousin says. I bet he has an interesting story to tell us."

He turned to the next agent. "Walters?"

"Sure. Jim Anderson generally oversaw the financial activity of the company, likely due to his degree in finance. He was in Oregon the week before his death for three days. He landed in Portland and virtually disappeared." He flipped through some papers.

"How so?" Jamille asked.

"There is no record of hotel rooms, car rentals, meals, credit card use; nothing," the agent replied.

"He used cash, then. Check his bank account and see how much he withdrew. Check his cell phone records and see who he called." Jamille knew the information was somewhere.

"We did. Can't find anything in the records except a $2,000 cash withdrawal from his personal checking account, and some calls here to Biotrogen."

"Personal account? Why not use the business account for a trip. Any trip could be explained as a business trip, especially alone to another state like this. OK. Do we know when he flew out?" Jamille asked.

"Yeah. His secretary said he had a 4 P.M. flight on Alaska Air. It wasn't on his calendar."

"Good. They probably have a daily route so check when that flight normally lands. Then get our office in Portland to do a quick door-to-door at the car rentals near the airport about the time the flight arrives. Maybe someone will recognize him. Get a copy of the security feed, too." He thought for a second. "I doubt that he went anywhere else by plane but check connecting flights during that time just in case," the agent nodded.

He turned to the next person. "Lisa? What did you find out about Lowell?" Jamille took a sip of coffee.

"Bruce Lowell spoke at a conference in San Diego two weeks ago. He then went to Houston for another presentation. Looks like he has been hitting the speaking circuit. Upon his return, he was planning some time off for a round of golf with some buddies. Had a tee time for . . . .

Wednesday the 13th at 4 P.M. He also had a hiking trip planned for the weekend." She flipped through some notes. "When the first notices from the FDA came through, he cancelled all of his appointments and formed a project team to prepare information for the CDC."

Richards popped up. "I wonder why he didn't form research teams to try and stop the problem."

"Maybe he thought getting data to the CDC was research enough and more important," Lisa replied. "The prep team had Leslie Singer on it, and two other employees. That's about it. Richards has the rest."

"Richards?"

"Not much here. Singer was a new employee at Biotrogen. She went through orientation and immediately worked on a project with Bruce Lowell. She was part of a three person team that brought boxes of documents to Lowell to prepare for distribution to the CDC. The other teammates said they were pulling files and samples for research on the medicine for Maskill's disease and running copies, scanning, and sorting the documents. Lowell would review the files and make sure they were getting the pertinent information ready for CDC and protecting the information that they had by taking copies of everything."

Jamille had a stern look on his face. "You said three interns were working with him?"

"No. Three analysts. Singer was the only intern. The other two have been here awhile."

"So, they were working with him in his office sorting documents and . . . ."

"No," Richards interrupted. "The secretary said they brought boxes and samples to him in his office and left them there. He sorted through them alone."

"Huh. I bet he did. So, they didn't work with Bruce sorting the documents, like side by side?"

"No. They brought the boxes to him, he would sort, and return it back to them to copy and refile. He was working in his office on the fifth floor, they were in the conference room on the third."

Walters jumped in. "Jim Anderson was also pulling some files for his office." He opened a notepad. "I didn't think much about it until Richards said Lowell was pulling files for the CDC. Anderson wasn't pulling files for the CDC; he was just pulling files. His secretary said he was working long hours taking a few boxes to his office and going through them."

"Was anyone working with him pulling files?" Jamille asked.

"No. His secretary said he was working on this project alone."

Jamille laughed.

"One more thing, boss. Jimmy boy had a trip planned to Cancun the same week he scheduled a flight to France."

"Traveling the world, huh?" Agent Walker asked.

"No. His flight to France would have been while he was in Cancun. He planned and paid for the trip to Cancun two weeks ago, then got a flight to France two days before he died. He never cancelled his trip to Cancun."

"There ya go." Jamille clapped his hands. "They were both covering something up." He smiled as he poured another cup of coffee. "Folks, we need to find out what they were hiding."

Carl, Bob, Alice, and several other people were setting around a table in the conference room at the CDC. There was a whiteboard in the corner of the room with scribbling that only a scientist would understand. Each person had a pile of papers in front of them on the table, along with a soda and some bagels. It was lunch time at the CDC, but no one was eating.

"I don't know what to say, Bob." Carl took his glasses off and laid them carefully on the table as he spoke. "We have no idea what is causing the mutations. We have studied everything we can think of with no breakthrough. My team is working tirelessly, but we keep hitting dead ends. We can not replicate the mutation. We can't find a common denominator amongst the samples. We can't find a source, a catalyst. We are venturing into the molecular structure of the cells searching for aberrations of any type."

"I understand." Bob looked at the doctor who, for the first time, looked defeated. His eyes swollen and red. He was unshaven, tired. "I think you need to clear your mind of this for a day. You need to take a day off and just regroup, Carl."

Carl slammed his fist on the table. "I can't." His outburst caught everyone off guard. Carl seemed shocked as well.

Alice placed her hand on his arm. "Yes, you can," she said softly. She looked at the other people. "We aren't doing ourselves any favor by burning out." She looked back at Carl. "Taking a day off won't mean the end of the world."

Carl looked at her. "Are you sure about that?"

They were all stunned for a second by the profound thought that maybe, just maybe this was something they wouldn't be able to control. What if it became contagious and went airborne? What if it was already? Carl, continued. "We don't know what we are dealing with here. Every second we waste causes more deaths."

"I hate to sound crass here . . ." Alice replied, " . . . . but we aren't doing any good if we are exhausted and miss something simple. It may cost more lives to delay our progress one day, but that's the harsh reality of what we are dealing with."

Bob stepped in and took control as he often did. "Set up your teams to work in shifts. No more that sixteen hours at a time." Bob knew he had to put structure to the idea or no one would follow it on their own. They were too committed, too stubborn to admit failure. They would, literally, work themselves to death if they thought it would help solve the crisis. "Carl. See if you can recruit some of the research doctors or scientists at Emory's to assist you. They can help cover your shifts."

Carl nodded his approval.

"Anything develop with the FBI investigation?" Alice asked.

Bob took a deep breath. "They believe the founders at Biotrogen were covering up something, possibly the medicine, but they don't know for sure. I have a conference call with them tomorrow morning at 10. I'd like both of you to join me, here." He pointed to Carl and Alice.

"We know it's not the medicine. We've run tests and there is nothing that indicates it is the cause of the mutations or deaths," Carl replied.

"Not only that," Alice jumped in, " . . . . we've pulled all of the medicine and the deaths continue to rise. We would expect to see some drop or slowing if it's associated with the cause of death."

Bob confirmed. "I agree. But we should at least discuss the situation, their findings, ours, and see if anything floats to the surface."

Alice continued. "The only thing we have is the cluster of events with no explanation."

Bob pushed himself back from the table and stood. "I know, Alice." It was one of the few times he dismissed Alice's comment or opinion, and she felt the sting from it. Bob continued, oblivious to his offense. "OK. Tomorrow. Here. Ten sharp." He paused for a moment. "Get some rest."

19Q

It was six P.M. The wholesale discount store had a variety of televisions, most with high definition screens. They were synchronized to play the same channel, giving the perception of soldiers marching in ranks. Every screen showed the same image at the same time, except one.

An older man was standing in front of a screen and changing channels. He flipped it to the local news. He had difficulty hearing, so he turned the volume up. Other people in the area looked over to see what he was watching.

". . . . *report from Mercy General Hospital.*" The man on the TV was sharply dressed, and looked very serious. The scene cut to Rebekah Crawford standing in front of Mercy Hospital.

"*Thank you, Roger. I'm standing in front of the emergency entrance of Mercy General Hospital in Eugene. A few days ago, Bill Hammond's daughter, Lisa, was brought to the hospital by ambulance after suffering a stroke of some type that resulted in her death. She was eight years old with no history of illnesses. Mr. Hammond was with his wife, Linda, in emergency's waiting room when she suffered a similar stroke, also dying.*" Pictures of both Linda and Lisa flashed on the screen. "*The tragedy here is that their son, John Hammond, died twelve days ago from a similar stroke. He had suffered from Maskill's Seizures, whereas his mother and sister did not.*" A picture of John flashed on the screen with his mom and sister.

The man who was watching said, "Oh no." A few people moved in closer to see. Others started to gather.

"*Our investigation has revealed fifteen people from our area have died from a similar illness. And that is only at this hospital.*" The camera pulls back to show Mercy General Hospital. The scene cuts away to a shot of Grace Moore entering the building. "*I tried to speak with the hospital administrator, Ms. Grace Moore, earlier today. She refused an onscreen interview, and said very little about the deaths citing 'patient confidentiality.' The one thing she did say was that the patients did not die from a disease. If it wasn't a disease, Jeff, then what was it?*" The camera closed in on the reporter. "*I'm Rebekah Crawford from channel eleven action news. Jeff?*"

"Good question, Rebekah." The screen switched back to the anchor. More people had gathered around the television. "*Rebekah's report indicated one of the patients suffered from Maskill's seizures. We have obtained two releases from government agencies that may relate to these deaths.*" The camera panned out to show a picture of the CDC. "*Last Tuesday, the Center for Disease Control in Atlanta, Georgia, issued an alert to doctors and medical practitioners stating that 3,162 reported deaths associated to Maskill's Seizures had occurred and that the situation was intensifying. The CDC asked for those in the medical community to provide information if any more deaths occur in their areas."*

Several people around the television gasped. One lady blurted, "My neighbor died from that."

The picture switched to the Food and Drug Administration headquarters. *"The second notice we intercepted was from the Food and Drug Administration, or the FDA as we know it. The FDA issued a recall notice of Inferon and Tegbatol—the two drugs developed by Biotrogen to combat Maskill's Seizures."* The camera switched to pictures of two bottles labeled with the names of the two drugs. *"The FDA believes these drugs could be causing the deaths, so if you have them in your house or are using them, please stop immediately and contact your doctor."*

The group of people around the television had grown considerably and some were whispering amongst themselves. The anchor continued. *"No one knows for sure what is causing these deaths."* The screen switched back to the pictures of the three victims. *"Hopefully, they will soon."*

"I think you are making the right choice, Bill." The lady smiled as she closed the door. Bill Hammond stood in the living room with his suitcase next to him.

"I appreciate this, sis. I didn't expect them to quarantine my house. I really have nowhere else to go."

The woman walked up and gave him a big hug. He barely responded. "Thanks. Where do you want me to sleep?"

"The first room at the top of the stairs. Here, I'll show you." She grabbed his bag before he could say no, and started up the stairs. "Right this way."

Bill followed her up the stairs, looking at the pictures on the wall. Deanna had pictures of all the family members. He stopped when he saw a picture of him, Linda, John and Lisa. He touched the picture for a second, took a breath, and continued up the stairs.

"Right here, honey." Deanna stepped aside and pointed into the room. She was quite the hostess. Being almost ten years older than he, she often acted more like a mom than a sister. She always took care of Billy, and what better time than now. He was hurting. She knew that she and her husband could help lighten the load and give him a reprieve from the constant phone calls and newshounds. No one would know he was there.

"There's clean towels over here. You can hang your clothes up and kick your shoes off. This is your room for as long as you want to stay."

"I . . . . I don't know how to thank you, sis." He put his suitcase up on the bed. "This means a lot to me."

"You can thank me by making this your temporary home . . . until you get things sorted out. I think it's a good idea to take a break and just try and get back into some routine."

"I am. I'm going back to work tomorrow. I'm kind of looking forward to doing something that occupies my mind. It's terrible just always thinking about it."

Deanna put her arm around Bill's shoulder. "Have you talked to anyone yet, like a counselor or something?"

"No. Not sure who I would go see." Bill was not one to share his feelings.

"Well, we had a tough time awhile back and saw a great counselor. Maybe he could help? I could get his number.."

"No. Thanks, sis," Bill said sharply, cutting her off. "Give me a few days and we can talk about it then. I think I just need a break." Bill sat down and took his shoes off.

"OK. Hey, I fixed salmon for dinner. Do you want me to call you when it's all ready?"

"Sure. I'd like that."

Deanna knelt down and gave Bill a big hug. "I sure love you. I'm glad you're here." She kissed him on the forehead.

Bill thought about the rifle muzzle leaning against his forehead two days ago. "So am I."

CHAPTER 18

Wednesday April 27
Deaths 6,233

"Ok folks. Settle down." The group was chatting about their research, discoveries, the upcoming NBA playoffs, and their families. They were a team that worked well together, and had endured much. Jamille was proud of his team and how diligent they were with following leads. He was confident that, at the end of the day, their work efforts would be successful. They had to be. Not only was he trying to solve a murder, likely two, but he had a strong suspicion the events of the Maskill deaths were tied to the deaths of these three people and this company. There were too many inconsistencies; too many questions that needed answers.

"OK. Let's see what we have this morning. Let's start with the research on . . . ." He stopped to look at the whiteboard . . . . "Mr. Wristen in Vacaville. Agent Walker?"

"He's dead." The room went silent.

Jamille froze. "Dead? Are you kidding me?"

"Nope. He died eleven years ago in a car accident." He looked at the papers and continued. "He was Jim Anderson's cousin, but that's where it ends. His wife had no idea a corporation was established using his name. He was never involved in any business activities with Mr. Anderson. They weren't even close cousins."

"So, a bogus corporation established by a bogus person to do what?" Jamille asked.

The agent next to Agent Walker answered the question. "To buy and sell wheat . . . organic wheat, to be precise."

"There must be something more. Why create a shell company to buy or sell organic wheat? What else did you find?" Jamille sat in his chair as he listened to the agent explain the research on the company.

"The wheat was purchased from organic farmers and sold to local markets through Tradekey. It appears a premium was paid for the crops. There was almost no margin. In fact, there was a loss on some of the sales, possibly because the market prices changed so quickly," the agent replied.

"That doesn't make any sense. Their prices should have adjusted as the market changed," Jamille commented.

The agent pulled out a sheet of paper and looked at it. "True, except they were buying the products two months before harvest at a premium." He handed the paper to Jamille. "We have a list of some of the purchases over the past three years. They were mostly the same farmers each year, same crop, same times, higher than market prices."

Jamille looked at the list. "Where were they sold?" Jamille asked.

"Local processing plants, all on the West Coast." The agent slid more papers over to Jamille. "There's the list of sales."

"Anything else?"

"Just cashier's checks made out to cash for several thousand dollars each. They came from a bank account under the shell corporation, so we are tracking them down as we speak." The agent took a sip of coffee.

"Good. I want to know where those checks went." Jamille was adamant. "Check the endorsements and the routing numbers. We need to know whose hands they passed through."

"We'll have it in a few hours, boss."

Jamille turned to Agent Walters. "What did you find out about Portland?"

"Turns out he did go there. We pulled the security feed and saw he went to Enterprise car rental. We confirmed with the employee he rented a car. The time stamp on the video and the entry in their system shows he used the name James Bry. He had a driver's license and insurance."

Jamille jumped to his feet. "Yes! That's what we like to hear. A good old cover-up-use-the-fake-ID link." He walked over to the whiteboard and wrote AKA James BRY next to Jim's picture. "What else?"

"The car logged in three hundred and sixty-seven miles over a forty-eight hour period, so he drove a ways. We don't know where."

Jamille walked over to a map of Oregon and Washington and pointed at Portland. "Draw a circle around Portland with a two hundred mile radius. That's the target area."

One of the agents commented, "It could be nothing, boss."

"Or it could be everything. We're not dropping any leads on this, especially when it involves some guy using an alias and paying cash from a shell corporation that was created using a dead man's name." A couple of agents snickered. Jamille was adamant. "Anything else on Jimmy Boy?"

The agent shook his head. "Nope."

"What do we have on the girl?" Jamille turned to Agent Richards.

"Nothing more, boss. All dead ends." A couple of agents snickered again. "No pun intended."

"Same here on Lowell," Agent Lisa replied.

Jamille circled the AKA on the whiteboard several times, then returned to his chair. "Well, we have something more here to work on. Keep digging. I want to meet again at six for a wrap."

The agents stood and left the room, while Jamille stared at the whiteboard. "Jimmy boy . . . talk to me."

Alice and Carl walked into Bob's office together. They looked rested and refreshed. It was almost ten and Bob had already gone through two pots of coffee and a half box of bagels. He looked up from his pile of documents as they walked through the door. "Well, good morning sunshine," Bob said.

"Yes," replied Alice. "It is."

"Why so cheerful? Did you find out something?" Bob asked.

"No. Just got some rest. It's still bad, Bob. More than six thousand so far. But at least I got some sleep and now I can think clearly again. I'm ready to solve this thing," she said.

"Me too. Slept nine hours like a rock," Carl said. "Amazing how a little rest can change your perspective."

"You should try it, Bob," Alice chided him.

Bob laughed. "I seem to do fine on five hours, thanks. Some people are just wired differently."

"Maybe so," Alice said, even though she didn't buy it. Bob was a workaholic; always had been, always will be. He would preach to them about getting rest, and then keep doing the opposite. Hypocrite, she thought. But she admired him as a boss, and loved him as a friend.

The phone interrupted their banter. "Agent Larson from the FBI on line two, Mr. Struthers." Bob pushed the button. "Struthers, here."

"Mr. Struthers, Agent Jamille Larson here with an update for you."

"Good. I have Alice Barker and Doctor Kruger with me. What have you found?" Bob was anxious to hear some good news.

"We've discovered a shell corporation licensed in Nevada under the name of a deceased cousin of Jim Anderson."

"Whoa, whoa, whoa." Bob was taken aback. "That's quite a bit in one sentence, agent."

"I know. It gets better." He continued. "The corporation was involved with purchasing and selling organic wheat through an online clearinghouse program called TradeKey. He used an alias named Jim Bry."

"Bry?" Bob pulled a small slip of paper from his pile. "One of my analysts found a slip of paper in a report. It was a trade on Tradekey electronically signed by James Bry."

"That ties into our discovery. I'll need that document. Can you ship it to me?"

"Certainly."

Jamille continued. "Good. The wheat was purchased from organic farmers and resold to processors located mostly on the West Coast."

"Did you say West Coast, agent?" Alice leaned forward in her chair.

"Yes, ma'am. Oregon and Washington and some in California. There were also some in Canada."

"Where in Oregon and Washington agent? Do you have a list of the companies?" Alice became very excited. She started going through the documents that she had in front of her.

"Yes, ma'am. The companies are mostly in central Oregon and central Washington. I am emailing you the list of companies where sales took place over the past three years. You should have it in a few seconds."

Bob turned to Alice. "Have Janice pull the email when it comes in." Alice grabbed her crutches and walked briskly out the door to get the list. Bob continued. "Go ahead, agent." He was taking notes excitedly.

"We also discovered Jim Anderson went to Portland for three days, rented a car under the alias, and paid cash. We don't know where he went or what he did. We are still checking on that lead."

Alice walked back into the room with the list. She sat back in her chair and studied the list as they continued to talk.

Jamille continued. "We also have some cashier's checks issued to cash. We are running endorsement verifications to back trace them through the banking system to see who cashed them, and where. We should know in an hour or two."

"These wheat sales to processors look like they might correspond to the cluster groups we have identified." Alice slowly lowered the paper. "We need to run this through our analytics right now." Alice grabbed her messenger bag and crutches and started for the door.

Bob called out to her. "I'll be there right after I wrap up here, Alice." She didn't reply.

"You stirred up some things here, agent. Anything more?" Bob asked.

"No, that's it for now. I'll call when I find out about the cashier's checks."

"OK. Thanks." With that, Bob terminated the call. "I need to update Randall about this situation." He stood to exit.

Carl looked at Bob. "Wheat?"

Grace Moore was meeting with her department heads in her office. Seven educated, intelligent doctors sat around a medium sized conference table. Grace was standing near the window. A large binder was setting in front of each person. A couple of people were scanning the pages when Grace started.

"This is becoming a dire situation. We have had twelve more people die from Maskill's type aneurysms in four days. We don't know why. The CDC does not know why." Grace grabbed a remote control and turned on the TV, then started the recorded newscast. "This was broadcast yesterday on the primetime news." Grace let the newscast play to the end and turned the television off.

"Ladies and gentlemen, we don't need this, but we've got it. This newscast will create a level of panic that we do not want to deal with right now. We have more than enough issues dealing with patients' treatment rather than to try and circumvent public panic. However, it's been tossed into our lap."

Grace moved to her seat at the table and continued. "I met with the hospital board last week. I briefed them on the deaths at the hospital and discussions with the CDC. I told them I believed we could face public panic over this situation and needed to prepare appropriately. The Board unanimously agreed we implement our disaster preparedness plan at the first sign of a possible public panic." Grace pointed to the TV. "That was the sign." She lifted a thick manual to show the group. "This is our disaster preparedness plan. There is a copy setting in front of you."

Each person looked at the manual. Some people opened it, others just stared at the size of the document. "Please turn to section sixteen . . . . Public Panic Preparation." Everyone turned to the section. "This section is how we need to prepare for a public panic related to an outbreak. You should have already reviewed this document from an executive level when you received it. Now, I want each of you to thoroughly read this section, and report back here in two hours with your plans on how to fulfill your tasks related to this topic and your respective departments." Grace scanned the group. "I have also approached the other hospitals in the area regarding this situation and their participation to create a consolidated triage center. They are very open to the idea. Whether they do or not will not affect our goal here." Grace paused for a moment to let this sink in to her team. "This is serious. It could be disastrous. We must be ready for the worst possible scenario."

One doctor raised his hand slightly and said, "May I ask what that would be, Doctor?"

"I don't fully know," she replied. "I suspect an absolute nightmare."

The door opened quickly. Agent Walker walked into Jamille's office. "We found it."

"Found what?" Jamille asked.

"Where Jimmy Boy's cashier's check went." He waived a copy of the check. "A crop duster in Antelope Oregon."

"Crop duster?" Jamille took the check copy.

Walker continued. "The check was of no significance since it was made out for cash. The endorsement on the back read Andrew Potter. We looked him up. He owns a crop dusting service called 'Potter's Field'."

"Call this Mr. Potter. I want to know what Mr. 'Bry' asked him to do for $10,000."

"Yes sir."

"Keep digging up the financials. There must be more stuff out there." Jamille gave the check copy back to Walker.

"There is. We've found several more accounts and cashier's checks. Getting copies now, boss." Walker was already heading out the door.

"Good."

"What do you think she found?" Carl was walking briskly with Bob to Alice's command center. She called them both and told them they needed to come to her office right away. Alice wasn't a drama queen. If she wanted them there right away, it was for something significant. They both hoped that it was the breakthrough they were waiting for.

They stepped through the door and saw Alice looking over several sheets of paper with two of her analysts. Next to her was a large map of the United States. On the adjoining wall was a map of the world. Both maps had red pins in them; thousands of red pins. There were seven large blue pins stuck in areas on the West Coast. There were a dozen yellow pins in the general areas.

Across the room was a bank of terminals with analysts seated at them. They had piles of papers, compact disks, coffee cups, and paper plates strewn about. At the far end of the room was a large whiteboard that took up most of the wall. It had columns and lines and numbers and locations written in codes and formats that only Alice and her team could understand. It was obvious to the two men that this room was the central command for sifting through tons of information coming in from all over the world.

"We've got it, Bob." Alice couldn't contain her excitement. "Look at this." Alice waddled over to the map using the table as her crutch. "We have been entering the locations of known deaths with these red pins. You can see here, here, here, cluster areas have formed. When cases occur in the defined cluster areas, we bypass them and just track the numbers separately in our database. These cluster areas account for 50% of the cases. We ran correlation analysis on everything we could think of to see if there was a common denominator; industry, chemical emissions, radiation. Nothing. Everything we ran came up blank . . . . except for one thing. Wheat."

"Wheat?" Carl asked. "Do you mean the wheat Agent Larson told us about?"

"Yes. The information we received from the FBI was that Biotrogen had a shell corporation established under a fictitious name. The corporation was involved with purchasing and selling organic wheat. We ran the list of processors that the corporation sold wheat to. The seven processors are the large blue pins in the middle of the cluster areas. Then we ran the farms that the wheat was purchased from. Those are the yellow pins. They are in the general areas, but not as well defined as the processors. Those are the only things that correlate to the cases and the cluster groups. Organic wheat bought and sold in these areas."

"That makes no sense at all, Alice." Bob walked to a chair and sat down. "How can wheat have anything to do with the changes we are seeing with the Maskill's patients?"

"Not only that," Carl added, "but that has nothing to do with the mutations of the 19Q chromosome. Even to suggest that it does is absurd."

"I know, I know," Alice agreed as she started to raise her voice. "I'm not suggesting anything. My job is to process data and see if correlations exist. They do. It's here." She was almost shouting as she slapped the map with her open hand. "I'm telling you what the data says, and it says very clearly there is a connection to the organic wheat and the deaths."

The room fell silent. Everyone stopped working and turned to watch the three leaders at the map. Carl was the first to speak. "I suppose it is possible tainted wheat could cause an illness or symptoms comparable to what we are seeing in the Maskill's patients, but we have the mutated 19Q chromosome that is unexplained. How does this fit with that?"

The people in the room returned to their tasks.

"Don't know, Carl. Maybe it is two different issues. Maybe they are connected in some unforeseen way. What we know is there is a correlation to the two issues," Alice answered.

Bob looked over the list of processors and farmers. "Let's call Agent Larson and see if we can get samples pulled from the processors or the end suppliers."

"What would we test for?" Carl asked.

"Chemicals, poisons, something out of the ordinary." Bob was grasping for answers. "Who knows."

"OK. Maybe we should have Agent Larson contact some of the victims' families and see if they have any products from any of these companies," Carl suggested. "Maybe we will find a link, there."

"Good thinking," Bob replied.

"There has to be something, Bob," Alice pleaded with him. "This is more than a gut feeling."

"Alice, I would never expect you of all people to react to a gut feeling," Bob smiled. "You are the queen of data mining. It is an absolute science with you; not guesswork or intuition."

Alice smiled. Bob knew her all too well.

"All right," Bob said. "I'll call Larson and have them pull samples of the wheat products from the processors and contact some victims' homes to see if they have any products as well."

"Good." Alice was relieved.

"Carl. I'll need you to get a group together to run analysis on the wheat. I would start with chemicals first, then go to organics." Carl nodded his approval. "At least we have something to start on. Let's hope it tells us something."

Captain Andy was tossing a ball for Frisky to catch. He loved playing with his black mutt. It was a good way for the dog to get his exercise in, and a good way for Captain Andy to enjoy someone's companionship, even if it was just a dog. But Frisky was more than 'just a dog' to him.

One time when Captain Andy was deer hunting in eastern Oregon, he was walking a small trail through a gully when a cougar decided to jump him from behind. The cougar landed on his shoulders and knocked him to the ground. His rifle flew forward as he fell on the rocks, breaking his ankle. The cougar spun and leaped forward onto Andy's back and sunk his teeth in the top of the left shoulder.

Frisky was a few yards ahead of Andy on the trail when the cougar attacked Andy. The dog always ran ahead of him, smelling everything, marking most bushes. He heard the commotion and immediately ran back to his master who was under attack. The dog growled and jumped on the back of the cougar, sinking his teeth into its hind quarter. It was just enough for the cougar to arch his back and try to reach the dog at his rear. His violent twisting body caused Frisky to fly off and land near a large boulder.

It was enough to allow Andy to get free of the beast and grab his pistol. In seconds he released the safety and shot the cougar as it was leaping toward the injured dog. Frisky saved the Captain's life that day. And the Captain saved the dog's life. Since then, nothing could separate them. Nothing.

Andy had just thrown the ball when the phone in his pocket rang. "Potter's Field," he answered.

"Hello. This is Agent Melvin Walker from the FBI."

"Sure it is," replied Captain Andy. He closed the phone and put it back in his pocket. "Kids."

Frisky brought the ball back and turned to the hangar to get a drink. Andy put the ball in his pocket and wiped his hand on his coveralls. "Slobbering mutt."

The phone rang again. "Potter's Field."

"Don't hang up! This is the FBI and this is very important!" The agent was desperate.

"OK. I'll play along. What can I do for you, agent . . . ?"

"Walker. Agent Walker from the Sacramento FBI office. I'm calling about a James Bry."

Captain Andy lost his smile when he heard the name. "Bry?"

"Yes. James Bry." Agent Walker wasn't sure if he would get any information from this guy or not. If he was involved in a conspiracy, he might run or destroy evidence. If he was upfront, he might cooperate. It was worth a try rather than going all the way there to ask him one question. "He apparently paid you $10,000 on Monday April 4th for something. He paid by cashier's check. We would like to know what he paid for."

"Why is that? Did he murder someone or something?"

"No. We think he was murdered. He was the victim. We're just trying to tie up loose ends here. Do you remember him?"

"Murdered? Wow. Yeah. I remember the guy. He had me do a dusting in a test field in Riley." Andy bent down and petted Frisky who just walked up to him and scratched on his leg for attention. "Seemed strange because it was a long ways off, but he said it was for a fertilizer test by the Oregon State University."

The agent paused. "I need to have someone come out and discuss this with you. This is really important."

"Hey, I don't want to get in any trouble here." Andy started to get nervous about the conversation. "The guy had court documents, an affidavit, everything I needed to show he had access to the land for the spray."

"I believe you. I'd like to send an agent from Portland. He can be there first thing in the morning. Will you be around?"

"Sure. I've got nowhere to go . . . . and nothing to hide."

"It's OK. I know the FBI causes some people to get nervous. Don't worry about it. We just need to ask a few questions, look at the documents you have, stuff like that. Do you still have the product there that he asked you to spray?"

"No. Used it all." Andy thought for a second. "Another strange thing was the way he asked me to clean the hopper in the plane afterwards. He had real specific instructions on what to use and how to clean the fertilizer out of the hopper and spray system."

"Do you have copies of those instructions?"

"Sure do. In fact, the instructions were to clean it once with solvents, wait ten days or longer, and clean it again with muratic acid. I haven't done the second step yet. I was planning on doing that today."

"You haven't?" The agent was excited. Maybe he found something.

"No. I figured if I had to shutdown my business for ten days, I may as well go Spring bear hunting, so I took a few days off. I was just going to wrap up this project and get back to dusting when you called."

"Great!!! Can my agent take samples from your application system when he arrives?" Agent Walker was obviously excited.

"Sure. Doesn't bother me, as long as I'm not accused of something here. I just did a job, and he paid me for it."

"No. No problems. It's easier for us to ask for your cooperation rather than bother a judge to have him sign a search warrant. It makes all of our jobs easier."

"Easy works for me."

"Great! I'll have our agent call you when he gets closer to your location."

Captain Andy closed the phone, pulled the ball out of his pocket, and threw it into the field. "Murdered, huh?"

CHAPTER 19

Thursday April 28
Deaths 7,742

The sun was shining directly into the driver's eyes as she maneuvered her way through the rolling hills. "Man that sun is just blinding."

"Stop whining. We'll be there in a few minutes." Agent Tom Lindsey of the Portland FBI office had the GPS programmed to give directions to 1467 High Mountain Road, Antelope Oregon; Potter's Field. The map on the GPS showed the arrow getting closer and closer to its target. "We only have a few more miles to go. High Mountain Road is the next right."

"Turn right two hundred yards." The GPS woman's voice said.

"See?"

"Yeah," the driver said, "but I bet she's better looking than you."

The car turned right and within a few minutes approached a small sign on the side of the road; 'Potter's Field.' The agents turned into the gravel driveway past an old farmhouse and headed toward the 'office' at the end of the large barn used as a hangar. They passed two young boys, maybe six years old, several yards off the side of the road, spinning in circles with their arms out like wings yelling, "crop duster, crop duster." They were both peeing.

"Did you see that?" Agent Lindsey asked.

"See what?"

"Those kids? They . . . ." Agent Lindsey stopped. "Never mind. You had to see it to understand." He laughed as he thought about what he had just seen.

The airstrip was dirt and gravel. The area around it was little more than a barren field. Frisky ran out to greet the car with his tail wagging and a ball in his mouth. He was ready to play. Captain Andy walked out of the hangar and approached the two agents as they were getting out of the car. "Well, you must be the FBI guys. Welcome to Antelope, Oregon."

"Yes, we are. Thanks." Agent Lindsey reached down and gave the dog a pat on the head. "Cute dog." He grabbed the ball and tossed it for the dog.

"That's Frisky, my co-pilot, navigator, and best friend." Andy put his hand out. "I'm Captain Andy."

"I'm Agent Tom Lindsey and this is Agent Jennifer Ramirez from the Portland FBI office." Andy grabbed Agent Lindsey's hand as soon as it came in reach.

Andy corrected himself. "I guess 'guys' isn't the appropriate greeting here, is it?" as he looked at Agent Ramirez.

"Probably not," Agent Lindsey said as he pulled his hand away and wiped it on his pants.

Andy wiped his hands on his pants. "Slobbering mutt."

"Yeah, I noticed." Agent Lindsey apologized. "Sorry." He wiped his hand again.

"He does it all the time, but I love him." Andy smiled. "So, you both have the same first names. That's odd."

The agents looked at each other puzzled.

"Agent; that's an odd first name." Andy slapped Agent Lindsey on the shoulder. "Get it? Agent . . . . I . . . . never mind." He turned and started walking toward the hangar. "You wanted to see the plane, right?"

"Uh, yeah." Agent Ramirez grabbed her briefcase from the car and walked briskly to catch up to Andy. "We'd like to see if we can get some samples of any spray residue that might have been left in the plane."

"Sure. It's over here." Andy led the agents to inside the hangar. It was a large metal building with three planes inside, along with a boat, tractor, and pieces of vehicles and various machinery. It was more than a hangar. It doubled as a garage, workshop, and indoor basketball court. "Like I said, I didn't finish the cleanout yet." Andy reached into his pocket and pulled out a couple of pages stapled together. "Here's the cleaning instructions. When I saw I had to wait ten days before a second phase wash out, I decided to go bear hunting."

Agent Lindsey asked, "Any luck?"

"Nope. Saw one run into the brush at sun up, but couldn't get a good track on him. It was raining, I was cold, and he was fast." Andy walked up to the AIRTRACTOR and slapped the wing. "Here ya go. Old Yeller."

"Great." The woman had her briefcase with her. It was an evidence kit that contained a variety of small tools for scraping, gouging, and such. It had plastic bags, cloth bags, vials, canisters; everything one would need to obtain and secure samples of most anything. "I'd like to disconnect some of these hoses and get samples from them."

Captain Andy walked over to the workbench near the plane. "Better yet, why don't you just take the hose. I have replacements that I can put on. That way, you can take it back and do whatever you want with it." He started to disconnect the hose from the hopper.

"That's excellent. Makes it a lot easier for us," Agent Lindsey replied. "Can we look in the hopper?"

"Sure," Andy said, "But I don't think you will find much in there. I washed it out pretty good."

"I think he's right, Tom," Agent Ramirez agreed. "Our best bet for any residue will be from this hose, one of the sprayers, and the outside of the plane . . . . here . . . ." Agent Ramirez pointed to the underside of the tail and continued. " . . . where the wind would cause residue to build."

"I'll pull some samples from there." The agents grabbed some plastic gloves, a face mask and bags from the case. Agent Lindsey pulled the gloves and mask on, pulled out his penknife and started scrapping the exterior of the plane into the bag. "I'll try not to scratch the paint," he said.

"Oh, a scratch won't hurt nothing. Do what you have to do." Andy handed the hose to the woman who was doctored up, and then he squatted down to pick up Frisky who was begging for attention. "Is this stuff dangerous or something? You look like a doctor. This stuff isn't going to kill me or anything, is it?"

"Nope, don't think so." Agent Lindsey put the hose into a plastic bag and labeled it. "We just have procedures and are always careful when dealing with something we don't know about."

"What's this all about, anyway?" Andy asked.

"This guy, Mr. Bry, was using an alias when he hired you. What did he hire you to do?" the woman asked.

"Spray fertilizer on a field in Riley. It's about two hundred miles south."

"One field two hundred miles away? That's quite a ways for you to do a job, isn't it?" Agent Lindsey asked.

"Sure it is. That's why he paid me extra. He said he wanted me to spray it because it was a small field and he wanted to make sure it was sprayed precisely. He couldn't take any chances for overspray or drift. They had to make sure it was only in that field so they could run the proper tests for the University. He knew I was one of the best dusters in Oregon." Andy was proud of his skills, and talking about them. "So, it didn't surprise me too much. He even had the affidavit from the court allowing him access from the landowner to spray there."

"Do you have the paperwork?" Agent Ramirez asked.

"Sure. It's in the office." Frisky jumped down as Andy turned to go to the office.

The agents carefully put their gloves and masks into a plastic bag, sealed it, and then placed the bag and samples in the briefcase. They followed Andy to his office at the end of the hangar. Once inside, Andy handed a few papers that he had copied for the agents. "Here's the copies of what he gave me."

The woman was polite. "We need the originals. There may be evidence on them, like fingerprints or residue. We will return them when we can. As long as you have copies for your business, you should be fine."

"Don't you need a warrant or something?" Andy asked.

"Only if you don't want to provide them voluntarily," Agent Lindsey said. "We are just trying to find out why this guy lied, used an alias, sprayed a field he likely didn't own or have permission to, what he sprayed it with, and why he's dead." He took a deep breath. "We'd like to get the information from you without having to go through a judge. If you cooperate, we don't need a search warrant. If not, then we do, and we will, but that is not the route we want to take. So, we are hoping we can just work together on this."

"Wow." Captain Andy pushed his ball cap back and wiped his brow. "That was quite a speech. Been practicing?" he chuckled.

"Sort of. It was a long drive from Portland." They both laughed.

Andy reached out and took the copies back, and handed the agents the originals from the file. "Here's the originals. I'm curious to find out all that stuff, too. I don't like being played."

Agent Lindsey put on some latex gloves, took the papers from Andy and glanced through them. "Nice job on the affidavit. Looks like a real notary stamp." He scanned the document. "So, the landowner is Bobby Joe Johnston?"

"Yeah, that's what I recall. Down in Riley."

Agent Ramirez glanced over his shoulder. "Looks like we should give Mr. Johnston, or whoever really owns the place, a visit."

Three large moving vans pulled up to the empty office space in the business complex at High Banks Road. Grace Moore got out of her car and walked up to the front of the building and unlocked the door. Two more cars pulled up and several people stepped out. They met Grace inside the empty, expansive area.

Grace glanced around the spacious area, took a deep breath, and took control. She handed each of her department heads a document of several pages. They started to flip through it as she spoke. "We talked about this yesterday and the Board agrees. We need a triage processing center for Maskill's patients. This is the place. The handout you have are estimations of patients, staffing, and a general view of processes. I need to have you review it, add your feedback, and make decisions about your respective areas. Questions come to me. We need this operational tomorrow."

Randy was shocked. "Tomorrow? That's impossible."

"No, it isn't," Grace corrected him. "I appreciate your concern, but there are no options here. You can develop the area, staffing and supplies while it is up and running, but I need patients to be brought here starting tomorrow. We can not have them continue to route through the hospitals. I don't care if you start off checking them in by hand, but we will process them here."

"Hospitals?" one person asked.

"Yes. Hospitals. All three area hospitals are going to use this facility as a Maskill's triage center. We aren't in this alone," she replied.

Grace surveyed the expansive area, started pointing in various directions. "Randy, we need signage to direct incoming patients through triage to treatment or release. Mark, we need a network wired in with a secure connection to the hospital servers. Dave, equipment. Everything for triage and treatment. Tables, beds, medical equipment, toilet paper, everything. Allison, staffing. Virginia, insurance processing. Gregory, we need patient screening protocol for the paramedics. They need to know how to identify a Maskill's patient in order to bring them here first." Gregory nodded. Grace continued. "I want this running twenty-four hours a day, starting tomorrow." Grace could see the overwhelming look on each person's face. "We can do this, folks. We have to do this."

One of the men spoke up. "What about contamination control? Do we need to create biohazard isolation areas?"

"Great question, Tom. Yes." Grace looked at each person, and continued. "I need complete patient quarantine from the general population once they are brought here. Treat this according to the CDC SARS Community Containment Isolation and Quarantine directive. When the patient is brought here, they will stay here."

The group was shocked. Grace continued. "This disease is deadly. We do not know exactly how it is contracted, but the fatality rate is 100%. We've lost two employees to this disease already. There is no room for error. It is escalating. And until we know what we are dealing with, we control and contain all patients. We can start small and expand if the need increases."

"What about security?" Tom asked.

"I've asked the governor to deploy a unit from the National Guard. They will provide security in cooperation with the Eugene Police Department and our Security Team. The other hospitals will also provide some security assistance if needed. Andrew, you will need to coordinate placement, containment, and control." She pointed to the back of the expansive warehouse. "We will need a division from the inception point to housing. I expect we will eventually need several hundred beds."

"Several hundred?" Dave asked.

"Yes. Several hundred, Dave. You can bring them in over the next few days. Contact the National Guard, forest work camp, and summer camps. Anyplace you can think to acquire them. Also contact hospitals out of the area if need be. If you have to, build them. I don't care how you do it, but we will need beds."

"Or coffins," Randy said solemnly. The group looked at him for a second. No one said a word.

"Or coffins," Grace confirmed. "We will need a staging area for the morgue. Doctor Allbright is already preparing for that." She looked to Howard who just smiled. "Folks, we have a lot of work to do. There is no budget. Make it happen."

The people disbanded. Several started to pull out their cell phones to make calls. Others started taking pictures. Grace watched as each person began to take charge of their respective areas. "God help us," she whispered.

Alice Barker was setting at the table studying several pages of printouts in her hands. She was flipping back and forth through the pages. "From what I can determine, wheat matures in one hundred and twenty days, give or take, depending on the type of wheat and location." Alice studied the map with the pins sticking everywhere, different colors, different sizes. She spun to the monitor and began typing, pulling up screen after screen and reading through sections of web pages. She had several windows open and was toggling back and forth.

"See. Here. 'The maturation of wheat.' It even shows by region and climate." Alice looked back at the map. "That would mean most harvests from the last crop occurred sometime around . . . . mid September."

The analyst scanned through the printouts. "The first event occurred here—first part of November in Eugene, Oregon." The analyst pointed to the city on the map which was a cluster area.

The two continued to search pages, review reports. The analyst pointed to several entries on the printouts. "It looks like the processors take thirty to forty-five days from harvest to shelf of their products. Much of that depends on what products they are creating from the grain, but an average of thirty-seven days."

Alice slapped the top of the desk. "That's it! It ties perfectly with our timelines."

Doctor Carl Kruger burst into Alice's lab. "Alice." Carl was obviously excited. "Bob wants to see us right away in his office. He said he has the key we've been looking for."

"The key? Let's go." Alice grabbed her crutches and a few papers, and in seconds they were out the door.

It was mid afternoon when the agents pulled up to the door of Bobby Joe Johnston's house. The small farm was nestled in a valley with the ranch house perched on a small knoll. It looked out over the dark soil, showing the first signs of the wheat planting emerge from the soil. Tiny green shoots thinly blanketed the field. The sun was baking the ground as the early morning rain had just watered it. It was perfect conditions for the wheat to germinate and take firm root in the Oregon desert.

Bobby Joe was setting in one of two metal rocking chairs staring out to the fields. He had his rifle next to him leaning against the porch banister. He was dressed in his overalls with a flannel shirt underneath. He was wearing socks. He hadn't shaved in a couple of days. His hair was uncombed. His face was drawn with circles under his red, swollen eyes. He looked disheveled and tired. Two glasses of iced tea were setting on the table between the chairs.

The agents stepped out of their rental car and walked up to the porch. Agent Lindsey spoke first. "Mr. Johnston?"

"Yeah." Bobby Joe stayed in his chair, looking out over his farm.

"We are from the FBI, sir. My name is Agent Lindsey, and this is Agent Ramirez."

"FBI? What do you want with me?" Bobby Joe glanced to the pair. He was short with them. He didn't like the interruption.

The woman explained. "Sir, we have reason to believe that a man had your crop sprayed several weeks ago without your permission. Do you recall seeing a crop duster spraying in or near your field?" She was polite and soft spoken.

Bobby Joe perked up a little. "Yeah. I remember about two weeks ago when I saw a duster flying low near the field. It was early in the morning. Me and Ethel were getting ready to have coffee . . . ." His voice trailed off.

Agent Lindsey continued the questioning. "Has anyone called or contacted you about wanting to spray your field, or when you were going to plant, or anything like that in the last month?"

The old man spoke softly. "Someone called about planting awhile back, but I don't know who."

"Is there anything you can remember about the plane?" Agent Ramirez continued.

"Yeah, it was yellow. Hadn't seen it around here before." Bobby Joe stared out over the field again, losing interest in the conversation.

Agent Lindsey continued with the questioning. "Is your wife here? Maybe she will remember something more about the duster. Can we ask her a few questions?"

Bobby Joe turned to the agents. "No. She died two days ago." He looked back to the fields.

"Oh. I'm sorry to hear that." Agent Ramirez apologized for them. "I thought the two glasses there were . . . ."

" . . . . for me and Ethel. They are." Bobby Joe paused. "You know, after fifty three years of a routine, it's pretty damned hard to just stop. Doesn't feel right. Not at all." Bobby Joe took a sip of tea. "Not at all."

"Mr. Johnston. I know this is hard. We are truly sorry. But we need to find out what's going on." The woman squatted down to get to eye level with Bobby Joe. "Sir, may I ask what happened to your wife?" She gently touched his hand.

Bobby Joe looked at her. "Doctor said she had an aneurysm or stroke or something. It was like her brain just started bleeding." He wiped his chin. "She was in good health. Then, this. No warning." He looked at Agent Ramirez with tears welling up in his eyes. "Your life can change in an instant, young lady."

"Sir, the duster may have had something to do with this," Agent Lindsey said.

"What do you mean?"

He continued. "If he was spraying something nearby, it could have been something that made her sick. We'd like to take some samples of your soil and run it through our lab just in case."

"You mean he could have killed her?" Bobby Joe perked up, ready to fight.

"We don't know," Agent Ramirez said. "We just know he was hired to spray something here, and two weeks later she dies. That is unusual, to say the least."

"Sure. Go get whatever you want. If this bastard is responsible, I want to see him suffer . . . like Ethel did." Bobby Joe stood up. He was ready for a fight. His life suddenly had purpose again; justice. "What do you need from me?"

"Where did you see the duster?" Agent Lindsey asked.

"South fence line. Over there between the hills. He was headed north."

"Can you take us to the area?"

Bobby Joe reached for his boots. "Sure. Just climb in my truck."

The three climbed into the old Ford pickup and headed to the south fence line. The agents took their evidence kit to gather some of the precious soil and sprouting wheat.

Doctor Carl Kruger and Bob Struthers were surrounded by several analysts, scientists, and doctors, some of whom were specially recruited to attend this meeting on very short notice. They weren't sure how to address the group of intellectuals. Bob walked up to the podium and opened the session. "Ladies and gentlemen. If you could all take your seats." He then walked over to the side of a big screen in the small theater. They were meeting at the Emory University School of Medicine main amphitheater. Among the guests were a molecular physicist, Dr. Norman Raynould, a Nobel Prize micro biologist, Dr. Imar Spaan, several key staff from Emory, and other geneticists, scientists, and analysts that had been recruited to join Doctor Kruger's team and the CDC over the past two weeks. The CDC executives joined them to share the information on their progress. Randall Sterling, Deputy Director of Infectious Disease from the CDC and Donald Sinclair from the Food and Drug Administration sat next to each other in the front row.

"Thank you for coming here this evening on such short notice. I am Robert Struthers, Assistant Director of the National Center for Emerging and Zoonotic Infectious Disease from the Center of Disease Control here in Atlanta. We have asked you here today to share information with you regarding the research we have conducted on the issue of increasing deaths associated to Maskill's Seizures. I would like to first thank Doctors Norman Raynould and Imar Spaan for joining us on such short notice. They are renowned in their respective field's molecular physics and micro biology, and flew here at my request earlier today. Gentlemen, thank you." The audience gave a polite applause and both doctors gave a slight wave of the hand. Doctor Spaan looked remarkably like Albert Einstein.

"Today, we have verified that more than seven thousand deaths have occurred and are related to chromosomes that cause the Maskill's Seizures." The slide show on the big screen recapped what Bob was covering with the audience. "For the benefit of those not involved with the medical community, Maskill's Seizures have generally been classified as a benign seizure resulting in headaches and minor hearing loss. Recently, the nature of the seizure has changed to become deadly as a result of multiple aneurysms located in the audio cortex of the brain. The seizures were historically associated with a genetic mutation of the 19q13.33 chromosome, type A, and could be identified and controlled through medicine developed by a company called Biotrogen in California." Bob continued through the slides. "We have obtained samples from the victims and have identified an anomaly with the victim's chromosomes, of which Doctor Carl Kruger from John Hopkins will address."

He turned the projector control over to Doctor Kruger to continue the presentation. "Thank you, Bob." Carl's voice echoed through the small theater. The acoustics were superb. "The 19Q chromosome, as we will call it by its abbreviated name, had a single mutation associated with Maskill's which Doctor Everett Maskill identified as type A. Our review of the victim's samples have revealed four more types of mutations, now called B, C, D, and E. Each mutation is slightly different that the others resulting in the various types." He paused for a second and took a deep breath. "We have no record of these mutations existing before four months ago. Nor did we have any explanation of why they exist now . . . . until this morning."

He looked to Bob who continued the presentation. "This morning I received a letter mailed parcel post from California." He changed the slide. A picture of James Anderson appeared. "The letter was mailed last week by one of the partners of Biotrogen, who happened to die on the day of the mailing. The FBI believes he was murdered and is currently investigating." The audience gasped, and a few murmurs occurred. Bob continued. "The letter confirms some of our assumptions developed through analytics performed in our 'data mining' division at CDC. Through the efforts of the FBI and our analysis, we determined there was a correlation between organic wheat grown in the Northwest and the genetic mutations of the victims."

One of the scientists blurted out, "How can that be?"

Bob quickly responded. "We don't know, yet. Give me just a minute to continue, and I will address questions at the end. If you have the whole picture, we may better understand how to respond." He advanced the slide to a few sentences from the letter. "The partner who mailed the letter, James Anderson, was preparing to leave the country. He had liquidated much of his stock holdings before the FDA announcement was made regarding Maskill's deaths and the withdrawal of the two medicines Biotrogen developed for Maskill's patients; Inferon and Tegbatol. On the day of his death he had a one way ticket to France in his pocket. We believe he may have written the letter I received explaining the circumstances of the Maskill's deaths before he fled the country. He mailed it parcel post, possibly to allow time to escape.

The letter is pretty detailed and lengthy. What I would like to draw your attention to are a few paragraphs in the letter explaining how they developed a product that causes chromosomal mutations."

Bob continued. "You can see here that Mr. Anderson states that 'Dr. Maskill discovered a method to chemically alter the genetic signature of a wheat chromosome at the molecular level.' He then states that the 'altered wheat chromosome became an active catalyst capable of changing the genetic signature of the 19Q13.33 chromosome into a type A mutation, again, at the molecular level to create the Maskill's disease.'"

"This is impossible!" Someone blurted from the audience. The guests started discussing the issue amongst themselves.

"Please, please! Hold on." Bob raised his hands to calm the audience. "We realize this is far fetched, but listen to what we have discovered so far. Please. Doctor Kruger."

Carl continued. "This is impossible . . . . from what we know today. However, Doctor Maskill was a scientist working at the molecular level. He had PhDs in both Chemistry and Molecular Engineering. We know that working at the molecular level opens multiple possibilities for changes that we may not understand today. Look what we have in regards to genetic science compared to twenty years ago? We have the complete Human Genome mapped and documented. This would not have been conceived then. Sixty years ago, DNA was unheard of. Whose to say what is or isn't possible when we refer to molecular engineering?" The audience quieted down and listened intently. Carl continued. "We are scientists. This letter suggests a new frontier of discovery; the ability to alter molecular structure through biogenetic influences. Ladies and gentlemen, I believe we are at the precipice of an extraordinary breakthrough of a new frontier."

A young man setting in the front row raised his hand. "How do we know the letter is accurate?"

Bob Struthers answered. "The man who wrote it had emptied his bank accounts and scheduled a flight out of the country. He was killed the same day. The purpose of this letter was . . . ." Bob paused. " . . . . was to ask for forgiveness for the deaths associated to Maskill's Seizures. The author was detailed in his explanation of events that led to the creation of Maskill's as well as some documents and records. His information was corroborated through our analysis, to some degree. I believe he was accurate, sincere, and remorseful. He explained in his letter that he was leaving the country and would eventually settle in a place where he could not be found because he could not face prison or the people that he may have harmed. He planned to continue research to try and treat the disease."

The audience was silent. Bob continued. "I will entertain any questions that you may have."

An audience member raised his hand and stood. "Do we have any evidence or samples of the proposed genetically altered wheat or what was used to alter it?" He sat back down.

"At present, no. Not in its raw form. We are in contact with the FBI and are in the process of obtaining residue from a recent chemical application to the wheat, as well as possible samples of treated soil. We have contacted the wheat processors and are retrieving samples of processed wheat that may help us analyze the mutation. We should have those by morning."

Another member of the audience raised their hand and stood after Bob acknowledged them. "Do we know if the chemical agent was applied to other plants or animals and, if so, what the outcome would be?" The person sat back down and waited for the answer.

Bob leaned over to Carl and whispered something. The audience was completely silent. Carl stepped forward. "We know other plants and animals or insects in the contaminated area would have received the chemical. We do not know if or how this could affect them." Carl paused, looked at Bob who nodded, and continued. "Since we know the chemical is able to alter the wheat gene and subsequently create a mutation in a human gene through ingestion, the possibility of the chemical either altering another type of plant or animal, and creating another mutation in humans or animals who ingest the mutation, is very, very high." The audience began to murmur amongst themselves, raising the volume. Carl spoke up. "Our concern is the same as yours. The chemical used to genetically alter the wheat could alter other plant or animal forms, creating untold chaos in the environment. If the chemical was sprayed in an open area, as we suspect, then everything it touched could be affected by it, regardless if it is plant or animal. We don't know what it is capable of impacting because we do not know how it works, yet. We plan to analyze other living organisms in the affected areas, but have not yet done so."

Bob stepped to the microphone to calm the audience down again. "Ladies and gentlemen, we just received this letter and we realize this is a troubling situation that we are in. We do not fully know the extent of the situation or possible outcomes. Right now, we believe the letter is accurate, that a chemical agent was used on wheat to cause a mutation transferred to humans resulting in an illness. Something changed to cause the deaths. Our focus is to determine what changed so that we may correct and reverse the illness. We will analyze the affected areas, but our first and foremost concern is addressing and reversing the continuing deaths associated with the wheat."

Bob advanced the slide show to the next slide. "The letter indicated there was a storage unit that contained samples of wheat from the original development of Maskill's. We have an FBI team on their way to retrieve the samples and reports stored there." Bob pointed to the slide, and continued.

"We believe our next step is the recall of all of the wheat products associated to this wheat if we are able to ratify the mutation. We have Mr. Sinclair here from the Food and Drug Administration today." Bob pointed to Mr. Sinclair who briefly raised his hand. "The companies that processed this wheat are few, the list is short, the products are limited, and the market is small. We should be able to stop the spread of this catalyst in a few weeks, if it is the catalyst. The difficulty will be the removal of products from consumer possession. This is always the case."

Bob changed the slide and continued. "We need to have teams assigned to these four tasks;" He pointed to the slide. "Analyze the wheat, the chemical agent, the medicines Inferon and Tegbatol, and the 19Q chromosome. Each of these is a piece of the puzzle, with no single answer." Bob leaned on the podium and addressed the audience. "It is imperative that we understand what has occurred and how to stop it. Otherwise . . . . we could be facing a dire situation of catastrophic proportions."

The audience was stunned. There was absolute silence.

Carl continued. "We are scientists. You are experts in your field. It is incumbent upon us to resolve this crisis. My team has already made great progress on the research of the 19Q mutations. However, we need your help to research these other pieces of the puzzle. We must understand what is happening so that we can stop it."

Dr. Imar Spaan stood. His wild hair made him look like a mad scientist. He had a slight Austrian accent. "Gentlemen, what you are inferring is unthinkable." He looked to the audience. "It is times like this when the scientific community needs to set aside differences, ambition, and pride and come together to pursue a common solution. Seldom are we called upon to address a problem of this magnitude." He looked back to the presenters. "You have my unwaivered commitment to help."

"Thank you, Dr. Spaan." Bob was sincere. "Anyone else who is willing to sacrifice their time and energy to join us, please raise your hand." The entire audience raised their hands. "Very well then. We need to assign teams for the four areas of research. I would like to take a ten minute break and resume to discuss the teams, team leaders, available resources and budgets, and project goals."

People in the audience stood and some exited the room. Others started to mill about. Bob and Carl walked over to Randall and Donald.

"Nice job on the presentation, Bob," Randall acknowledged. "You too, Carl. I'm pleased you are a part of our team."

"Thank you. Looks like we have a good start."

"Yes, we do," Randall said. He turned to Don Sinclair standing next to him. "Gentlemen, this is Donald Sinclair, Director of the Center for Food Safety at the FDA."

Don shook hands with Bob and Carl. "Nice job, fellas."

"Thanks," they said in unison.

"This is quite troubling, to say the least," Don said. "If you can provide the evidence, then we will have no choice but to recall the products. There is a process, you know."

Bob spoke first. "We do." He had been through this before, and once with dismal results. Don wasn't at the FDA then, so he had no history of the prior failure that Bob pursued.

Donald was looking at the large group of people milling about. "We need to make absolutely sure before we pull the trigger on this, Randall. No mis-steps here."

Randall replied, "None," as he looked at Bob.

"Good." Don smiled as he grabbed his briefcase and notes. "Now, if you'll excuse me, I need to catch my flight. Randall, I expect to be hearing from you soon."

Randall patted Don on the shoulder. "Yes, very soon I'm sure."

Agents Lindsey and Ramirez were driving back to Portland after a long day. They had been to Antelope to gather samples of spray residue, and then to Riley for samples of sprayed soil and wheat shoots. The samples were secured in their evidence kit inside the metal canisters and plastic bags. It was late in the evening and their five hour drive was but half over when the call came in.

"Agent Lindsey here. Yes. We retrieved samples from the crop duster and the farm. We scraped residue from areas of the plane as well as a hose that led from the hopper to the applicator. Yes, he is storing the plane until further notice. The soil is in plastic bags. Yes, we used gloves and masks. What's this all about?"

There was a long pause. "What? Are you joking? No, sir." Agent Lindsey was obviously agitated.

"What's going on?" The woman asked. Agent Lindsey held his hand up to stop her while he listened intently on the phone.

"Yes, sir. I understand. We will, sir." He slowly closed the phone and stared at it.

"What the hell is going on?" Agent Ramirez could tell something serious was up.

"We apparently have something from the plane and the farm that could . . . could be very deadly if we came into direct contact with it."

"So, we used the precautions to gather the samples. We were gloved and masked. What's the big deal?"

"This stuff is unlike anything they may have seen. It changes the genetic structure of something. Like mutations," he said.

"So what. Andy was fine. He wasn't a mutant or anything." Agent Ramirez laughed at the absurdity of the moment. "In fact, he looked pretty good to me."

"Yeah? Well don't forget Johnston's wife just died," Agent Lindsey said sharply.

The woman stopped laughing, and the two looked at each other. Agent Ramirez spoke first. "What do they want us to do?"

"Drive straight to the center. No stops except for gas. Contain as though highly contagious."

"Why don't they send a chopper to get the stuff if they are so concerned?" she asked.

"They're thinking about it."

The two agents looked at the road and drove silently toward the FBI center in Portland.

CHAPTER 20

Friday April 29
Deaths 9,446

"Mr. Struthers. FBI on line two."

Bob pressed the speaker phone button. "Struthers here."

"Bob. Agent Jamille Larson here."

"Agent Larson. Good to hear from you. What's the latest?" Bob didn't have time to waste. He wanted to hear something positive from the agent.

"We've retrieved the residue from the plane and obtained soil samples from one of the affected farms. Our office is delivering the samples to you today. You should have them by 4 p.m. eastern time."

"That's great." Bob was thrilled with the news. "I think this will be the key to us solving this problem."

Jamille paused for a moment. "I have a question."

"Shoot."

"Can you tell me a little more about what this stuff does?"

Bob could sense the concern in Jamille's voice. "Sure. We don't fully understand it yet, but it appears that it is an active chemical that causes the genetic structure of the wheat to mutate and become a catalyst for further genetic mutations in people when consumed." Bob had been living with the issue everyday for weeks, so much so he made the statement as though it was almost nothing to be concerned about.

"Are you kidding me? How does it need to be consumed?" Jamille asked.

"Ingesting, from what we know so far. Why do you ask?"

"Oh, you know, just curious. One of the agents that gathered the samples from the plane and the affected farm wanted to make sure she wasn't going to grow another eye or something." He laughed nervously.

"Did they take precautions?"

"Yes. They gloved up and used face masks."

"I wouldn't worry about it. It looks like it has to be consumed over a period of time to alter the genetic structure of a particular chromosome. Our estimates are about thirty to sixty days of consumption before the recipient chromosome breaks down and changes. We are still running tests and analyzing the chromosome, but that is all we have so far. Having the chemical is one of the pieces we have been missing."

"Well, makes me feel a little better. Thanks."

Bob got back to the topic at hand. "Is the FBI securing wheat samples from the storage unit?"

"Yes. We have a team going to the unit in Sacramento as we speak. They will basically empty the unit to our office in Sac, and forward the wheat samples to you. I'm not sure when you will get them. You might be receiving several Christmas packages from the FBI today."

"I sure hope so. Christmas in April is fine with me." Bob laughed. "It's about time something is going our way. We just received the samples of wheat from the processors earlier today. Now we can compare those to the old wheat samples from the storage unit. It feels like it's all coming together."

"You have quite a job to do. I don't envy you at all, Bob."

"Thanks. Keep me posted. And if your agent starts growing another nose, call me. I want to know." Bob heard Jamille laugh.

"Sure will," he said.

It was late afternoon when Bob Struthers and Alice Barker walked into the lab where Dr. Carl Kruger and Dr. Imar Spaan were discussing the results of their tests with three analysts.

"OK. What do you have?" Bob asked.

Dr. Spaan began. "We received the samples of the wheat and have identified the three types according to their development cycle. They are prior to original mutation, after original mutation and recent mutation. Doctor Spaan walked over to the whiteboard. "Sample A is the original wheat with no genetic mutations. This has given us the base to work from."

"It's a starting point that we can compare backwards to determine changes. The difficulty is that the wheat genome has not been fully mapped," Carl added.

"Correct," Doctor Spaan confirmed. "The sample of the original mutation was a tetraploid wheat. It has four chromosomes. We call this sample B. The most recent mutation is a hexaploid wheat. It has six chromosomes and shows a different mutation. This is sample C."

"What does that mean?" Bob asked.

Carl and Imar looked at each other. Imar answered his question. "It appears the genetic structure of the wheat has mutated from sample B to C because the type of wheat changed. The chemical agent attacked the wheat chromosome differently in the six chromosome wheat as opposed to the four chromosome wheat. This resulted in the further deadly mutation of the 19Q chromosome."

"You mean just changing the wheat type could be the cause for people dying?" Alice asked.

Imar responded. "The wheat type and the chemical agent. There were two more chromosomes that the chemical was able to effect."

Bob realized the implications of Imar's statement. "Then, if this chemical could dramatically change the chromosome of a new wheat type, would it be possible to change a chromosome of, say, another plant?"

Carl took his glasses off and looked at Bob. "We don't know for sure, but we believe it is very possible."

"Quite," Imar added.

The room became eerily quiet.

"Do you know which specific harvests this mutation is attributed to?" Bob asked.

"Yes," Carl replied. "We have plotted the wheat to the harvest and have a clear picture of which wheat from which harvest is involved. We know the wheat, the farms, the crops and the dates of the harvest. We can show that the wheat harvested from a farm has changed dramatically from harvest to harvest. Doctor Raynould is analyzing the molecular structure of the samples."

Bob thought for a minute. "Seems to me we have enough evidence to show that this wheat is somehow causing the genetic changes resulting in Maskill's type deaths." He looked at the group. "We don't have an absolutely clear connection, but all of the pieces of evidence show links eventually to the deaths. I doubt that this wheat would have passed FGIS inspection standards. I think this is what Don Sinclair needs for the USDA to recall the products."

"We better get this to Randall right away," Alice said. "You know we need his support."

Bob smiled. "We already have it. I'll get Randall down here within the hour. Get your information ready, and prepare it for the FDA. We don't have any time to waste here."

The new Maskill's triage center was a joint venture of three local hospitals in the area. In just twenty-four hours it was fully operational with an emergency entrance established to receive patients by ambulance separate from the main entrance, just like a hospital. The ambulance drivers wore protective clothing, masks, and gloves. They would pull up to the new double doors and hospital staff would come out to receive the patient. The ambulance crew tending to the patient and hospital employees wore full, yellow hazmat suits. They had rubber gloves, masks, oxygen, and protective shoes. Once the patient went into the hospital, the ambulance crew would go through decontamination near the entrance.

The new emergency ward consisted of forty beds and various equipment. The patients were brought in, assessed, treated, and often moved to the makeshift morgue in the back of the building. Those who were alive were wheeled into beds after stabilization. The patients were separated from the rest of the operation by a large, dual pane plexiglass wall covered with long, black drapes. No one could see in and observe the hospital staff in hazmat suits roaming the area checking on patients.

Family members were guided to the "lobby" where they would have to wait without seeing their loved ones. Two National Guard troops were stationed at each entrance and exit. Two police officers were walking through the crowd of people.

Four receptionists were lined up at the tables with makeshift partitions separating them for "privacy." A long line was snaking its way through the lobby toward the door. An elderly lady struggled through the crowd with her walker and up to the front of the line. "Excuse me, miss?" The elderly lady interrupted the young woman typing on the keyboard.

The young lady looked up, quite perturbed. "I'm sorry. You'll have to wait over there until I can get to you." The receptionist pointed to the crowded lobby where all the seats were taken. There were so many people of all ages and walks of life. Several were crying. Others were reading newspapers or watching the newscast on the television. Babies were crying. The elderly lady looked at the crowded lobby and back at the receptionist. "How long will this take?"

The receptionist was annoyed by the interruption and the unanswerable question. "Listen, I told you, I don't know. You need to just wait over there. Someone will come out and tell you what is going on with your brother."

"My husband," the lady corrected her. "Henry. My husband."

"Right." The lady turned to the young man she was helping while she placed some papers in a large stack. She continued to enter information into the computer. The elderly lady used her walker to steady herself as she slowly worked her way across the crowded lobby. No one offered her a seat. She weaved her way through the throng of people, and out the door past the National Guardsmen. There were people standing outside along the walkway, on the grass, smoking, talking, crying. The elderly lady continued down the sidewalk. She stopped under the shade of a large maple tree that was in bloom. She looked up at the new, green leaves. They were beautiful against the blue sky with white, billowy clouds.

Another ambulance could be heard approaching the triage center. It soon turned off its siren as it drove past the front of the building. The elderly lady watched as it pulled into the emergency entrance and unload another victim.

The lady lowered her head and cried.

The lab was quiet. Everyone was either working on their assigned task, or discussing their progress with an associate. Doctor Kruger was meeting with Doctor Imar Spaan and Doctor Norman Raynould in his office at CDC. Doctor Kruger had been working on the project tirelessly, and was revered as an equal to CDC's management staff. He was the leader of the genetic research of the samples, both wheat and human. He and his team made great strides to understand the developing mutations. They identified the varying mutations of 19Q, but continued to be baffled as to how they occur.

Doctor Spaan was a renowned micro biologist. His work with cellular structures and biomedical applications was cutting edge in his field. His understanding of cell development in all living organisms may lead to an understanding of how one genetic mutation could alter a gene of a recipient host. It was unheard of, but happening.

Doctor Raynould was one of the foremost molecular physicists in the world. For the CDC to acquire him as one of the team members was a coup beyond description. He was a natural leader. His insight to the molecular attributes of the host and recipient cells was critical to the success of this venture. He was capable of determining even the slightest variations of cell structures at the molecular level.

The three scientists had just returned from the meeting with Randall Sterling convincing him to pursue a recall of all products associated with the wheat through the FDA. This was a significant step. They pleaded the case that the wheat was the cause. Why was another question to be answered another day. If they were correct, the number of deaths will begin to slow and give them some breathing room to pursue their research without the additional stress of people dying. The score was now Maskill's; 9,446—Scientists; 1.

"Gentlemen," Carl began. "You did an excellent job of presenting your information to Randall."

"Thank you, Doctor Kruger, but you took the lead. You should be credited for our progress thus far," Imar said.

Carl replied, "I'm not ready to take credit for anything until we stop this thing. We need to know about that chemical."

Doctor Raynould responded. "Until I receive samples of the chemical agent used to alter the wheat gene, and the original wheat samples, I have little to go on other than establishing a molecular base for the 19Q cell structure in both the victim and the resident and the current wheat samples we received from the processors."

"We expect to receive the chemical agent later today or tomorrow," Carl assured him. "The additional wheat samples from storage should be here as well. I will make sure those samples are delivered to you as soon as we receive them."

"Then tomorrow will be a new day with new data," Doctor Raynould said.

CHAPTER 21

Saturday April 30
Deaths 11,309

Doctor Norman Raynould was peering into the microscope when Bob walked in. Several analysts seated along three tables also were peering into microscopes. A centrifuge hummed in the background. "Have you received the chemical samples of the spray, doctor?" Bob asked.

"Yes, thank you. They came in late yesterday." He put his glasses back on and pushed away from the microscope.

"What's the status?" Bob wanted answers. Everyone wanted answers.

Doctor Raynould took a deep breath. "We've been able to isolate the chemical compounds and run spectrum analysis on the elements. The process is tedious since we don't know what we are looking for. At present, our goal is to break down the elements and map them accordingly. Then we will test for interactions, cause and effect if you will, amongst the compounds."

"So, no idea what this is or why it works like it does?"

"No. Not completely."

"What do you mean, 'completely'?" Bob asked.

"We have mapped most of the elements of the chemical and it looks as though it has a new element in it . . . a new synthetic element."

"Are you telling me we might have a new element in this chemical? One that is not on the standard periodic table of elements?" Bob was astonished.

"Yes. That is exactly what I am saying." Doctor Raynould walked over to this desk and pulled a pile of papers from a stack on top. He returned and tossed them on the table top. "This is a summary of the research thus far from the lab. We are less than halfway through the samples using three electron microscopes. We have already found a questionable element in this chemical that we have yet been able to identify."

"Look, I'm no chemist, but I know we have a list of elements already defined and accounted for. How can a new one just show up?"

"It is a synthetic element; man made." Doctor Raynould walked over to the whiteboard and erased a large section. "As of 2011, the table contained one hundred and eighteen chemical elements whose discoveries have been confirmed. The first ninety-four are found naturally on Earth, and the rest are synthetic elements that have been produced artificially in particle accelerators. Some of the isotopes of elements that were first discovered synthetically have since been discovered in trace amounts on Earth as products of natural radioactive decay processes. The primary determinant of an element's chemical properties is its electron configuration, particularly the valence shell electrons." The doctor drew numbers, circles, orbits and arrows as he spoke. It was like he was teaching a college class.

"Hold it." Bob raised his hand to stop the doctor. "You are way over my head here." Bob felt so inadequate in the presence of such brilliance. "Can you bring this down a couple of notches on the IQ scale and tell me the meaning of all of this in laymen's terms?"

"Certainly." This wasn't the first time Doctor Raynould had received such a request. He paused for a second to consider the best way to phrase an answer. "The best way to put this is that elements are determined to a large part by the orbits of electrons and number of electron shells in the molecule. We have a new molecule with a new electron orbit and new number of shells. It does not fit into the table."

Bob was silent. He stared at the board. "What are the implications of this discovery, doctor?"

"I don't know. That is what I am attempting to determine."

CHAPTER 22

Monday May 2
Deaths 15,368

Bob Struthers was seated at his desk reading the FDA notices of recall, one after another. He just met with each scientist for an update of their research. Doctor Raynould's discovery of a new element was most troubling. The idea that a new element could be created by man and introduced into the environment was unsettling. The very notion that it could cause some type of genetic mutation in living organisms was overwhelming. *What has science gotten us into,* he thought? *Are we creating our very demise as a species?* It was the first time Bob felt that he may be a part of the problem and not the solution.

He continued to glance at the FDA notices, one after another. He and his team of scientists presented enough information to Randall and the FDA to recall all of these products. There were eleven companies involved thus far; 500,000 bushels of wheat, harvesters, manufacturers, distributors and suppliers. Bob hoped he was right. The evidence suggested he was. He had to be. He imagined the number of people who would be displaced, unemployed from this event. He also imagined the number of lives that would be saved.

Recall—Firm Press Release

FDA posts press releases and other notices of recalls and market withdrawals from the firms involved as a service to consumers, the media, and other interested parties. FDA does not endorse either the product or the company. Organic Hills Corporation Involuntary Recall of Certain Lots Of Garden Of Grains'® Organic Wheat Products Due To The Presence Of Unknown Substances

Contact:
Lisa Barclay
Phone: 303-555-1345

FOR IMMEDIATE RELEASE—May 2, 2011—The Federal Drug Administration announced that it is taking the precautionary measure of recalling all lots of Garden Of Grains'® Organic Wheat Products due to the presence of unknown substances found in the products.

Consumers run the risk of serious or life-threatening reactions if they consume these products.

The recalled products were distributed to food stores nationwide. The recall affects all products distributed by Garden Of Grains'® with the following lot codes:

Garden Of Grains'® Multi Grain Sea Salt Tortilla Chips (9 oz)
Unit UPC code # 163-00134
Lot codes: 03SEP10, 08SEP10, 19SEP10, 24SEP10

Garden Of Grains'® Multi Grain Bread (16 oz)
Unit UPC code # 163-0732
Lot codes: 08SEP10, 24SEP10, 25SEP10, 01OCT10 and 22OCT10

Garden Of Grains'® Multi Grain Crackers (16 oz)
Unit UPC code # 163-0922
Lot codes: 08SEP10, 25SEP10, 26SEP10, 22OCT10 and 23OCT10

The lot code can be located on the right side of the upper front panel of the individual package.

The recall was initiated after it was discovered that the product contained an unknown substance.

Consumers who have purchased any products covered by this recall are urged to return them to the store of purchase for a full refund. Consumers with questions or concerns please call 1-800-555-4244, during extended hours from Monday to Friday 9:00 am—9:00 pm EST and on Saturday and Sunday from 10:00 am to 6:00 pm.

This involuntary recall is being conducted by the U.S. Food and Drug Administration.

PRODUCT RECALL NOTICE

PRODUCT
Garden Of Grains'® Multi Grain Bread (16 oz)—Unit UPC code # 163-0732
Lot codes: 08SEP10, 24SEP10, 25SEP10, 01OCT10 and 22OCT10***Certified Organic***Country of Origin: USA***". Recall # F-0533-2011

CODE
Garden Of Grains'® Multi Grain Bread (16 oz)
Unit UPC code # 163-0732
Lot codes: 08SEP10, 24SEP10, 25SEP10, 01OCT10 and 22OCT10***Certified Organic***Country of Origin: USA***". Recall # F-0534-2011

CODE
Garden Of Grains'® Multi Grain Crackers (16 oz)
Unit UPC code # 163-0922
Lot codes: 08SEP10, 25SEP10, 26SEP10, 22OCT10 and 23OCT10***Certified Organic***Country of Origin: USA***". Recall # F-0535-2011

CODE

RECALLING FIRM/MANUFACTURER
Organic Hills Corporation, Madras, Oregon, by telephone on April 22, 2011 and by letter on April 22, 2011. FDA initiated recall is ongoing.

REASON
There is an unknown substance in the product.
VOLUME OF PRODUCT IN COMMERCE
69, 084 lbs
DISTRIBUTION
Nationwide

19Q

The store in Eugene, Oregon was busy. The city made famous by Nike and the University of Oregon's history of track was a bedrock of residents geared toward healthy and organic lifestyles. That explained why a large percentage of the cases involving Maskill's deaths were in this metropolitan area. This was the store to shop at if you wanted anything organic. This was the Mecca of green living, or dying, as the case may be.

Jimmy John's Organics, or JJO's as the locals called it, was always bustling on Saturday mornings. On this day, however, there was a handful of people walking the empty aisles with many shelves emptied of common, well known products; all of the Garden of Grains wheat and wheat products produced by Organic Hills were gone, as well as several other well known organic companies' products.

The large sign at the entrance generally listed the day's specials. Today, however, it listed the products of death.

"We regret to inform you that there is a major recall of all organic wheat and wheat products for the following companies."

The companies were listed in alphabetical order. At the end of the list was the statement;

"We regret any inconvenience that this may have caused you. Please ask a JJO employee for additional information about the recall."

Below the sign was a brochure holder with a printed list of companies, a copy of the FDA recall notice, and contact phone numbers to call if you had ingested any of the wheat products in the past four months or if you had any of the symptoms of Maskill's Seizures.

A young lady walked up to the sign and started to hit it with her fist, and cry. Several people just watched.

Two police cars were parked at the entrance to the hospital. Around the corner a crowd of people were gathering near the makeshift emergency room entrance. Several people were yelling to be let in. Others were yelling their loved one's name, trying to find out what was happening. Some people near the street were carrying signs that read *"This is God's punishment"* and *"Maskill's is AIDS."*

Grace Moore was parked a block away observing the crowd growing by the hour. News teams were scattered about the area, cameras rolling. A National Guard truck pulled up to the front of the entrance and several men jumped out, rifles in hand. They formed a line across the front, and slowly started to push the people back. "Please, step away from the entrance folks," A policeman shouted.

The crowd slowly retreated.

An ambulance siren could be heard approaching the makeshift hospital. As it neared the entrance, the driver turned the siren off. The people outside watched the ambulance speed into the emergency parking lot and get in line behind two other ambulances.

"Please folks, clear the entrance," the policeman said.

The driver jump out of the ambulance dressed in protective gear and ran to the back as the paramedic inside swung the door open. He was dressed in a biohazard suit. A hospital employee met the paramedic at the back of the ambulance. He, too, was dressed in a biohazard suit. They pulled the stretcher out and the legs folded down. The patient was a man, unknown age, with blood covering his face and side of his head. Blood was on the blanket that covered him. He looked like he had been in a car accident, but he was another Maskill's victim.

Other hospital staff came outside in their yellow biohazard suits. They started to roll the patient toward the door.

A shot rang out. The crowd in front yelled and some scattered. Others fell to the ground. Another shot rang out. No one knew where the shots were coming from. The hospital staff ran inside with the patient and locked the doors to the entrance. The National Guardsmen leveled their rifles, but had no idea who the enemy was. People were yelling. Guardsmen were barking orders for people to stay down. The policemen were crouched looking in all directions. An ambulance sped away.

Grace watched the scene unfold. She lowered her head and wept quietly. Newscasters rushed to the side of the building. Guardsmen ran across the grounds to the emergency entrance. Chaos filled the streets.

After a few minutes, Grace composed herself. She started her car and drove off.

Bill walked up to the front door and hesitated to open it. It seemed like he should be ringing the doorbell or knocking, not just walking in. It was his sister's house, not his. Even though he had been there for a couple of days, he couldn't shake the feeling of being a stranger. They didn't understand. They were empathetic and sincere, but they had no idea what he was really going through. The anger, frustration, uncertainty, questions were overwhelming. So many questions. He was glad he was back at his job in the mill. The hum of the saws and smell of the cut timber gave him a sense of solitude. He felt invincible when he was working in the mill, though he remembered his injury well.

Deanna greeted him as he stepped through the door. "How was work?"

"Good. It feels good to be back to work." He sat his lunch pail on the ground and piled his hat and jacket on top. He sat down to take his boots off. He could hear the television on in the kitchen. Deanna liked to listen to the small television as she cooked.

"Leo will be home soon." Deanna reached over to take his things piled on the floor. "Here. Let me take these." Bill put his hand out to stop her. "I'll take care of it, sis." He continued to unlace his boots.

Deanna was persistent. "I can just take these . . ."

Bill slammed his hand on top of the jacket. "I've got it." He glared at his sister for a second, then caught himself. "Uh, sorry." He went back to unlacing his boots. "Just a bit edgy, I guess."

"I guess." Deanna started into the kitchen and then stopped. "Do you want me to call you when dinner is ready?"

Bill didn't look up. "Sure." He continued to unlace his boots as Deanna walked into the kitchen. She turned the television up and started washing pots and pans.

"*. . . . and all products from Organic Hills Foods, Natasha. The FDA believes the products may be the cause of the seizures and deaths we are seeing throughout the country.*" Bill took off his last boot and slowly stood, listening to the television. "*So far the CDC reports more than 10,000 people have died as a result of these terrible seizures.*" He walked closer to the kitchen. "*There have been 242 deaths in Lane County so far. Everyone hopes this will stop the spread of this terrible disease. Natasha?*"

Bill thought about his family that he lost.

"*Thanks, Al. Just to recap, all foods processed by our local company, Organic Hills, should be removed immediately. You may return products to your store for a full refund. For a complete list, please visit our website at . . . .*"

"Organic Hills," Bill said.

"What was that, Bill?" Deanna stepped out of the kitchen drying her hands. "Did you say something?"

"Uh, I was just saying I need to find my pills. The anxiety pills the doctor gave me. Have you seen them?"

"Yeah. They're in the upstairs bathroom." Deanna walked back into the kitchen.

Bill went upstairs to his room, and closed the door.

CHAPTER 23

Tuesday May 3
Deaths 17,499

It was three A.M. in Eugene, Oregon. Hardly anyone was on the street. A car pulled up to the AMCE Fastener and Supply Company on W. Sixth Avenue and turned their lights off. The driver sat in the car with the window down, and listened. The cool air was not enough to keep him from sweating. He was nervous, tired, but determined to follow through with his plan. He had to. It was the only way to stop this terrible plague from spreading, so he thought. If only someone had done this sooner. Maybe his family would still be alive.

Bill Hammond looked around, carefully looking for any sign of life. None. It was dead quiet. A light mist was falling, creating a shadowy glow in the streetlights down the road. He opened the door and slowly climbed out, looking around as he did. He opened the back door and grabbed a two gallon gas container from the floor of the back seat. He quietly closed the door and pulled the hood of his jacket over his head. He started walking down the street toward the Organic Hills processing plant just two blocks away.

Bill walked briskly to the back of the building and knelt down in the tall grass. He took a deep breath and, as he exhaled, the warmth of this breath turned to a cloud of vapor. It was chilly, but he was sweating profusely. He noticed his hands were shaking. He took the lid off the gas can and splashed the gas along the back of the building. He had seen this done in movies, but never expected he would be in this position. He was soon to be an arsonist. He knew it was the right thing to do. Someone has to stop them.

He was sheltered from the street and out of the lights, tucked between two buildings. He figured he would have about two minutes to run back to the car and get away before the flames grew enough to be noticed by someone driving by in the area. He pulled a stick match out of the box. His hands stopped shaking as he struck the match. "You bastards," he said as he threw the match onto the ground at the edge of the building.

The flame was immediate and intense. Bill was shocked to see the huge fireball climb up the side of the building. He stumbled backwards to avoid the intense heat. The fire raced along the edge of the wooden building. In seconds it had engulfed most of the exterior wall and was traveling around the corner. Bill dropped the gas can as he spun around and ran down the alley and toward his car, splashing mud on his shoes and pants.

On the next street, a policeman was typing in an illegally parked car's license plate when he noticed a flash in front of him. He looked up to see the backside of the Organic Hills Processing Center burst into flames. The building was directly across from him on the other side of the alley. He grabbed his radio and called the fire into dispatch as he sped his car around the corner. That was when he noticed a figure running down the alley and across the next street.

He called for backup.

Bill was muddy, winded, and in a panic. He saw the police car speed down the back street with his lights on. It was just a block away and coming in his direction. Bill's heart was beating so hard. He was winded and scared. He reached his car as the police car rounded the corner. Bill fumbled for his keys as he opened the door to his car and jumped in. The police car pulled up facing his vehicle and blocking it in. The officer yelled over the car speaker. "Stop right there!" The car's lights were flashing and siren wailing. Bill could hear another siren in the distance, indicating another car was quickly approaching. He didn't know what to do. Could he get away? Would they shoot? He started his car and jammed it into reverse. The tires spun in the mud making a high pitched whine. Bill accelerated desperately trying to get away causing the car to dig deeper in the mud and swing to the side of the ditch. The second police car pulled up behind him and blocked him in as his tires spun and the car slowly slid into the ditch.

He was trapped. There was nowhere to go. His heart was beating wildly. He thought he was going to pass out. Bill lowered his head and gripped the steering wheel tightly. He knew he was caught. He didn't want to hurt anyone. He just wanted the company to stop producing death.

He turned the car off and raised his hands out the window. The officers yelled orders for him to step out of the car, lay down on the ground, face first, and spread out.

Bill slowly opened the door with one hand. He leaned his head out with his hands up and glanced at the officers at each end of the car. Their guns were drawn and aimed at him. They were nervous, excited, yelling orders at him one after another. He slowly fell to his knees and spread out face first in the mud as ordered.

The officers approached him, guns drawn and aimed at his head. One officer put his gun back in his holster, pulled out a set of handcuffs, and kneeled on Bill's back. A sharp pain went through his ribs and chest. The officer twisted his arms behind his back and handcuffed him while the other officer kept his pistol aim at Bill until he was secured. As they raised Bill to his feet, one officer read him his rights. They placed him in the patrol car as a third and fourth car approached the scene.

Bill sat in the car and watched the officers taking notes as two fire trucks rounded the corner.

Organic Hills Processing Center continued to burn out of control.

It was early Tuesday morning at CDC. The team leaders and key scientists were gathering for their daily update. Sandy brought a fresh fruit plate, bagels, a variety of cream cheeses, and several coffees to choose from. She knew the team had worked hard and seldom took breaks. She, too, had worked long, hard days supporting the chaos of the CDC investigation into the Maskill's deaths. She knew it was time for a mini vacation in the office. She put some Hawaiian music on the CD player and turned it down low. She had whole, fresh pineapples at the center of the meeting table along with several fresh flowers and a lei at each seat. Palm trees, an ocean beach and waves were drawn on the whiteboard with the words, 'Welcome to CDC Hawaii' written across the top.

Each team leader smiled as they walked into the room. "I need a vacation," Bob replied. "Thanks, Alice."

"Oh, it wasn't my idea to put this on." Alice pointed to Sandy as she was doing the hula while leaning on her crutches. "It's her fault!" Everyone laughed at the comment.

Bob commented, "Then she needs a raise for this 'fault'."

"My pleasure. Call if you need anything more." Sandy smiled as she walked out the door. Carl followed her every step with his eyes.

Alice nudged him in the ribs to break his attention. "Park your peedle, buddy and let's get to work."

Doctor Spaan had a puzzled look, not understanding what she meant. "Peedle?" he asked. The group ignored him. They were lost in their conversations.

"That was quite nice of your secretary to put this celebration together for us," Doctor Raynould said. "However, I am not sure what we are celebrating."

"We are celebrating the recall from the FDA Norm," Bob replied.

"I don't plan to celebrate anything until we stop the deaths from occurring," Norm responded. He put some fruit and a bagel on his plate.

Bob seemed a bit frustrated. "I understand your concern, Norm. But we have made some progress. We wanted to have some good food and atmosphere at our daily meeting this time. The goal is still the same."

"As it should be," Alice said. "We have almost 18,000 deaths. The rate is escalating." Alice glanced through her notes. "The areas of concentrations haven't changed much. We are receiving more reports down the West Coast."

"Thanks, Alice." Bob took a sip of coffee. "I heard from a colleague of mine last night in Eugene, Oregon. Grace Moore. Their hospital is overwhelmed by the increase in deaths and public panic. They set up a Maskill's triage processing area offsite to screen and treat patients for three hospitals. They are trying to keep the general public at the hospitals from seeing the volume of inflicted patients coming to Emergency. She said it is quite chaotic there."

Doctor Spaan sighed. "It must be frightening."

Alice continued. "This is hitting everyone. We've had three CDC families affected by this disease."

The group became very quiet.

Bob cleared his throat. "This morning, we start a new. I expect to see some slowing of the death rate in a few days. If this holds true, then we have to consider how to prevent this from spreading."

Doctor Spaan was first to respond. "I'm not sure we have many options. If the wheat is the cause and the product recall works, then we need to make sure it stops there. The only way I can see to prevent future contamination of plants is to sterilize the ground from which they came." They realized the implications of what Imar was saying and became eerily silent. Doctor Spaan continued. "It is not difficult for me to make the leap to sterilization. I can tell by the looks on your faces that this is a surprise."

"Surprise is an understatement, Imar," Alice blurted. "Don't you think that's pretty extreme?"

"Maybe, but the number of deaths is also extreme," Imar replied. "Almost 18,000."

Carl joined in. "We don't know what has mutated beyond this wheat, whether it can reproduce or not, or if it can mutate other life forms, such as bacteria, insects or animals. We have no idea what this stuff is capable of. I agree with Imar. Extreme situations call for extreme actions. We need to do something."

"You've pulled the products from the market, isn't that a good enough start?" Alice asked.

"No. I agree with Imar. This can't spread. It has to stop . . . here . . . now," Bob replied.

"You're going to need more evidence than this if you want to sterilize the fields," Carl said.

"We will have it if the death rate drops," Bob replied.

CHAPTER 24

Thursday May 5
Deaths 22,022

Agent Jamille Larson walked into his office with his Starbucks coffee and roll. It was a nice spring morning in Sacramento. He turned on his computer and opened the window shades. He sat at his desk and scanned some of the internal mail while his system started. He opened his email program and scanned the subjects. One caught his attention.

"FGIS Wheat Testing Program Notice—URGENT"

He opened the email.

United States Department of Agriculture
Grain Inspection, Packers and Stockyards Administration
Federal Grain Inspection Service
Program Notice FGIS-PN-10-22 04-28-11
NATIONAL WHEAT SAMPLE COLLECTION PLAN FOR ANALYSIS OF GENETIC DEFECTS
1. PURPOSE
This notice outlines procedures for collecting wheat samples to analyze for genetic defects.
2. BACKGROUND
The Grain Inspection, Packers and Stockyards Administration, Federal Grain Inspection Service (FGIS), under the direction of the United States Department of Agriculture (USDA), is ordering the testing of all wheat samples, domestic and imported, for genetic defects. From April 29, 2011 and ongoing until further notice, FGIS and official inspection

agencies will collect and forward wheat samples to the Technical Services Division of the USDA.

"Well, I'll be," agent Larson chuckled. "Looks like they got the government to check all of the wheat." He sat back in his chair. "This is going to wreak havoc on the commodities markets." Jamille leaned forward and continued to read the notice.

CHAPTER 25

Sunday May 8
Deaths 29,654

The daily briefing at CDC was not as jubilant or relaxed as the week before. The team members were exhausted. Little progress had been made in any of the areas of research. They knew the victims were dying because of a mutated gene in the 19Q chromosome, and they knew the wheat was causing the mutation. They knew the wheat type change corresponded to the outbreak, but they still had no answers about the chemical agent that was sprayed on the wheat, why it created different mutations in different wheat, or how to correct it.

Still too many questions, not enough answers.

Bob addressed the group. "Look, folks. We have tried our best to understand what is happening here. I know you are the best and the brightest in your respective fields. But, we haven't made any progress this week. I'm sure it feels like we are still at square one to some of you."

Doctor Kruger was first to speak. "To a large degree, we are way past square one, Bob."

"I know we are, Carl. But we still do not know how this chemical changes the genetic structure of the wheat, or how that transfers to a mutation in the recipient." Bob said. "We only know that it does."

"Bob, we have identified several of the factors causing the deaths," Carl said. "We know that the change in the wheat type is the reason for the new mutations. We know the chemical agent affected the wheat types differently resulting in new mutations. We have evidence to show the wheat is currently in stages of varying mutations, so the chemical must have a prolonged effect on the wheat, breaking down the genetic structure over time resulting in the new mutations. These new mutations must be having an effect on the acceleration of deaths. I agree that knowing how they relate is still a puzzle. But this is very much like trying to cure AIDS in a month. Do you remember that thirty years ago the CDC made the first report of the disease?"

"I do," Bob replied. "That date is etched in history. June 5th, 1981. It was five cases in San Francisco that has grown to thirty-three million people worldwide."

"That's right," Carl replied. "It has taken years and there is still no outright cure or vaccination for AIDS, but we have more answers and more treatments."

"We don't have years, Carl," Bob said. "So far we have almost 30,000 deaths. Even people we know are being affected by this. It is hitting everyone."

"But we got the FGIS to conduct genetic sampling of the wheat. That is a huge step, Bob," Carl retorted.

"I think we are making good progress, Bob." Alice handed out another graph showing the daily deaths. "The daily death rate has dropped for the past few days. It looks like the product recall may be taking affect."

The group looked at the graph. The graph showed a steep rise as the daily deaths escalated. Then, it peaks and slowly starts a decline. It was a typical bell shaped curve. Norman spoke first. "This is great news, Alice!"

"It is if it continues," Bob cautioned. "We have had aberrations before that showed as false progress. I can see why Alice isn't too excited about this trend, yet. If it continues . . ."

Alice interrupted. " . . . . then Ya Hoo! If it continues."

"I think we should send this to Randall right away," Carl said. "This is what he needs to move on a sterilization program. I think it clearly shows the impact of the recall."

"We normally see a drop like this, then a bump back up," Bob said. "But if it continues for another week, it should be evidence enough for him, I would think."

"It seems that the government has been pretty responsive to our requests thus far," Doctor Raynould added. "The notice from the FGIS indicated they are going to test all wheat for genetic defects."

"That's true, Norm," Bob replied. "That is a two edged sword. The testing will be cumbersome and expensive, which will drive up the cost of wheat and possibly other commodities. They can do spot tests, and focus on organic wheat to keep the costs and market impact down. We don't want to create an unnecessary scare with regular wheat. It would have a dramatic impact on the economy."

"Well, if it saves lives, so be it," Alice said.

"Here, here," Carl agreed.

"Easy for you to say," Bob chided. He walked over to the window and pondered his next statement. He didn't want to get into a discussion about the implications of a worldwide wheat scare. He knew something like that could devastate markets, industries and economies throughout the world. Wheat is a major staple and commodity for several countries, including the U.S. A worldwide scare would be devastating.

"Gentlemen . . ." Bob turned to the team . . . "and Alice . . ." He smiled. " . . . . you have done a remarkable job. Even though we do not have the breakthrough we need, your efforts have been remarkable. Your comment about AIDS, Carl, really hits me. This could be something that takes years to unravel. Let's hope not. Though I am extremely disappointed that we have not discovered how the mutations occur, we know that they do. I believe we will, in time, understand how this chemical works."

"Until then, let's hope the USDA will move on the sterilization program," Carl said.

"Carl, it's more than the USDA. This may very well involve the highest levels of most of the government agencies." Bob paused. "To be honest, I'm not sure who to contact with something like this. I've never encountered a need to request a sterilization program of this magnitude." He looked over at Alice. "How many farms changed their wheat type, Alice?"

Alice scanned her notes. "Seven."

"Doesn't seem like very many, Bob," Carl noted. "Maybe a few acres here and there.

Alice ran her finger down the list. "All are outside of populated areas . . ." she paused. " . . . . except two farms bordering the town of Quincy, Washington."

Carl perked up. "That's near the Gorge amphitheater, east of Moses Lake. Nice area. I recall going to several concerts there to see some pretty big name bands."

Alice smiled. "Great place! I went to Creation Northwest for several years there. What an amazing venue!"

"OK, kids," Bob interrupted. "How many acres were affected near Quincy?"

Alice looked back over her notes. "This can't be right."

"What?" Bob asked.

"It shows three hundred and forty." Alice put her notes down. "I thought they were all small sprays."

"Maybe they didn't spray all of it," Imar said.

"Doesn't matter, Imar," Carl replied. "All of it will need to be sterilized."

Bob leaned over to see what Alice was looking at. "That's a pretty large area. Are there any more large sprays like this?"

"Doesn't look like it."

"I'm really concerned about this," Bob said. "It's one thing to have a small, localized spray in a field. The likelihood of drift or overspray is significantly reduced. But a spray this large can easily have both of those occur."

"What are you thinking, Bob?" Carl asked.

"I think we should see if Jamille can dig up the crop duster and find out specifically where and when he sprayed. We can determine if there is additional risk to the outlying areas or not."

"But it shows the date of the spray right here," Alice said.

"That doesn't tell us the local weather or wind conditions at the time of the spray. The pilot will know what it was like, and hopefully will remember any issues that arose during the spray that he had to adjust for," Bob replied.

"Well, let's hope Jamille can track this guy down and tell us something. Otherwise, we could have a major issue here," Carl said.

"I agree, Carl," Bob said. "We could."

A large eighteen wheel truck rolled up to the driveway at Potter's Field. Captain Andy walked out to greet him. He thought the truck was using his driveway as a turn-around as many large trucks do. This one, however, was empty. The driver stopped and climbed out. A passenger stepped out of the other side. A black SUV rolled up behind him and parked.

"Gentlemen. To what do I owe the pleasure of this visit?" Andy was smiling and enjoying the day, as he well should be. It was a sunny spring day in Antelope, Oregon.

"Andrew Potter?" one of the federal men called out.

"Yessiree, that's me. And who are you, pray tell?"

The truck passenger walked over and extended his hand. "William Thornton from the Department of Agriculture, sir."

"Glad to meet you. What can I do for you?"

"You had a visit sometime back from a couple of FBI agents getting samples of a chemical from your crop duster, correct?"

"Yes, I did. They took a hose and some applicator nozzles, and scraped the hopper and skin. Why?" Frisky ran up to sniff the stranger's leg, and he shoed him away with his foot.

"The plane showed positive signs of the chemical. It's pretty dangerous stuff." Thornton took out some papers. "I have a court order here to take possession of your plane, sir, so we can thoroughly rid it of the chemical agent." He handed the paper to Andy.

"Take it?"

"Take it." He pointed to the truck. "On that truck. Today." Two men stepped out of the SUV.

"Oh." Andy looked at the paper, the two agents, and the truck driver. "Looks legit." He looked around and back at Mr. Thornton. "Guess I'd be a fool to try and stop you, eh?"

"Yes, you would. Please don't. We don't need trouble. We just need your plane."

Andy looked down to Frisky, whistled, and snapped his fingers. Frisky ran and jumped into his arms. "Mama didn't raise no fool. I've had my share of 'fun' in Viet Nam. I certainly don't need it here in my front yard." He smiled. "Do I get paid for my time lost from business since this is my main piece of business equipment and livelihood?"

Thornton smiled. "Certainly. I've been authorized to compensate you for your loss."

"Good. I expect a good 'compensation' for my hardship."

"Of course."

Andy pointed to the hangar. "She's over there."

"Thanks." The driver climbed back into the cab of the truck. Thornton waived the truck over to the hangar.

"No problem. Just make sure you clean her up real good before you bring her back. She's due for a good wash."

CHAPTER 26

Tuesday May 10, 2011
Deaths 34,732

It was nearly seven in the evening. Bob was just loading his evening work into his briefcase. He would often run reports during the day of a variety of analysis, and then peruse them in the evening in the peace and quiet of his living room. The past month at CDC was grueling. The ongoing task of trying to figure out why the mutations occurred was overwhelming. But he continued to keep the perspective that they were making progress, albeit slowly. They knew the change in wheat type resulted in a new mutation. How it was affected by the chemical was baffling.

Bob's cell phone rang as he started to the door. "Bob here."

"Bob, this is Jamille."

"Jamille. I've been expecting your call. What did you find?" Bob walked to the chair by the window and sat down, looking out over the city as Jamille began the conversation.

"Quite a bit. It's not good news, either." Bob sat up and pulled a notepad to him. "I found the crop duster. He lives close to Quincy. He remembered the spray because of the cleaning instructions that Mr. 'Bry' left for him."

"Bry, huh? He used the alias again."

"That's not all. The duster didn't clean the plane as instructed." Bob sat upright as Jamille continued. "In fact, he didn't clean it at all."

"What?" Bob stood as he heard the news.

"He didn't clean it, Bob. He said since it was just fertilizer, there was no need to go through all those hoops for some scientist test. So, he just rinsed it out."

"Did he have any sprays after that?" Bob already knew the answer, but he had to ask the question.

"Plenty. Seventeen."

Bob was stunned. "Where?"

"I have the list. They were all right around the area. But there's another problem."

Bob became irritated. "How can there be anything more?"

"He had some over spray on the first two applications; the primary spray and the next spray."

"Over spray? How much?"

"A lot. The wind was whipping around and he said he over sprayed into a couple of fields and may have drifted toward the city of Quincy. He said it was no big deal because it was just fertilizer and there were no structures or people in the immediate area."

"How large were the first two subsequent sprays," Bob asked?

There was a moment of silence on the phone before Jamille answered. "Almost seven hundred acres."

The phone was silent as Bob sat back in his chair and let the news soak in.

"Bob?"

"Yeah. I'm here. I'm just . . . I . . ." Bob took a deep breath to refocus. "Jamille, we need to get samples of the soil, crops, and . . . ." Bob thought for a second. " . . . . and some insects from the three spray zones."

"Did you say insects?"

"Yes. Insects. We've discovered this spray can mutate differently on different types of wheat, so now I question if it can affect other living organisms."

"You didn't ask for this before. Why now?" Jamille asked.

"Because we thought they were small sprays, primarily affected plants, one type of wheat to be exact, and the possibility of an insect or animal passing it along has never been seriously considered."

"And now?" Jamille asked.

"Now, I don't know. We have at least two types of wheat that this affects and, if it is sprayed on other plants . . . . I don't know. I think we need to explore the possibility. If we are going to address an area of this size, we better get some more evidence and data." Bob was worried the chemical could do more harm than they initially believed. They needed to know how it affected the other crops.

"OK. I'll get my team on this right away. Any idea what type of insects you'd like to have?"

"Earthworm, most definitely. The genome has been mapped of the worm. Other than that, grasshoppers, beetles, or ants or whatever. Can you send the specs on the sprays so I can do an overlay to see how much area was affected?"

"Sure. I'll send that in a few minutes. And I'll get your insects, too."

"Thanks, Jamille."

"You're welcome. Sorry for the bad news, Bob."

"Thanks."

Bob closed his cell phone and walked over to his desk and pushed the button on the phone.

"Yeah, Bob," came the answer.

"Carl. We have another problem."

"What is it, Bob?"

"Not good. We need to talk. I'll be right down." Bob disconnected the call and started out the door.

CHAPTER 27

Thursday May 12, 2011
Deaths 39,314

The samples of plants and insects arrived at CDC yesterday afternoon. The samples were segregated and identified by area of spray. Some were from the primary spray area. Others from the subsequent sprays. There was alfalfa, onions, tomatoes, broccoli, grass, and a few flowering plants. The samples of insects included grasshoppers, ants, beetles, and some earthworms, just as Bob had asked for.

Carl received the samples and re-classified them accordingly. He knew that there was too much work and not enough time to thoroughly research possible genetic changes amongst all of the samples. Some could take months. He was tasked with deciding what to test first.

Carl knew that any sample he chose had to have mapped genomes to compare current samples to. The decision was easy; the earthworm and the alfalfa from the subsequent sprays. He was very please to see they had earthworms. He reached down and lifted the wiggling worm into the air. "I bet you have quite a story to tell young fella . . . uh . . . lady . . . . uh . . ." He chuckled and placed the hermaphrodite[5] worm in a plastic container.

"OK folks. Here's what we have." Several analysts gathered around the table. Carl continued. "We need to see if there are any genetic aberrations to these samples. If you find anything, anything at all that is questionable, I want to know . . . . yesterday. All other testing stops. This takes first priority. I want twenty-four hour shifts working on these samples. Break up into two teams and have at it. Dennis and

---

[5] Hermaphrodite-contains sex organs from both sexes.

Angela—form your teams and let me know who is doing what. Any questions?"

The room was silent. "OK. Let's go." Carl turned and walked out as the analysts discussed their team and sample assignments.

CHAPTER 28

Friday May 13, 2011
Deaths 41,374

The CDC command center was quiet. Imar, Carl, Bob, Alice, and Norman were setting around their meeting table this morning, the same as they had done every morning for almost a month now. A month. A very long month. No one spoke. There were several documents in front of them. A plate of fruit and some rolls sat untouched. It was obvious that they were all upset by the information just shared with them.

Alice spoke first. "Carl, are you sure about your findings?"

"Yes, Alice. We double checked the results. There are mutations in the alfalfa, some insects, and some of the plant samples obtained from around the primary, secondary and tertiary sprays."

Bob cleared his throat. "Then that means we have a wide area of infestation and mutation effects on other plants and insects."

Carl confirmed. "It does."

"Then this . . . . chemical . . . . is . . . . is capable of mutating most anything it comes into contact with," Imar said.

Norman disagreed. "No, Imar. I don't think so. The insect mutation could be caused by ingestion of a plant."

"What about the earthworm, then?" Imar asked.

Norman smiled. "Ingestion of the soil."

Carl interrupted. "But we don't know for sure."

"No, we don't," Alice agreed.

"If the insect could be affected by ingesting the soil, then that would mean the chemical does not need a host to create a mutation to pass along to a recipient, as we previously thought," Imar said.

The group froze. Imar was right. That means anyone who came in contact with the chemical could be subject to its effects if ingested.

"That wouldn't classify it as a contagion, would it?" asked Norm.

"No," Bob replied. "It isn't passed along from one host to another."

"If it can affect a recipient without passing through a host, then whose to say it couldn't become a contagion," Alice said.

"Hold on, now." Bob raised his hands to settle everyone down. Their thoughts were beginning to run wild with the possibilities that this chemical, whatever it was, could become active and transferable between victims. "We have to stay focused on the task at hand, and that is to determine how these recipients became infected and the nature of the change. Just because a worm is affected doesn't mean it is deadly or will become a problem."

"Doesn't mean that it won't, either, Bob," Alice retorted.

"Agreed." Bob said as he diverted the topic. "Now, we know something has a mutation, but we still do not know how. Only that the chemical is involved."

"So far, the only common link that we have verified is that the spray affects the plant and the plant affects the living organism, in particular wheat and alfalfa." Norman said. "And we have plenty of correlative evidence to support that."

"We do," Carl confirmed.

"I think we need to gather our evidence and present the case to Randall to move forward with a sterilization program," Bob said. The idea that almost any living organism could be affected by this chemical was upsetting to Bob. He felt they had to take action right away to try and stop this from spreading any further.

"I agree, Bob," Alice said. "This graph shows a steady decline in the new deaths after we recalled the products." The updated graph of the daily death rate showed a dramatic decline in numbers. The bell shaped curve was more dramatic and clearly showed the positive impact of the product recall. "We're beating this thing, Bob."

"Alice, I appreciate your enthusiasm, but we are only winning the battle; not the war." Bob turned to the rest of the group. "Until we know exactly why this chemical causes the mutations, and how it is transferred into a recipient host, we are far from done. It could pop up anywhere, or possibly transfer through reproduction."

Imar responded. "I'd hate to think what would happen if that was the case."

"It would be unimaginable," Imar said.

"It would," agreed Carl. "This is a horrific chemical. The possibilities are becoming quite overwhelming."

The group was silent for a moment as they pondered the utter catastrophes of the various scenarios.

Alice broke the silence. "Isn't today Friday the thirteenth?" Imar looked at Alice, puzzled. The group started chuckling.

"I don't believe that stuff," Imar rejected.

"Pure nonsense," said Carl with a laugh.

Bob interrupted. "OK. Let's get this information together for tomorrow. I'm going to call a meeting with Randall and Samar."

"Pulling in the big guns, eh?" Alice joked.

"Yep. May as well get the Director on board. This is something he will need to take to the top level of government, possibly all the way to the White House." Bob was writing some notes on a pad. "We're breaking new ground here, folks."

CHAPTER 29

Saturday May 14, 2011
Deaths 43,237

The conference room was large with glass walls on two sides. It was a large, corner room on the top floor of the Center for Disease Control in Atlanta, Georgia. A large rectangular wooden table with leather chairs sat in the middle of the room. Whiteboards, projection systems, all of the elements of a high level board room were present. The table was littered with cups, binders, papers, pens, and cell phones.

Samar Inghall, the Director of CDC, was impeccably dressed in a dark suit with red tie. He sat at the head of the table with Randall Sterling, Deputy Director of Infectious Disease. The three scientists, Doctors Spaan, Kruger and Raynould sat along one side of the table. Alice and Bob sat across the table from them. The remaining chairs were empty.

No one was talking. Everyone was looking at the picture of the chromosome on the screen except Carl Kruger. He was standing behind his chair addressing the audience. "There are now six types of the 19Q chromosome that we have confirmed." The slide advanced to a picture of the six X-type chromosomes. "We have determined that the five mutations have occurred from two types of wheat that was treated with a chemical agent developed by Biotrogen. Dr. Spaan, if you will." He handed the controller to Dr. Spaan.

"Thank you. You heard the report from the FBI about the murders and cover up at Biotrogen. We received samples of wheat from the FBI that were stored by one of the victims, and performed extensive tests on them. The wheat was a tetraploid variety with four chromosomes. Our comparative analysis of the wheat recently harvested and sold through the Biotrogen shell company revealed a hexaploid wheat variety with six chromosomes. We compared that to the wheat samples that were originally used in the creation of the chemical agent years ago and it shows significant variances. What we have discovered is that both wheat varieties have mutated, and the Hexaploid is the most recent wheat variety that is continuing to mutate."

"This is quite troubling, to say the least," said Samar, with a slight Indian accent.

Bob stood. "It is. To bring this together thus far, the FBI has confirmed the existence of a shell company to hide the application of the spray, harvest of the wheat, and distribution to processors. We have tied the time frames for all of that to the mutations of the wheat by harvest, the mutations of the 19Q chromosome and birth of the Maskill's deaths. It all fits."

Doctor Spaan continued. "We have the primary mutation in a tetraploid wheat variety that resulted in Maskill's, and subsequent mutations in the hexaploid varieties that have resulted in the aneurysms and deaths. The chemical that was sprayed on one wheat variety created Maskill's, while being sprayed on the other variety created deadly mutations in non-Maskill's patients."

"Have you identified the chemical and how the wheat is mutated?" Raymond asked.

"I'll let Doctor Raynould answer that question. Doctor?" Bob handed the controller to the Doctor, who advanced past several slides. He stopped at a picture of a molecule.

"What we have discovered, sir, is a new element," he began.

Samar was shocked. "A new element, from the table of periodic elements?"

"Yes," Doctor Raynould replied. He educated the group about the periodic table of elements and that this chemical contained a new, synthetically man made element. "We have discovered a new molecule with a new electron orbit and valence shells. It does not fit into the table."

"Do you know how that happened?" Samar asked.

"No, we don't," Bob answered. "Everett Maskill was, by far, a genius. We are attempting to understand more of the chemical, but at present it eludes us. What we know is the chemical caused the original and subsequent mutations of the wheat."

"We have evidence to show the wheat harvested from particular fields caused the deaths," Alice added. Bob advanced the slides to the graph of daily Maskill's deaths. Alice pointed to the graph which depicted a dramatic drop in the death rates since the product recalls. "We recalled the products associated to the wheat from specific fields involved with the spray. You can see the death rate drops significantly after the product recalls."

"Yes, I see." Randall was pleased to see the drop. "But you don't know what causes the wheat to mutate?"

Bob corrected him. "We know what, Randall, not why."

"And the mutation is transferred to the recipient through ingestion, causing a secondary mutation in the host?" Samar asked.

"That is correct, sir," Carl confirmed. He looked to Bob who nodded, and continued. "We also have discovered it goes beyond humans . . . .sir."

"Meaning?" Samar asked.

Randall answered. "They have confirmed mutations in earthworms and grasshoppers, so far."

"That's right, Randall," Bob confirmed. "We retrieved samples of insects from an area of spray and conducted some genetic tests on them. The results indicate both types of insects obtained had genetic mutations. We believe it is the result of the chemical spray."

"How can this be?" Samar asked.

"The mutation is transferred through ingestion, at least that is what we believe. The grasshoppers would have ingested the mutated grains or grasses; the earthworm the soil," Carl explained.

Samar thought for a few seconds, digesting what he had heard. "Then, the mutations to insects could have been occurring for some time now. Years."

"Possibly so, but we don't know for certain," Bob said. "Most of the sprays are in localized, concentrated areas. There may be insects or small animals that have been 'infected' over the years. We do not know what the ramifications are. They could pass the mutation to following generations through birth, to other living organisms through the food chain, or just die like the current human victims. We don't know."

"And the mutations can occur without passing through a plant host to the recipient, such as with the grasshopper?" Samar asked.

"It appears that is possible, but we have not confirmed that, yet," Bob replied.

"There's more, sir" Alice interrupted. "We found mutations in additional plant types; onions and alfalfa, to be specific."

"How? I thought the original intent was to create the disease specifically through wheat?" Samar asked.

Alice continued. "It was. One of the crop dusters did not properly clean his plane of the agent, thus applying it in subsequent sprays in the area." Alice advanced through a couple of slides. "Here. You can see that the fields he sprayed cover approximately twelve hundred total acres in and around Quincy, Washington. We pulled samples of plants in the areas and confirmed mutations had occurred . . . . in alfalfa and onions."

Samar leaned forward looking at the map of the Quincy area with large splotches indicating the spray zones. "Do we know where the alfalfa has been distributed to, or what the end result is of any animals ingesting it?" he asked.

"No. We just discovered this yesterday. We have asked the FBI to track down the distribution of the alfalfa and the end user. This may well lead to a recall of beef, milk, who knows," Bob explained.

"We have to stop this thing now," Randall said. "It can't spread any further either by application or transference."

"We have stopped the application, Randall," Bob said. "What we don't know are the implications of continuing transference through the food chain."

"What do you suggest?" Samar asked the group.

Randall answered. "Sterilization of the plants and animals in the affected areas."

Samar thought for a few seconds. He stood and walked over to the windows. All eyes were on him. He turned to Randall. "That is not easily accomplished."

"I understand. But we see no other option. It is imperative that we stop this from spreading. We believe sterilization is the only way to accomplish that," Randall replied.

"Very well." Samar walked back to his seat. "I can see where we can sterilize the smaller areas of infestation, but Quincy is troubling. It is more than one thousand acres. What do you propose there?"

"Eradication," Bob replied.

The room went silent. No one said a word for several seconds. Samar spoke first. "That is pretty extreme, Mr. Struthers."

"So are forty-three thousand deaths," Alice blurted. She caught herself. " . . . . sir."

Samar glared at her. "Yes that, too, is extreme, Ms. Barker. I agree. But to eradicate an entire community? He took off his glasses, and leaned forward. "The information you have presented is quite compelling, but not absolute. I will need more information, more evidence."

"Sir, everything lines up," Bob said.

"Well, it might line up for you, but it doesn't for me. Not yet," the Director replied.

Bob Spoke. "Sir, with all due respect, time is our enemy. I understand there is a process that you must go through. I would ask that you expedite it if at all possible."

"I understand, Mr. Struthers. If we are talking about sterilizing several thousand acres and several farms and ranches, then we, the United States government, will be expected to be absolutely sure of the threat, and to compensate these people in some way. From the evidence you have presented, I don't dispute we have an urgent situation that requires immediate action. I believe sterilization may be appropriate to the smaller affected areas. I'm just not convinced that eradication of a large area is the proper solution for Quincy. I need more evidence."

"I understand," Bob replied. "We will continue to gather information and evidence. Again, I just ask you to expedite the process if at all possible."

Samar seemed irritated at Bob's persistence. "I need to get it approved through our governmental process. Nothing will happen for at least a few weeks."

Bob spoke up. "Sir. Our concern is that this chemical agent may cause significant environmental damage. If it is able to mutate plants, which can adversely affect humans and insects, there is no telling what it may do to the environment."

"I understand," Samar said loudly as he glared at Bob for his persistence. Everyone was silent. Samar lowered his voice and continued. "But we do not have the right to take away someone's livelihood, their home without due process and absolute evidence. We can't just circumvent the constitution. It isn't like we were under attack from aliens or something." He chuckled at the absurdity. Several people at the table joined in.

Doctor Raynould spoke. "But, sir, we *are* being attacked by an alien." The room quieted. "The new element that we discovered is an alien to what we know. What it is possible of doing is what we don't know. If it is able to alter the molecular composition of plants, it could possibly alter the genetic composition of bacteria. If so, and it became an airborne contagion, it could be catastrophic."

The room fell silent.

Samar broke the silence. "Thank you for your opinion, Doctor. I understand. I will set up a meeting in Washington as soon as possible. I want all of you to clear your calendars and make sure you can attend." He paused as he collected his thoughts. "I believe the information you have presented is evidence that we have a serious situation occurring that must be stopped. I just need to make sure we are proposing the right solution to accomplish that." He started to gather his papers, signaling the end of the meeting. He looked at Bob. "Continue to get the additional evidence I need to make the case."

"We will," Bob replied.

"Someone from my office will be in contact with each of you for the Washington meeting." He looked around the table. "If there are no more questions, we are adjourned." He picked up his papers and stood. The meeting was obviously over.

CHAPTER 30

Monday, May 16, 2011
Deaths 46,419

The courtroom was full. The gallery of wooden benches had people setting elbow to elbow. The media was across the back of the room in the last row. The jury box with twelve high backed cloth chairs sat empty.

On the left side of the room, across from the jury box, sat a long wooden table. The prosecuting district attorney sat on the right end with his assistant to his left. To the left of them were the defendant's attorney and the defendant, William Hammond.

Bill was wearing an orange jumpsuit from the Lane County Jail. Since his arrest for arson, he has been in jail. Though his crime was a first offense, it was serious; Arson 1. It was a measure eleven crime punishable with a mandatory sentence of seven years and six months in prison if convicted.

Bill sat at the table with his hands folded on top of his wife's bible. His legs were shackled. Though he was not considered to be a violent man, he was seen as being highly distraught by the deaths of his family. He was on suicide watch and considered to be a severe flight risk in court. He knew what he had done. He planned it. He didn't shirk away from it when asked. When the judge asked him how he pled last week, he was quick to say, "Guilty."

His defense attorney believed he could get him off or significantly reduced charges if he could show how distraught he was from the deaths of his wife and two kids. He wanted a jury that he could play with their emotions and likely get reduced charges. But Bill didn't care. Not anymore. He knew he did wrong and dragging this through the courts would just prolong the nightmare.

Deanna and her husband were setting in the front row behind Bill. Bill never looked back. He knew she was there, but just stared at the bible on the table top.

"All rise." Everyone in the courtroom stood as the judge entered from the back door wearing a long, black robe. She was in her mid fifties, silver blond hair with glasses. "The honorable Melissa LeFevre presiding." The judge sat in her chair behind the elevated platform allowing her to look down on everyone in the room. "Please be seated."

The judge began. "This is case number 51-11-3448; the State of Oregon versus William L. Hammond. Are the parties present?"

"The DA and the defendant's attorney stood. The DA spoke. "We are, your honor."

The judge looked over some papers. "Very well, then." The men sat back down as the judge continued. "William Hammond, please stand."

Bill stood to his feet. His legs were weak. Deanna quietly wept in the back. Everyone knew he would be going to prison. They just couldn't believe it.

"Mr. Hammond. The charge against you is Arson 1. You have pled guilty before the court to this charge. It is my duty today to impose sentencing for this crime. Do you understand?"

Bill looked up at the judge. "I do, your Honor."

The judge continued. "Sir, this is a difficult case. The loss of your family is tragic. I understand what led you to take matters into your own hands. But we live in a civil society where our laws and courts dictate and administer justice; not the citizens through vigilante actions. Though the court empathizes with you for your loss, I have no choice than to sentence you to . . . ." The judge glanced down at some papers and then back up to the defendant. " . . . . seven years and six months of correctional custody at the Two Rivers Correctional Institution."

Bill lowered his head. Deanna wept. The crowd made a collective gasp and people started whispering.

"Bailiff, please take Mr. Hammond into custody. This court is adjourned." The judge banged her gavel, stood and exited the courtroom as the bailiff took hold of Bill's arm and escorted him out of the room carrying his wife's bible.

CHAPTER 31

Sunday, May 22, 2011
Deaths 52,630

The work crews were running about, tearing down the plexiglass wall, removing partitions, pulling out cable, and removing the signs. The noise of the saws, drills, hammers, and material being moved echoed through the building. There were no patients, no doctors, no staff. Just contractors, everywhere.

The moving trucks were lined up on both sides of the parking lot and streets. Grace Moore and Alan Gobel were watching the dismantling of the temporary Maskill's triage center and morgue of Mercy Hospital.

The number of patients with Maskill's related seizures and deaths dropped dramatically over the past ten days. The chaos waned as fast as it surfaced. The few number of patients were easily accommodated by the three hospitals in the area through their regular channels.

"I can't believe what we have just been through, Alan." Grace had her arms folded, watching the bustling activity. "Not even a full month."

"Remarkable, Grace. Absolutely remarkable."

The bustling activities reminded her of the marketplaces in some of the foreign countries that she had traveled. People were moving in all directions. A different type of managed chaos. "It's difficult to grasp that more than two thousand people died in this county from that dreadful disease."

"It is. But, Grace, it wasn't really a disease, you know." Alan looked at her. "It was a whole lot more than that."

"I know, Alan. That's what still scares me." Grace's phone vibrated and she pulled it out to look at the text. "Sorry. Looks like I need to get back."

"Not an emergency, I hope," Alan said.

Grace chuckled. "After this," Grace waived her hand toward the dismantling of the processing center and continued. " . . . . nothing is an emergency. Just an inconvenience."

CHAPTER 32

Tuesday, May 24, 2011
Deaths 53,872

It was noon. The large laboratory was full of people celebrating the news. The team leaders were mingling with the analysts. A huge cake made in the shape of a large chromosome was on a table surrounded with white paper plates, plastic forks and blue napkins. A banner hung above the cake.

> "See You
> Team 19Q"

Next to the cake was a small sign that read:

> Deaths reported 24 hours—243

Under the sign was a graph of the reported deaths showing the success of the product recall.

The champagne bottles were intermingled with the sparkling cider. Soda cans littered the desks and tables. Confetti was on the floor. Balloons were floating against the ceiling being pushed around by the air flowing out of the vents. It was a celebration. And Bob Struthers was struggling with it all.

Alice held up a soda can and banged it with a marker. "Ladies and gentlemen, can I have your attention, please?" The room slowly quieted down. "Thank you. Thank you." Alice looked around the room. "As you know, the Secretary of Agriculture . . . ." Alice paused and cleared her throat, and continued. " . . . . and the Vice President authorized the sterilization program as of last Saturday." The audience gave a hearty applause with a few cheers. Alice continued. "This is our 'going away thank you celebration party' for all of the great team leaders we had working on the 19Q project, as we call it." The crowd applauded, some cheered and whistled. "Bob, can you step up here, please?"

Bob blushed and shyly walked up to the front of the audience. He forced a smile as Alice put her arm around his waist and leaned on one crutch. "Bob, you have been a great leader through this nightmare." The audience again applauded.

"Bob held up his hands, one with a drink in it, and quieted down the crowd. "Thank you, Alice, and everyone . . . ." Bob didn't want to squelch the celebration with his real thoughts of their progress. He continued. " . . . . but the credit really goes to these guys." Bob pointed to Carl, Norman, and Imar. "These three scientists have made great strides with solving the Maskill's dilemma." The crowd again applauded. He turned to the three men. "I am honored to have had the opportunity to work with such brilliant minds." He bowed gracefully to them.

Carl walked over and shook Bob's hand as the crowd applauded again. He turned to the audience. "Thank you, everyone." He paused as they quieted down. "It has been a pleasure, and I use the term loosely, for me to be able to work here on this challenging project. Even though we do not have all of the answers, I know we have laid the ground work in a new science that will eventually reap great results for mankind." The audience applauded and cheered. He continued. "The end result may not come for years, but it will come. I just regret that the time has come for me, and Norm and Imar, to leave." The audience gave a collective "Aw." "But we leave knowing that all of us contributed much to the solution of the Maskill's deaths. Thank you for that opportunity."

The audience applauded as Carl and Bob shook hands. Imar and Norm walked over to the group and they each shook hands and patted each other on the back.

Randall Sterling and Samar Inghall walked into the room as the celebration was at its peak. Alice saw them enter and worked her way over to greet them. "Samar, Randall." Randall had a strained smile on his face. "Hello, Alice. Looks like a party," he said.

Bob saw the three together and joined them. "Samar, Randall. Glad you could make it back in time."

Alice pointed to the table with the punch and other drinks near the cake. "Come have a drink."

"Thank you." Bob started toward the table as Randall grabbed his arm to stop him. "I wanted to let you know there is no decision from Washington yet regarding Quincy." Bob and Alice lost their smiles. Randall continued. "We reviewed the information and decided to conduct further testing of the living organisms in the area before we decide how to address the . . . . 'situation'."

"Any idea how long?" Alice asked.

Samar answered. "No. Could be awhile. The testing will be conducted in Washington." He looked around the room. "We can still disband the team here. Some members may be asked to join the new research teams, though."

"Well, we did what we could. It's up to them now," Bob said.

Samar agreed. "Yes, it is. This is more complicated than any of us imagined."

Randall looked around the room with a smile. "Your team did an amazing job in Washington."

Bob smiled. "Thanks. It isn't every day you get a chance to share your insight and knowledge with the Secretary of Agriculture, Secretary of the Interior, Homeland Security Director . . ."

Alice interrupted. "And the Vice President."

Samar chuckled. "Yes, the Vice President. It was quite a contingent I must say."

"I'm just thankful they agreed to do the sterilization," Alice exclaimed. "It took them a few days, but we got it."

"Yes, we did. None of us on the committee want to deprive any citizen of their right to property. We had to agree to use eminent domain as a matter of national security," Samar said. "We will compensate them fairly, but some families will lose the heritage their ancestors built. It is another layer to this tragedy."

"It is," Alice agreed.

Imar and Norman noticed Samar and Randall were chatting with Bob and Alice. They walked over and shook their hands. "Have you come to wish us a bon voyage?" Imar asked.

Randall smiled. "As a matter of fact, we have." Randall stepped to the table by the cake. "Ladies and gentlemen. May I have your attention, please." The crowd quickly quieted down. "Thank you. Director Inghall and I would like to take this opportunity to thank all of you for a job well done." The crowd applauded and a few people whistled. Randall continued. "There have been more than fifty-three thousand deaths from the Maskill's mutations, as we now call them." The crowd became silent. "Many lives have been lost. Families have experienced horrendous tragedies. But your efforts have resulted in the cessation of the Maskill deaths, and in a very short time I must say. To that, we say thank you."

The crowd broke into applause again. Several people walked up and shook Randall and Samar's hands. Everyone was smiling. Everyone was happy.

Except Bob. He walked over to the side of the room and watched the celebration. He felt like he was on the outside looking in on someone else's party. He knew, deep down inside, that they did a remarkable job of working through this catastrophe and made great discoveries. They were a fabulous team and brilliant minds. It pained him to know they failed.

The 19Q team was being dismantled.

Two sheriff's cars pulled up to the front of the house in Riley. They were closely followed by a black SUV with tinted windows. The two deputies stepped out of the sheriff's vehicle and walked up to the porch. One looked back at the SUV and three people stepped out, all dressed in suits. One of the men nodded to the deputy. The deputy turned and knocked on the door.

The door opened. "Mr. Johnston?" the deputy asked.

The middle aged man behind the screen door responded. "Yes."

"I'm Deputy Sanchez. This is deputy Miles. We are here on an urgent government matter, sir."

"Is this a joke or something?" the young man asked.

"No, sir. It is not." The deputy was serious. "It involves your farm, sir."

The young man opened the screen door and stepped onto the porch. "Hold it. This is not my farm, yet. It's my dad's."

"Oh. I see. Is he available?" Deputy Miles asked looking around.

"No. He died last week. Suicide."

Deputy Sanchez responded. "I see. I'm sorry for your loss, sir. May I have your name, please?"

"Sure Earl Johnston. What's this about anyway? Who are they?" Earl pointed to the men by the SUV who were watching them.

The deputies looked at each other. "They are from.... the government, sir. Top levels," Deputy Sanchez replied. "This involves your dad's farm and the crops he raised. Do you have a moment that we can talk about this?"

"Sure. I guess so," Earl said. "What do you mean it involves his crops?"

Deputy Sanchez pulled a piece of paper out of a folder. "Sir, this is an order from the federal court. It orders the residents of this property to vacate immediately for safety reasons." Deputy Sanchez handed the order to Earl.

Earl took the paper and glanced over it. "Why? What do you mean 'vacate'?"

Deputy Miles looked to the men by the SUV. "I think these gentlemen need to answer that question for you."

The deputies escorted Earl to the SUV, one on each side. As they walked up, one man put his hand out to shake. "Hello. I'm Jim Kowalczyk. I'm from the Department of Agriculture."

Earl didn't shake his hand. "I'm Earl. Can you tell me what's going on here?" he said as he waived the paper, obviously getting more agitated by the moment.

"Sure. This land was recently sprayed with an unknown substance about two months ago. We know that it is dangerous and possibly deadly, but what it is exactly we don't know. This order is for you and the residents to immediately vacate the premises while we . . . . correct the problem."

"What do you mean, 'correct the problem'?" Earl asked.

The man cleared his throat. "We need to sterilize the soil, sir."

"Are you joking?" Earl became upset and started to raise his voice. "This is a farm. You can't just come in here and sterilize the place."

"Look. You are not alone in this." One of the other federal men said. "We have several farms and ranches that have to be sterilized."

"I don't care." Earl was mad at the idea.

"The government has exercised eminent domain on this place," one of the agents said. "You will receive just compensation for this place."

"I don't want your just compensation," he said as he threw the paper back at the agent. "You know what you can do with this."

The agent didn't flinch. He stared at Earl. "You don't have a choice."

"Like hell I don't." Earl turned and started to walk back toward the house. One of the men grabbed him, put his arm behind his back, and forced him against the vehicle. Earl struggled, and tried to kick and twist his way free. The other man pulled out handcuffs and cuffed Earl in the yard. Earl started yelling for his wife.

"Listen, I'm sorry we have to do this, but we have orders to clear this place immediately," Kowalczyk said.

"Orders? Orders from who?" he yelled.

"The White House."

One man opened the door and they pushed Earl into the SUV and slammed the door. The deputies started back to the porch.

A woman appeared at the front door. "Earl. What's going on? What's the yelling about?" She rushed out onto the porch, only to be stopped by both deputies. "Ma'am. Please," Deputy Sanchez said as he held her arms. "This is a difficult situation. Please just wait a moment."

"What's going on? Why is Earl in that car?" She was becoming frantic.

"Ma'am. We have orders to empty this house. Today," Miles said.

"Why? What's wrong?" She could hear Earl yelling from inside the car. "What are you doing to my husband?"

"Please, set down." The deputy forcibly sat her in the chair. Agent Kowalczyk walked up to the porch. "He can explain."

"What's going on here? Why are you doing this? Who are you?"

"OK. Just wait a second and I'll explain. Sorry we have to do it this way. We have an order from the federal court, and directions from the highest levels of government, to clear this land today." Agent Kowalczyk raised his hand before the woman could ask more questions. "About two months ago this farm was sprayed with an unknown substance that must be neutralized. The only way to do that is to clear the farm and sterilize the soil for three years."

"Three years? What are you talking about?" Nothing made sense to the woman. Her husband was in an unmarked car, yelling. These men were telling her she had to leave. Why?

He continued. "The government is exercising eminent domain, ma'am. They are taking possession of your farm and will compensate you more than fairly for it."

"You can't do that," she said defiantly.

"Oh yes we can, and we are," Kowalczyk shot back.

The lady stood and tried to run to her husband. Deputy Sanchez grabbed her arm and forced her against the wall. The other deputy assisted him with getting the handcuffs on her. They led the screaming woman to the second patrol car. Once in the car, she yelled, "I'll fight you in court you bastard!"

Kowalczyk looked at her and smiled. "In this case, ma'am, it's too late." He closed the door.

The deputies went back to the house to make sure no one else was there as they took a series of pictures.

The road was blocked off by black SUVs a quarter mile in each direction around the farm near Riley, Oregon. Hundreds of people, including news trucks, police, and citizens of Riley watched from afar while dozens of men with large contractor's trucks, trailers, generators, and supplies were frantically installing an eight foot chain link fence with a razor wire top around the field. The foreman of the project was in a golf cart circling the perimeter, barking instructions to the contractors as they started on opposite ends and joined the fences in the middle. It looked like a modern version of the transcontinental railroad meeting at Promontory Point, Utah; except the golden spike was missing.

The contractors would complete a section and quickly mount signs on the fence every fifty yards.

United States Government Property
No Trespassing
Violators will be Prosecuted to the
fullest extent of the law

DANGER
These premises are a hazard
to human health

CHAPTER 33

Wednesday, May 25, 2011
Deaths 54,312

The bulldozer rolled up to the front of the house. The driver was wearing a hazardous materials suit of yellow rubber, mask, and hood. He maneuvered the bulldozer to face the porch. He looked back at the SUV. The man dressed in a black suit stood by the car and gave the 'thumbs up' to proceed. His gas mask made him look like a bug in a suit.

The porch was clear except for the two metal rocking chairs gently rocking in morning breeze and the small table. The bulldozer driver wondered who had sat there, the years they spent together. He could picture an older couple watching the crops grow, the children and grandchildren playing in the yard under the huge oak tree. The tire swing slowly turned as the breeze blew it in circles.

The bulldozer inched toward the house crushing the pansies and roses planted along the front picket fence, which snapped and cracked under the weight of the dozer. Black smoke billowed from the exhaust as the diesel engine revved. The huge metal blade slowly rose into the air as it approached the defenseless house. The dozer was ready to strike.

In minutes, the house was a pile of rubble. The dozer scooped up large bucket loads of the house, furniture, trees and shrubs and emptied them into a deep hole that was dug hours earlier. Pictures of the family fluttered in the wind. Several people encircled the area wearing gas masks and gathered the papers flying in the breeze. One man picked up a picture of the family reunion. It was the entire Johnston clan posing across the porch and steps back in 1996. Six generations. He tossed it into the bag.

Scoop after scoop, the lives and the heritage of the Johnston farm went into the hole with the sound of breaking glass, cracking wood, and broken lives. Once the buildings and plants were flattened, the farm animals euthanized, and everything loaded into the hole, the dozer pushed pile after pile of dirt over the top creating a small mound. After several hours of scraping and pushing, the house, barn, shed, animals, tree and tire swing were completely gone. There was no trace that they ever existed except for the mound near where the Johnston house once stood. The dozer lifted a large boulder and placed it on top of the mound, almost representing a monument to the farm that was wiped away.

Over the next two days, all of the farms and small ranches associated to the Biotrogen spray were gone . . . . except those in Quincy, Washington.

CHAPTER 34

Thursday, May 26
Deaths 54,627

The crop duster flew low and fast over the farm. It was early in the morning, a perfectly still day for the duster. Conditions could not have been better. The pilot maneuvered the plane with ease, cris-crossing the field and releasing his spray layer after layer until all of the land was saturated with the sterilizing agent. The plane roared over the chain-link fence where the signs still spoke of the dangers that lay behind them.

A second crop duster soon followed, again crossing over the field as it released its payload. The insecticide was lethal. There was no chance that any insect in this area would survive. Even small animals would quickly succumb to the poison. The spray drifted down across the barren land and coated the boulder setting on the mound where the Johnston farm once stood. It created a slick sheen that glistened in the sunshine.

The government wanted to make sure nothing would live in this field for months. The plant sterilizer and the insecticide were two of the most powerful known. What once grew organic wheat now housed death.

The land was now government property. It was completely encircled with a chainlink, razor wire fence. It was classified with the department of agriculture as a 'dead zone'; a piece of land that will never be used again, and where nothing will ever grow.

CHAPTER 35

Sunday, May 29, 2011
Deaths 55,016

The long lines of cars stretched out of town in two directions; one toward Moses Lake, the other toward Wenatchee. Quincy sat almost in the middle of the two cities. The entire population of Quincy was leaving, every one of them, by order of the United States Government. Several thousand people were packing what they could in a very short time, and heading to a safe area designated by the National Guard and United States Army. It was very likely they would return to their town, but the condition of their homes and buildings would be unknown until after the bomb was detonated and they had a chance to survey the damage.

A Humvee drove past the sign welcoming visitors to the city. It read, "Opportunities Unlimited." Soldiers in uniform were scattered everywhere. Camouflaged vehicles, trucks, and trailers were stationed throughout the city. Groups of soldiers congregated at key stations to discuss the evacuation. They didn't know what they were evacuating the people for. They didn't care. Orders were orders. And they were good soldiers. They were instructed to not use force except only as a last resort, and to make sure every living person and pet were removed from the area.

The command vehicle pulled up to the curb in front of city hall; a small building with two flags flying in the front. The large city water tower stood magnificently behind the building. Major General James Ritchie jumped out of the vehicle and walked briskly up the walkway followed by his assistant, Lieutenant Rigby. The General was wearing camouflage fatigues with two stars on each collar, the 101st Airborne insignia on this shoulder, shiny boots and a cap. He was carrying a satchel under his arm. He was greeted by the mayor, several local policemen, and a news crew.

Major General Ritchie pointed to the news crew. "Get them out of here."

A news woman with the microphone held it out to the General. "General, can you tell us what . . ."

With one swift move, the General grabbed the microphone out of the woman's hand, unplugged it and put it in his pocket. The woman was aghast. "This is a military operation, ma'am," General Ritchie smiled and said to the woman, "You need to leave now . . . unless you want me to take your camera, too."

The young lady spun on her heels as her cameraman lowered his camera and left.

The General reached into his pocket and handed the microphone to the policeman. "Here, I don't need this." He walked past the policeman and into the building followed by his aid and the mayor. The policeman stood looking at the microphone. He looked at the other policemen, glanced around, and tossed it into the bushes.

The mobile command of the 101st airborne had taken control of Quincy City Hall.

Someone in the room yelled, "Atten-hut!"

"At ease, people." The General walked over to the head of the table and tossed his satchel onto it. He stood there looking at the map to his right. His aid sat in the chair next to him and opened the satchel. "Where are we with this operation, Sergeant?"

"Sir." The Sergeant was in his mid forties, built like a rock, and stood tall. Several tours of Iraq and Afghanistan wore like a story across his weathered face. "Ninety percent of the town has been evacuated." The Sergeant glanced down at his notes lying on the table. "There has been some resistance, but our troops were able to extract the people without casualties. There have been no reports of significant injuries, sir."

"Fine." The General glanced through some notes. "When will we be ready, Sergeant?"

"Wednesday, sir. We are allowing citizens until zero hundred hours Tuesday to vacate. We will conduct a grid search Tuesday of the target area insuring it has been cleared."

"Weather cooperating?"

A Major in the room spoke. "Yes, sir. Heavy rains expected all day Wednesday into Thursday. We will have effective rainout, sir, reducing the contamination perimeter significantly."

"Outlaying areas?"

"There is a mandatory evacuation downwind for ten miles," the Major said. "Even though we expect the rainout to contain the fallout, our troops have informed me that all residents will be relocated to temporary facilities near Moses Lake until the area is safe to re-enter."

"Perimeter security?" the General continued.

The Captain next to the Sergeant spoke. "Secure, General. We have blocked off all roads leading to the target area. Troops have been stationed every hundred yards encircling the impact zone." He walked over to the map posted on the whiteboard. There were several concentric circles centered just to the northeast of Quincy. "For the twenty mile circumference, we have three hundred and fifty stations." The Captain circled the area with his finger. "This is the entire blast zone. A three hundred and forty kiloton bomb will exert fifteen PSI[6] for just over a mile from this point." The Captain pointed to the center of the circles. "From there we have five PSI at two miles, one PSI at five miles." The Captain paused. "Quincy is in the two PSI range, General."

"I see, Captain." The General studied the map. "The target is maximum coverage of the affected area?"

"It is, General," the Captain confirmed.

"Can you please tell me what all of this means?" Mayor Kitty Andrew had lived in Quincy most of her life. She was near eighty years old with white hair and a worried look. She was elected Mayor because everyone knew her, and she knew practically all seven thousand people in town. The Army came into her town and took over, and forced everyone out. All she knew was that there was some potential disease that had to be eradicated. "What is a PSI? What are the circles for?"

"Ma'am, we have quite a bit of work to do here," the General said dismissively. "Why don't you go outside and.."

"Excuse me, Mr. Major General Sir!" Kitty stood defiantly in the General's face. "This is my town." She said as she poked the General on the shoulder. "I am a citizen of this great country. I was born here and I will likely die here. I expect you to have the decency to tell me what in the hell is going on . . . . sir!"

The General started to get angry, then realized he was being accosted by a ninety pound pit bull of a woman. A big smile crossed his face as

---

[6] PSI—Pounds per square inch.

he looked down to her and said, "Yes, ma'am." His aid looked at the Captain curiously. The Captain lowered his head and smiled, making sure the General didn't see him.

"Thank you. Now," Kitty turned back and pointed to the map and continued. "…what do these circles represent?"

"Blast radius, ma'am," the General said. "The first circle is the greatest impact. It is fifteen pounds per square inch of pressure. That means everything in that range will be completely and utterly destroyed."

Kitty lowered her head and composed herself.

"I realize this is hard to take, ma'am," the Captain said as he placed his hand on her shoulder.

Kitty looked back up at the map and pointed near the center of the circle. "That's my family's homestead." A tear rolled down her cheek. "I was born there."

The people in the room suddenly became uncomfortable. Kitty wiped away her tear and continued as though she was not fazed. "And the rest of the circles, General?" She was back to being Mayor.

The General softened his voice. "The middle ring is elimination of life with destruction of most civilian buildings. The severity of damage diminishes to the outer ring, where there is elimination of plant life but moderate damage of buildings. It is five miles from the target . . . . ma'am. It is highly probable that part of Quincy will be gone, ma'am."

"Gone?" Kitty could hardly believe what she was hearing. She turned to the Captain. "Gone?"

"Yes, ma'am," the Captain replied. "We expect so."

"I don't understand why you have to wipe out a town for this. There must be a better way to . . ."

The Mayor was cut off by the General. "Ma'am, there is no other way. If there was, we would use it. All I know is that I have orders to fulfill, and I will do so."

"Orders?" she cried. "Orders? From whom? Who told you to wipe out my town?" The Mayor's face was red with anger. Tears rolled down her cheeks. "Who?" she demanded.

"The White House, ma'am." The General turned and started to the table to get some papers.

Kitty reached out to stop him, crying. "You can't do this."

The General pulled his arm away. The Lieutenant put his arm around Kitty's shoulder and firmly held her. "Ma'am," he said. "I think it's best if you and I go outside and talk this through." He gently, but forcibly, led her out of the room.

"Captain. I want Potassium Iodide issued to all humans within fifty miles of here."

"Yes, General."

"Sergeant!" The General called. "Move this command center to the outer perimeter."

"Yes sir." The Sergeant saluted, wheeled about and left the room.

"Captain."

"Yes, General."

"You have a town to secure."

CHAPTER 36

Wednesday, June 1, 2011
Deaths 55,121

The weather was miserable to some; perfect to others. It was raining steadily. A low front was swirling counterclockwise off the coast of Canada pulling the warm, moist tropical air in from Hawaii. It was a wet storm providing ample moisture to soak Seattle and carry on to the interior of the state. Quincy was in for a drenching.

Downtown Quincy was still. It was a ghost town. The cars that normally drove by the city park were gone. The playgrounds sat empty. There were no dogs roaming the streets. The only sound one could hear was the clicking of the street lights as they changed colors for no cars.

Highway 28 was closed at Palisades Road SW and Highway 283. Highway 281 was closed at interstate 90. The remaining country roads were closed a minimum of ten miles from the city. Military personnel were stationed at each roadblock, fully armed, with two tanks. No one was allowed past the roadblocks. No one.

From the point of each roadblock, two soldiers were stationed one hundred yards apart in a vehicle or ATV encircling the entire perimeter. A Humvee with a mounted 50 caliber machine gun was stationed every 1,000 yards.

A gray, unobtrusive modular building sat at the corner of a field about three miles out of town. It had no windows and two doors. It was positioned next to a power line. Military vehicles were scattered throughout the field. Soldiers were placed as sentries at various points around the building.

Inside the building was Major General Ritchie. He was seated at the head of a table facing the large map with concentric circles around Quincy. The Captain and Major were seated at the table with the General

19Q

looking over some documents. The Sergeant and several other soldiers were scattered throughout the room talking on phones and radios.

One of the soldiers turned around to face the men at the table. "General. It's Lieutenant General Mire from the Pentagon, sir."

"Put him on speaker."

"Jim. Doug, here." The voice over the phone was clear and forceful.

"You're coming in loud and clear. I have you on speaker in Ops."

"Fine. Operation Clean Sweep is a go." Everyone in the room froze.

"Roger. Operation Clean Sweep is a go for twelve hundred hours," the General repeated.

"God's speed." The line went dead.

The men in the room looked at the General, waiting for the order.

"Gentlemen. I wanted all of you to hear the green light. We are about to detonate a nuclear bomb near a city in the United States of America." The General stood to his feet. All eyes were on him. "There is a significant threat to human life in this area. The threat is some type of virus that is causing mutations in plant and animal life. I don't fully understand the specifics of what is happening here. I don't need to. What I need to know is that the President has directed us to take this action. He, and his advisors, believe this is the best, most efficient, most appropriate way to deal with this threat. In one hour, we will be dropping a 340 kiloton B61 low level nuclear bomb three miles northeast of Quincy." The General looked at each soldier in the room. "Fallout contamination in the area is significantly reduced because of the weather. However, there is a high probability the town will be rendered useless. If the force of the blast doesn't destroy the buildings, the SREMP[7] will likely fry everything in the area. We have not been charged to protect the town, but to protect the people . . . and a nation. Sergeant."

"Yes, sir."

"Status of the sweep?"

"Clear, sir. No humans or pets are in the blast zone."

"Good." The General sat down. "Well, then. We have one hour."

The pilot was strapped into the F16 Falcon cruising at mach one. He was headed west toward Quincy. The clouds below were full of moisture

---

[7] SREMP - Source Region Electro-Magnetic Pulse which is produced by low-altitude nuclear bursts.

and riding low in the air currents. The ceiling was just 2,500 feet. The pilot would have but a few seconds to release his payload and speed out of range. This was the first time he ever dropped a B61 nuclear bomb. It was also the first time he ever bombed a city in his own country.

The pilot checked in. "Red Viper to command."

"Go Red Viper." The General listened to the radio transmissions to the tower and his command center simultaneously. Everyone in the room was listening. He was watching a live broadcast from the nose of the plane. All he could see were clouds below the plane, and blue sky above.

"I am one minute from target."

"Roger, Red Viper. One minute to target," came the reply.

The men in the room looked at the General. The General looked at the map and a radio operator to his right. The operator shook his head 'no.' The General took the mouthpiece to the radio. "Roger that, Red Viper. This is General Ritchie. Alpha alpha zulu tango niner. Clean Sweep is still a go."

"Affirmative, sir. Alpha alpha zulu tango niner. Clean Sweep is a go," The pilot repeated.

The General turned away from the mouthpiece. "Major, prepare for shutdown."

"Yes, sir." The Major turned away and spoke into a handheld radio. He was giving instructions to his team to perform an entire shutdown of the electrical services to the building. Several soldiers in the room started to shutdown their systems, knowing they would not be needed in the next sixty seconds.

The pilot dove through the clouds and popped out underneath them. He was flying so fast the rain had no impact on his visibility. The screen showing the plane's view instantly went dark, then opened up to show the ground below flying by at supersonic speed. Everything was a blur, but recognizable.

The seconds ticked away.

The pilot's voice crackled over the speaker. "Red Viper to command."

"Go Red Viper."

"I am thirty seconds to target. I repeat, thirty seconds."

The General looked to a radio operator, who shook his head 'no.' "Roger that, Red Viper. Clean Sweep is still a go. You have a green light. I repeat, you have a green light," came the reply.

19Q

One of the soldiers at the blackened terminal whispered, "God, help us."

The pilot responded. "Affirmative."

The plane roared over the hills and fields, breaking the sound barrier as it tore through the rain just under the clouds forming a visible cone around the aircraft. The sophistication of the equipment made it almost impossible to miss the target, regardless of where it was, how high or fast the pilot flew, or what the weapon of choice was.

In this case, it was a B61 low level thermo nuclear bomb. With 340 kilotons of explosive power, it would utterly destroy any living thing within a two mile radius. Nothing would survive.

As the plane approached its target it slowed below mach one. The video transmission of the area became instantly clear. The hills and fields were soaked with rain. A few houses and barns could be seen in the foreground.

A long cylindrical object ejected from the underside of the plane. A parachute immediately deployed, and the object decelerated to less than fifty miles per hour in two seconds. It slowly floated toward the ground.

The people in the room watched the video transmission in horror as a small truck backed out of a barn. The plane engaged its afterburners and accelerated rapidly breaking the sound barrier as it easily surpassed mach one again and disappeared in the clouds. The video transmission instantly blurred and went dark.

One of the analysts turned to the General. "Did you see that?" he asked.

"I did. Continue." The General never changed expression.

The cylinder gracefully floated toward the ground, gently swaying side to side in the light breeze. At two hundred feet, the bomb detonated.

CHAPTER 37

Sunday, September 11, 2011
Deaths 55,986

The warm morning sun was beating down on the barren field in eastern Oregon. Where the Johnston farm once stood there was nothing but rock and dirt. A rabbit crossed the barren landscape scurrying to get away from the shrieking hawk circling above. The fence around the perimeter of the farm stood tall, unwaivered. The signs remained clear, visible. The trees at the corner of the property were dry and dead.

A sparrow fluttered over the fence and into the 'dead zone.' The bird pecked at the ground but found nothing. It hopped toward a large rock and pecked again. It used its beak to pick up a dead grasshopper lying on the ground. A gust of wind blew the dust into the air and the bird flew off.

A small, green wheat stalk had worked its way out from under the large rock on top of a mound of dirt, and waived gently in the breeze.

THE END

AFTERWARD

I hope you enjoyed my first venture into the realm of storytelling via a book. When my wife, Rikki, went on vacation to Italy with her mother and two sisters, I was alone for three weeks. I just had surgery on my ankle and was laid up, hobbled, near helpless and most definitely bored. I wanted to read a good book, but it seemed there were few authors who could hold my interest with science, education, suspense, and accuracy.

I had this idea for a book plot in my head that had to come out. I shared it with my son, Joshua, who said it sounded pretty cool. I started researching the vast material on genetic engineering spread throughout the internet. The amount of material is enormous; content fascinating; implications shocking. I found myself engrossed in the topic and hungry for knowledge. In a matter of three weeks, I drafted the majority of the book.

The idea of genetic engineering is nothing new. Man has engineered genetics for thousands of years. If someone grew a huge tomato, someone else would want the seeds to replicate the produce. We have seen people graft one type of plant or species to another, creating boysenberries, tangelos, flowers of multiple and varied colors, large chickens, huge pumpkins, and on and on. Genetic engineering the manual way.

Since the discovery of DNA, genes, and chromosomes, the science of genetics has grown exponentially. The advent of computers has provided the means to genetically map many living organisms. Libraries of information have been created and connected throughout the world providing the science community with instant retrieval of information from anywhere in the world. We are venturing into a new, vastly unknown area; genetics.

Scientists have explored a variety of applications for genetic engineering. The health industry screams for solutions to birth defects, deadly diseases, and human suffering. Just as apparent is the food industry with a multitude of research to maximize production of crops and animals. This is nothing new. It is only becoming sophisticated. The possibilities are limitless; ramifications unknown. For example, scientists are exploring ways to have strawberries create a type of antifreeze in the berry to make it freeze resistant. It may prove to be freeze resistant, but what are the implications to the human body, especially if consumed over a long period of time? Will it increase cholesterol, thin blood, cause cancer, or cause arteries to explode?

Or take the Africanized honey bee. A docile insect mutated into a fierce defender of territory now prevalent in North America. What started out as an experiment in a distant continent resulted in a problem with an entire industry in a foreign country.

It seems we, as a people and society, are susceptible to rapid deployment of new diseases. This may be due to the shrinking of our world through technology and transportation. Everyone is connected to everyone, and traveling thousands of miles is nothing to humans, animals, insects or bacteria. The introduction of AIDS in 1981 was a blip on the radar that evolved into one of the most fierce diseases known to mankind. Five men in San Francisco with some type of weird pneumonia evolved into thirty-three million infected people in thirty years. Almost two million dead in the United States alone. The numbers are appalling.

Genetic engineering is not a new field, but is becoming a sophisticated science. As the science evolves, there is no doubt new sciences will be discovered from a variety of tangents. It will never stop. There is no right or wrong in regards to the pursuit of genetic engineering. Each camp is able to effectively defend their position with fervor and passion. This book is not to make one decide which side is right or wrong; only to think.

BIBLIOGRAPHY

http://www.ama-assn.org/ama/pub/physician-resources/medical-science/genetics-molecular-medicine/news.page

http://arkansaswheat.org/

http://www.ncbi.nlm.nih.gov/pmc/articles/PMC531654/

http://en.wikipedia.org/wiki/Food_irradiation

http://www.hopkinsmedicine.org/geneticmedicine/

http://www.ncbi.nlm.nih.gov/pmc/articles/PMC57745/

http://www.tzuchi.com.tw/file/tcmj/95-v18n5/18-5-392-396.pdf

http://www.sec.gov/answers/ipodiff.htm

http://www.sec.gov/answers/ipodiff.htm

http://en.wikipedia.org/wiki/Genetic_medicine

http://www.ornl.gov/sci/techresources/Human_Genome/medicine/medicine.shtml

http://www.ncbi.nlm.nih.gov/pmc/articles/PMC2835984/

http://rarediseases.about.com/od/geneticdisorders/a/genesbasics.htm

http://en.wikipedia.org/wiki/Solar_flares

http://en.wikipedia.org/wiki/Air_Tractor_AT-300

http://www.owgl.org/index.cfm?show=10&mid=8

http://www.sandiegosymphony.org/copleysymphonyhall/

http://www.neuroskills.com/brain.shtml

http://www.conferencealerts.com/seeconf.mv?q=ca1ix388

http://www.stonybrook.edu/cme/

http://www.icmb.utexas.edu/facilities/

http://www.dailymail.co.uk/health/article-1134412/Two-minute-inhaler-treatment-ease-misery-migraine.html

http://en.wikipedia.org/wiki/Wheat

http://en.wikipedia.org/wiki/Chromosome

http://www.genecards.org/cgi-bin/carddisp.pl?gene=PNKP

http://en.wikipedia.org/wiki/Becker%27s_muscular_dystrophy

http://en.wikipedia.org/wiki/Effects_of_nuclear_explosions

http://www.cdc.gov/maso/pdf/CDC_Chart_wNames.pdf

http://www.cdc.gov/ncidod/sars/guidance/D/pdf/d.pdf

http://www.pbs.org/newshour/extra/features/july-dec06/ddt_9-18.pdf

http://meyerweb.com/eric/tools/gmap/hydesim.html

http://en.wikipedia.org/wiki/Periodic_table

http://nuclearweaponarchive.org/Usa/Weapons/B61.html

http://quincywashington.us/quincy/

http://www.fas.org/nuke/intro/nuke/emp.htm

AUTHOR BIO

Gerald Rainey is an avid reader of science and historical fiction. His first book, *Free from the Love of Money*, aided those in serious financial straits. He currently lives in Springfield, Oregon.